Hereditation

J.P. Smythe was born in London, but has spent most of his adult life living in south Wales. When he isn't writing novels or short stories, he writes computer game scripts. *Hereditation* is his first novel.

Hereditation

J. P. Smythe

Parthian
The Old Surgery
Napier Street
Cardigan
SA43 1ED

First published in 2010
© J. P. Smythe 2010
All Rights Reserved
ISBN 978-1-906998-09-7

Editor: Lucy Llewellyn
Cover design by Tim Albin www.droplet.co.uk
Inner design & typesetting by Lucy Llewellyn
Printed by Gwag Gomer, Llandysul

Published with the financial support of the Welsh Books Council.

For your FREE eBook follow these simple steps:
1) find the password: 3rd word on page 11
2) log on to www.parthianbooks.com
3) add 'Hereditation eBook' to your shopping cart
4) add the password when prompted
5) select 'Free order only' option at the checkout
You will then receive an email with a link to your free eBook

British Library Cataloguing in Publication Data
A cataloguing record for this book is available from the British Library.

For my mum and dad

Prologue

The final parts of his family's story were fragmented and cluttered. Maynard sorted, read and discarded them as Erwin, his brother, sat in the living room amongst the towers of papers and books and minutiae. Maynard had all but stopped caring. Sometimes he sat at the piano and put his fingers on the keys and pressed them gently, so gently that they barely made a sound. He wrote letters that he would never send, and watched the incoming mail pile up in the hallways. He went to the library and searched for as much as he could find on all of his ancestors, piecing together the actual dates of their births and deaths.

Through all of this he watched Erwin collapse. Maynard watched dust settle on him, the air full of the stuff, caught in the rays of light coming through the windows. It clung to what was left of Erwin's hair; to his shoulders, to his shoeless feet. Erwin spoke to himself more, mumbling as he built the living room up. He began tearing the books on the shelves apart, yanking the pages out to build his towers, sticking them together with water, smoothing the edges. Maynard didn't argue. Instead he gave him more pills, more of the vitamins, more of the painkillers. Erwin never complained of any pain, but Maynard thought that was because he was protected against it by his diligent nursing.

'I'm feeling better, I think,' Erwin told him one morning. Maynard knew that he was lying. He realised, as he looked at him in the tired light of the morning, that his brother wasn't long for the world.

Part One

'That which we do is what we are. That which we
remember is, more often than not, that which we would
like to have been; or that which we hope to be.
Thus our memory and our identity are ever at odds;
our history ever a tall tale told by inattentive idealists.'

Ralph Ellison

1

Maynard Sloane's dreams were slipping away from him day by day. He stood in his office, rigid – for his boss liked the regimented appearance of the army in his employees – and listened as he was picked apart, his behaviour dissected by a man who didn't care about him on an individual level, but had a financial investment in his ability to do his job.

'It's in your constant whistling,' said his boss. 'It feels like you couldn't care less about the work that we're doing here.' He smoked, and drank liquor constantly, and he jabbed at the air with the over-sized fingers that he didn't use to hold his over-sized cigar.

'It focuses me, helps me think,' Maynard said. His job – the job that he got paid for, that he wore his suit and sat at his desk for – was as a junior lawyer. He had been through years of (very expensive) education to get there, and he hated it. What he loved were the pieces of music and the poems and the stories that he wrote in his head as he co-signed documents and listened to his clients discuss the legal ramifications of their purchases. 'At home I like to compose music, for fun. It relaxes me.' His boss snorted at that.

'I have a son, around your age,' he said, 'and he's in the army, builds bridges for them. He's on a project out in Arizona, working on an aqueduct. Do you know what an aqueduct is?' He poked at Maynard's chest with his thick, stubby finger, the cigar ash fluttering down to Maynard's shoes. Maynard knew. His brother, Erwin, was an engineer, officially of buildings, working at a mid-level construction firm in the city. Unofficially, though, his interest ran to construction in all forms, all shapes and sizes, and the amount of books that sat on the walls of their library at home on the subject was dizzying. 'He's paid thousands,' said Maynard's boss, 'and he just goes out there, designs it, whips it up; then they build it, and he moves on. His design! And through all of that, Maynard, through the architectural side, he's a trained, regimented soldier. Uniformed. He lives a productive life, Maynard, and he's thrilled with it. We're all thrilled,' he said, with a look of pride. 'And do you think he whistles?' He waited for an answer, but Maynard didn't give one. 'Of course he doesn't, because – crucially – whistling isn't productive. Get back to work. I'd hate to see your talent wasted.' He put his cigar out in the ashtray on Maynard's desk, an ashtray kept there at his own insistence, and solely for his own use. He didn't notice the fists that Maynard was making under the lips of his jacket sleeves.

That evening, Maynard passed a group of men in army uniforms marching through the park, whistling as they marched. He listened to the rhythmic thudding of their boots, and he stared at their expression-free faces, and wondered if any of them ever dreamt of anything different.

Erwin was already home by the time Maynard walked in. He could smell the stew the second that he walked through the door – lamb, he guessed. Erwin liked making stews: they consisted of a simple lists of ingredients, and were difficult to get wrong. 'Hello,' Maynard shouted, 'I'm home.' He walked into the kitchen, grabbed an apple from the table and went to take a bite.

'Don't,' Erwin said, 'dinner's on the way.' Erwin was still in his overalls – what he referred to as his 'uniform' – a tatty set that hadn't been washed in weeks, mainly due to his laziness. The outfit was stained with oil, blood and dust, all embedded in the grain of the cloth, but Erwin barely ever noticed. He stirred the pot, throwing the smell around the kitchen. 'I hope you're hungry,' he said. Maynard nodded, sat at the table, and pulled his shoes from his feet.

'I need new shoes,' he said, peeling the sole back from the leather. 'This keeps getting looser.'

'I told you,' Erwin said, 'take it to the cobbler, get it fixed.'

'I haven't had time.'

'There's always time to take care of oneself.'

'Says you, with the grime still on your face,' Maynard countered. They both smiled. Maynard left the kitchen to head upstairs and change. The floor of the house was freezing cold, a result of their getting rid of all the carpets when their father left. The house had been, previously, awash with colour, as Ezra – their father – liked carpets from exotic places, even though their mother never did. As soon as he left, they were one of the first things to go, leaving a mixture of hardwood and stone floors, which needed (but never received) a polish. Maynard felt the floors in the house through the many holes in his socks. Despite all of their skills, their mother had never shown them how to darn; getting her to do anything productive was a chore at best in those days. At the top of the stairs Maynard noted that that the vase they kept on a plinth there was full of dead flowers, something that the mother might have fixed, in times gone by. Evelyn – for that was her name – wasn't the woman that she used to be. They excused her inactions and eccentricities as an offshoot of the traumas she had gone through with divorce. Thirty years, Maynard reasoned, is a long time to throw away, so Maynard had researched the effects of stress and trauma on people of frail disposition. The symptoms described in the books – listlessness, anger, confusion, palpitations – sat perfectly with his mother's. He decided that she was suffering from what was referred to as a 'mental breakdown'. This rendered her quiet – nearly mute – most days and often she would just sit and stare. She occasionally froze and juddered, like a shiver, and blamed it on the cold, but they sometimes saw it happen even when she wore a scarf and gloves. (Erwin, for his part, had been convinced that their mother had an illness referred to in those same medical books as 'St Vitus' dance', until the doctor gave her an all-clear.) The fact that the flowers were still there could be argued as being just as much their fault as hers; perhaps if they bought them for her more often, Maynard thought, she would remember to throw the old ones away.

The mother's door was slightly ajar. That meant either that she was up and out of bed – an occurrence that had become increasingly uncommon – or that she had fallen asleep without reminding Erwin to shut it. On more than one occasion her sons had returned from work to find her hoarse and ruddy, noiselessly yelping to the empty house and having run her throat ragged from calling for somebody to shut the door. Maynard went to peer in, to close the door if she was resting, to talk to her if she wasn't.

'Mother?' he asked, and she didn't answer. There was no snoring – she usually snored – so he went into the room, slowly, so as not to wake her if she was asleep. She was lying on top of the bed-sheets, her arms by her sides, flat, palms up. He took in her skin, pallid, grey: her veins, at the surface, swollen; her hair, or her lack of it, the strands that were still stuck to her scalp little more than wisps of smoke. (Her hair had been, when their father left them, the first part of their mother to go. They didn't know what caused it (because her doctor didn't believe in stress-onset alopecia), but they knew that she had been a proud woman, and still was, in her own way. She had been blonde, when she was younger.) 'Are you awake?' She still didn't answer, and Maynard began to sweat. He concentrated on the veins in her wrists, trying to see if they were pulsing, or even trembling, anything to suggest that her heart was still doing its job. He knew that he would have to touch them, and, if she was dead, make a declaration, as if he were a doctor. He tried to reason with himself, thinking that she always looked dead when she slept; but he knew that one day she would be, and why shouldn't it be today?

'Ask Mother if she's ready for dinner,' Erwin shouted up the stairs, but Maynard didn't respond. He stood there, by the foot of the bed, stared at her hairbrush, her head, her pale nightgown, and couldn't move. He saw himself in the room's solitary mirror, an outline of damp colours in the dusty glass. The mirror was a regal, floor-standing affair covered in (now-peeling) gold leaf, an anniversary present from his father, and, as he stared at it, he wondered if everything ended up like it had, like his mother had; alone, fragile, cracking.

It was their thirteenth wedding anniversary, and Ezra Sloane had forgotten. He had woken as usual, gone to work, slipped out in his lunch break and browsed in the antique shops, an extended lunch. His next client – Mrs Juniper, the wife of the current manager of Sachs, and riddled with cystitis – wasn't until three, so he had decided to take it easy. Amongst other purchases (a new hat and umbrella, some wine – French), he had seen the mirror in the window of one of the more expensive shops. He had purchased it without hesitation or haggle, thinking that it would look nice in his office. He was admiring himself in it when his secretary stepped in to advise him that Mrs Juniper had arrived, and that his wife had sent a card adorned with red hearts and cherubs. He wrapped the mirror with a solitary red ribbon (actually tape designed for holding clamps shut, but it didn't look it) and presented it to an overjoyed Evelyn that night at dinner, as they drank his French wine. Before bed, he contemplated – quite forgetting about the hat and umbrella – what he might ever get to have just for himself.

Maynard wondered if he could just leave his mother's body there, let Erwin find her later. He wondered what that period of time might do to her; he had never seen a dead body before. How quickly did they decay? Suddenly, he saw her index finger seem to vibrate, and all he could think was that she had entered the first stages of rigor mortis. He had read about people twitching after they died, minutes, even hours later. They could sit up suddenly, or grab the arms of their loved ones, or, in one extreme case that Maynard had read about, even bite the hand of the coroner that was working on them. (This was Maynard's worst dream: his mother's body settled with an internal bath of blood at her bottom half, her back swollen and bloated from an excess of plasma, her previously bony and protruding shoulder blades buried, enveloped under the fat sack of skin that did nothing but carry her blood, now, her hands shooting upwards, grabbing at him for one last maternal embrace.)

'Maynard? Is she alright?' Erwin appeared in the doorway and saw his brother just standing there, crying. Erwin ran to his mother's side, grabbed at her, and she coughed, slapped his hands away. She moaned. 'Let's leave her,' Erwin said, ushering Maynard (who looked pale and terrified) out of the room. Erwin returned to his cooking, and Maynard sat on the stairs for a few minutes before going to his piano and setting to work on a piece of music that would become a symphony, and that he would spend much of the rest of his life working on. Erwin spoke to him from the kitchen but Maynard didn't hear a word over his own large, clumsy sighs of relief, and the thud of his fingers on the piano keys that he was playing with far too much pressure.

2

Erwin Sloane spent his life doing one of three things: he worked, being the family's principal breadwinner (mainly because Maynard's junior position got them very little money); he designed things – buildings, inventions, vehicles, things that would never be made but existed first in his head, and then on paper; and he read magazines and newspapers. His father had promoted newspapers as a source of information for him when he was a child, and Erwin had taken the idea and run with it. He subscribed to a number of newspapers and magazines, and kept the ones that he thought meant something. An entire corner of his room was made up of those, towers, nearly as tall as a man, of the printed media. He never read them; he just like to know that they were there, for posterity.

Erwin loved – and had the distinct advantage of being excellent at – his job. He had trained under Jonathan Orton, a mechanical engineer who had helped work on the Kitty Hawk after its maiden flight, and, as his career progressed, came highly recommended by everybody that he worked with or for. Many in the trade had started to vouch for him purely based on word of mouth. The money was excellent, even though he was still not his own boss, and still told what to do, and when to do it. The job didn't leave him enough time to split between a social life and his family, and so since his father had left, he had chosen to travel home straight after work; his mother needed him, he reasoned. One particular day, however, he and his collagues had come from a job that they all hated, it being overly stressful and tiring, and made worse by a supervisor who pretentiously called himself 'The Captain'. That was why, when his workmates asked him if he fancied a drink that evening, he said 'yes'.

It had been months since he had socialised with them, and they all drank faster because of it, egging him on to match them. It had been, they noted in jest, even longer since he had been with a woman.

'Perhaps tonight!' one of his workmates shouted as they entered the bar – St Christopher's, by the river – but Erwin knew that he had no intention of finding anybody.

Erwin's first – and only – love had been named Myra, and she had been a seamstress that he had met when his last set of overalls fell apart completely. He would lie in her bed, in her apartment, and he would read as she wound her stockings on. She always wore stockings. They lived most of the days of their short relationship as if they were married, and happily at that. Then, one day, Erwin drew her as she dressed. He sat on her bed with his sketch pad and laboured, and then showed her the final result, a picture that was all angles, closer to a building sketch than a lover's portrait. She left him a week later, and would, when telling her friends why, say that it was because he offered her no excitement, and she was too young to not want unpredictability; this wasn't true. She had never met his family, the number one source of arguments between them, as she asked if he was ashamed of her, and he placated her with gifts that he felt were affectionate and she felt were trite. 'She wanted more than I could give,' he told Maynard. Maynard nodded, but didn't ask why he didn't just bring her home, then. 'Next time I won't make that mistake.'

They began with shots of whiskey and steaks, both served colder than they would have liked, but, collectively, they were not the type to complain. They had just finished eating – and were contemplating moving onto brandy and cigars – when Erwin saw Lia for the first time, running in, late for work. She apologised to the other members of staff, pulled her hair back in a scarf, tied a dusty apron around her dirty cream skirt. She looked foreign, Italian or Spanish, Erwin thought. He was, if it was possible on such a short glance, in love.

The evening went on, but she didn't serve their table, instead staying mostly behind the bar. When it came time for his round, Erwin turned away their waiter and went to the girl instead. He wasn't shy; he just didn't want the others to see him talking to her, as he could already hear the mocking tone of their voices. He asked for the drinks, and then, offhandedly, asked her name.

'Lia,' she said.

'That's a good name,' was his reply. He couldn't stop staring at her as she unstacked tumblers for the table, and poured the drinks. He had, he believed, never seen anybody pour drinks as beautifully as she did it.

'My mother would have liked you for saying that,' she told him, 'it was hers, as well.'

Lia Emanuela Di Bennato was the product of the most protracted labour that anybody working in New York Central Hospital had ever seen. Over a period of three days her mother, Lia Sr, pushed and squeezed the reticent baby from her womb. Lia, however, had claws, and wouldn't let go. No matter how many drugs the doctors passed into Lia Sr's system she would not come out. They flooded her with tranquilllisers, hoping to knock the baby out, and she would not leave. They decided to try a caesarian, a risky procedure given that the birthing had already begun, and she shifted her body further inside her mother so that she could not be reached by the probing hands of Dr Henry Kisswood. They tried a two-pronged attack, and she turned breach, sideways on, lodging herself in as tightly as she could manage. They kept Lia Sr open almost an entire day. At one point, Dr Henry swore that he could see Lia staring up, laughing at him. Eventually, she succumbed. They pulled the baby out, placed her in a cot to the left of Lia Sr's bed, and she fell into her first sleep away from the umbilicus. After a fashion, Lia Sr awoke. She turned over, feeling no pain, and saw her child lying silent, sucking her thumb. So relieved was she, she died.

Lia's father, Vito, picked her up the following morning with his own parents, Mamma and Papà Di Bennato. They lived together in the bottom floor of a brownstone on 47th. Vito was the manager of a restaurant by day, a small place called Laguna. He ran it most all of the day, whilst his mother cooked in the kitchens and his father ran the floor. They took little baby Lia to the restaurant with them, wherè she took part in the activities of the day. These would be, variously, as she grew: a specials holder (sleeping at the foot of a large black board); a tip collector (people were instructed to leave their tips in her cot); and the baby Jesus in the annual nativity. Then, one day, Laguna's owner announced that he was selling the restaurant. 'The business is dead. It's worth nothing. I'm finished. I am throwing it away.' Vito reached over and offering a consolatory handkerchief. Thirty minutes later the deeds to the restaurant had been passed over to Vito, and he decided to name it after his favourite saint.

'If you name it after somebody that people respect, they will come and eat there.' He was right, and they were soon busy, turning the fortunes around. They even gave the portly ex-owner a job managing the kitchens. Vito's fortune was turned around. Lia, when she came of age, left the safety of the restaurant environment to go to school, where she excelled in most subjects. She was a popular girl, and incredibly pretty. She discovered at an early age that her looks could get her anything she wanted, batting her eyes at boys who hoarded crayons and swamped sand-pits. Her beauty stuck; as she developed, she learned even better ways to use it. In class they would be tasked with writing a story about their holidays, and she would delegate the responsibility to any of the willing boys who sat around her at play-time. They would be taught a new type of sum, and there was always some young boy willing to show Lia how he did it, to do hers for her, to make sure that she got a good mark in her homework. They would have to learn their nine times tables, and one of Lia's suitors would swap a completed and correct test with her failure. By the time she was sixteen she had perfect grades throughout her education, and yet actually knew very little. She left school then, having gained a score in her standardised aptitude tests that shamed her entire family: a number so low that they never spoke of it again regardless of the context, lest it remind them of her failure. Her father sat her down and took her hand and held it firmly on the tablecloth that Lia would, later in life, remember her entire family by.

'You come work at the restaurant again until you get your heart's desires, eh? It's a good life.' She nodded, knowing that it would make her father happy.

Lia and Erwin chatted as long as they could, small talk, until Erwin, terrified that his workmates might finally notice and ruin everything for him, made his move. 'Can I take you out?'

he asked. She stepped back and looked him over.

'Yes,' she finally replied, 'but don't let my father know.'

'Who's your father?' Erwin asked, and she pointed to the owner, sitting in the corner, a man called Vito that everybody in New York seemed to know.

'Why don't you call for me tomorrow? I have the night off.' She scribbled her address on a napkin and passed it to him. 'Come for me about seven.'

'Thank you, miss,' Erwin said, and took the tray of drinks back to his workmates. Lia smiled at the thought of him calling her 'miss' for hours, and Erwin was sure that he could see her in the corner of his vision for the duration of his walk home.

Erwin barely slept that night, thinking about her as he lay in his bed, and then wasted the next day sitting in the kitchen, thinking about reading, thinking about going out, thinking about Lia. He ate with Maynard, home from work for his lunch-hour, nodding and smiling his way through their conversation, only half listening, and wishing that the day would race past. He left as soon as it got dark, far too early for the time it would actually take him to walk to hers, stopping only at a florist's to buy roses, the most expensive that they sold. As he turned onto her street, half an hour early for the date, he saw droves of Italians flooding the porch outside what he took to be her house. Fearing the worst (a habit which, like Maynard, he had gained since they began looking after their mother) he ran to the weeping people, all dressed in their blacks.

'What's happened?' he asked. 'Is Lia okay?' A woman, shrunken and elderly, looking for all the world as if she had been in training for this moment her entire life, grabbed at his arm.

'It's Vito! He's dead!' she howled. Erwin found Lia sitting at the kitchen table.

'You look nice,' he said. He didn't know how else to start.

She was dressed as if for their date, a black dress with roses dotted around it. He put the flowers on the table, and she smiled at them. If it had been a normal date, he would have remarked on the coincidence of him bringing roses, and her wearing them.

'I'm sorry, Erwin,' she said. She had the smallest hint of an accent, he noticed, when she said his name, just New York Italian, but an accent nonetheless. 'You didn't expect...' she waved a hand emphatically around herself and searched for a way to finish the sentence, '... all of this. You didn't expect this.' On every surface sat a food container of some sort, all covered with paper or film. Erwin could smell every dish, lasagnes and pies and bakes and stews. 'I don't know what I'm going to do now,' she said, 'now I'm all on my own. I can't even think straight.'

'You can stay with me,' Erwin said, not thinking as it came out of his mouth. He repeated it, to confirm both that he meant it, and that he said it in the first place.

'What? I can't.' She took the corner of the tablecloth, a bright yellow gingham pattern, and rolled it between her fingers, and then they sat there silently in the kitchen with the strong smells of other people's home cooking mingling together.

'You can,' Erwin told her. On the way back to the Sloane house they stopped at the cobbler's, because he had a key cutting machine, and the Sloanes kept no spares. All the way Erwin's stomach rumbled, and he wished he had asked if they could take some of the food that they had left to rot away on her old work-surface.

Maynard was sitting in the living room humming his symphony – of which he had just written another few bars, taking it slowly but methodically (or, some would say, aimlessly) – when he saw Erwin and Lia coming up the steps, hand in hand. He rushed out to the front door, flung it open.

'What time do you call this?' he joked.

'This is Lia,' Erwin said, and Maynard took her hand, pumped it comedically. 'Her father just died.' Maynard kept his mouth shut and dropped her hand. 'This is Maynard, my brother.'

'I'm sorry for your loss,' Maynard said eventually. 'If there's anything I can do to help?' Lia nodded her thanks. He looked just like his sibling, she thought, but slightly chubbier, less polished around the edges; despite being younger, he looked like a rougher version, a preliminary drawing.

'I'll show you around,' Erwin said, and led her into the hallway proper, in the shadow of the staircase. 'This is it,' he announced.

'It's nice,' Lia said. She was being polite. The house was overly dark, musty, cold and oppressive, and needed some real care. It looked like the house of two men with better things to do than clean, and the air tasted of the dust that hung perpetually around everything. Nothing in the house was influenced by any sense of taste, the furniture being little more than an expensive hodge-podge of items that barely worked together. All the art in the house – and there's wasn't much – was tepid and mediocre, bought from shops with no idea of the value of each piece. Erwin led Lia into the kitchen, which was white, but grey and yellow in the sad light from the tiny back window.

'This is where I cook,' he said. He took meat from the fridge and started cleaving on the chopping board. 'I hope you like stew?'

'Oh, I'm not hungry,' Lia replied. She reached into her handbag and pulled out the tablecloth from her old house. She spread it and put it over the table, then fastened it with an elastic band around the edge, like they did at the restaurant.

'You don't mind?' she asked. 'It was my father's favourite.'

'No, no,' Erwin said, stripping the bones. 'Make yourself at home.'

The tablecloth had been given to Vito by Lia's mother on their first date. Her mother had always been told to be grateful when a man gave you a gift on a date; she panicked as Vito handed her flowers, and told him that she had gotten him a present as well. 'I got you this,' she said, and ran to the kitchen where she grabbed the tablecloth from a drawer. Vito loved it, and when the time came to outfit his restaurant, he took inspiration from the colour scheme that she set on that first date. At school, Lia was chastised for saying that her favourite colour was 'yellow and black', and refused to pick just one.

Erwin emptied the meat into a pot, threw in hastily chopped carrots, cauliflower, swede, potato.

'Do you often cook?' Lia asked.

'Not always,' he replied. 'Most of the time, but not always. When I'm late, Maynard sets the stew going.'

'Not your mother or father?' She watched as Erwin clammed up, and realised, briefly, how little they both knew about each other, and yet, here they were.

'My father left,' he said, 'and my mother is ill. She doesn't come downstairs much.'

'What's wrong with her?'

'Let me show you the rest of the house,' Erwin said instead of answering. This was one of his worst traits, a habit of changing the subject bluntly if he didn't like the way that the conversation was going. It wasn't rudeness, per se; more an inability to think of ways to speak about things that he didn't want to speak about. They went to the living room first, Erwin leading the way. 'Sometimes we'll sit in here and listen to the wireless.' He indicated the ugly, clumsy box of wires and dials in the corner.

'What sort of wireless is that?'

'I built it, for Maynard to listen to his music on.' Lia investigated it, fiddling with the switches and dials on the front. 'He's very creative; he writes things, plays piano, that sort of thing.'

'That's amazing. Do you do those things as well?'

'No,' Erwin sighed. 'I can build things, though. I know how things work. It's just as much of a skill, I think.'

'Oh.' They then headed up the stairs, past the mother's room. 'Can I meet her?' asked Lia. Erwin shook his head.

'She's asleep. We should whisper, so that we don't wake her.' Next door was Maynard's room, but Erwin took Lia's hand and hurried her along, flinging open the next door. 'Bathroom,' he said proudly, 'I installed it myself.' She nodded, less impressed than he would have liked (because it was, again, tasteless, a horrendous suite of faux-antique curlicued pattering), so he ushered her into his room.

It was at odds with much of the rest of the house; at first glance it was utterly featureless, stark to the point of being almost empty. The bed was coated in thin cream sheets, perfectly matching the cream of the walls. The thin metal frame of the bed was painted off-white, stained over time by cigarette smoke.

Ezra used to sit, before he abandoned them, on the end of Erwin's bed, and discuss gynaecology with him whilst smoking long, thin cigarillos. This started in Erwin's childhood and ran well into adulthood, a ritual that they shared. Neither told Maynard about it, and he always went to bed first – as a child, because he was younger, and as an adult because his work started earlier than Ezra's or Erwin's, and he didn't function well without sleep. Ezra would have discussions with Erwin about how their lives were going, and they would always end with Ezra telling his son how proud he was of him, something that he never said to Maynard. This, for Erwin, made it an especially meaningful compliment. Of course, Ezra never told Erwin about his affairs, which rendered many of the conversations that they had riddled with lies; when he told his son that he was happy in his marriage, Erwin always assumed this to be the truth, right until the day that Ezra walked out on them.

The only feature in the room was the tower of magazines.

'You can sleep here,' Erwin told Lia, pulling back his sheets – both as an invitation, and a way of checking that they were clean. Since the mother's decline, laundry had taken something of a back-seat. 'I'll sleep on the couch.'

'We can both sleep up here, if you like. If it's easier.' She was trying to be as unobtrusive as possible, not wishing to get in the way; he read too much into it. He tried to kiss her and she moved her head to one side, leaving him to brush against her cheek. 'I don't know if this is right, so soon,' Lia said. Erwin put his hand on her shoulder, consolingly, and sat next to her. She leant into him, and they held each other. Erwin noticed his magazine on his bedside cabinet and wondered why he had not read it yet. He held her for a while, until his stomach gurgled louder and louder and he went to finish making the dinner.

The stew was served clumsily. Maynard and Erwin had extra portions, and Lia claimed that she wasn't hungry, using her grief as an acceptable excuse (though in reality she thought the food bland, tasteless, and lacking in seasoning; Erwin was not, she now knew, one of life's great cooks). When they had finished eating, Maynard excused himself, heading towards the piano. The symphony – though still ill-formed, broken, missing chunks – was beautiful and sad and powerful, and Lia went to stand next to the piano as Maynard played. When he was finished (or had reached the point that he hadn't written past, yet), she asked how long he had been playing.

'Forever,' he said. He stood, mocked putting coat tails behind his back – Erwin smiled, having seen him make this jokey gesture many times before – then started playing again. 'I can't get past this first section,' Maynard said.

'It's beautiful.' Lia was thinking about her father as she listened. The music, she decided, sounded very sad.

After he had played it three or four times, and deliberated in between attempts about where to take it, trying new runs and playing with the timing, the chords, Maynard announced that he was going to bed. He hugged Lia as if she had always been there living with them, and then retreated up the stairs, almost running. Lia went to the kitchen and cleared the table, soaked the pan in the sink, and then went upstairs with Erwin.

'I have an early start in the morning,' he said. He rescinded the bed to her, putting himself on the cold floor. She changed into her nightdress in the bathroom, and turned the light off when she returned. Erwin was already in his space, lying parallel with the bed, the sheets pulled over his body, tucked in at the sides like a cocoon. She climbed over him to the bed, slid under the slightly musty covers. 'You're lovely,' he said, through the darkness.

'Thank you,' she said, and then she heard him move, push himself to his knees. He came closer through the darkness and kissed her softly on the lips, gently. It was, she thought as it was happening, barely a kiss at all, more just lips touching and then parting, followed by Erwin's furious apologising as he retreated.

'There's nothing to say sorry for,' she said. She heard him

pull the sheets up, grunt to himself. Within minutes he was snoring. Lia lay there for hours, thinking about the walls and her father. She drifted into near-sleep over and over, never letting herself settle in, and as soon as the light starting creeping past the drabness of the curtains she got off the bed, stepped gingerly over Erwin, and went downstairs, hungry for something that wasn't Erwin's stew. In the kitchen she found bacon, cheese and grits, and she started the process of cooking the meat as her father used to, fried over an incredibly hot stove, then left it to stand when crispy, and set the grits to boil. Whilst they cooked she went into the living room – a room that Ezra Sloane had, before he abandoned them, referred to as 'The Library' – and worked her eyes across the bookshelves. They were floor-to-ceiling units, built into the walls, with more books stuffed onto them than she had ever seen in a home before. And she didn't recognise a single title or author on most of the shelves. Gray's *Anatomy of the Human Body*. Moore's *Principia Ethica*. Darwin's *Origin of Species*. Temkin's *The Falling Sickness*. She took one down from the shelf, blew the dust off, and attempted to read the first page, but found it to be full of words she didn't understand. Finally, after finding a section of fiction that consisted of language that she at least understood, she returned to her boiling water. There, sitting at the kitchen table already, as if waiting for her, was Erwin's and Maynard's mother.

The older lady didn't speak, at first, and Lia didn't want to scare her, so she sat down opposite her, smiling her best smile.

As a child, Lia was a horse-rider. Not being rich it wasn't something that happened regularly, but when they had the money and the cause – birthdays, for example, Lia's father would take her out to the country and she would trot around in

*circles for the best part of the day. Once day they were up-state
to meet a supplier, Lia going with her father for the ride. In a
field by the side of the road they had seen horses, wild, and Lia
had been desperate to meet them. They had approached the
horses slowly, as Lia was warned that running up to them
excitedly might make them back away. 'They are scared of
everything,' her father warned her, 'even a bit of paper trapped
in a hedge. You must be as careful with them as you would with
even a small china replica of the horse.' She was, and they let
her pet their noses, and ate mints from her hand.*

Lia walked across the kitchen slowly, acting as if she hadn't
noticed the mother. She turned up the heat on the grits and
was grating cheese when the mother spoke up.

'I haven't had bacon in an age,' she said. Her voice was
like bees, Lia thought, a humming in it, low and vibrato.

'Would you like some?' Lia was aware that she was
nervous, for some reason. The mother was perfectly well
turned out – Lia hadn't known what to expect – but she was
neat, wearing a bathroom robe, something white underneath
it, a scarf wrapped around her head, holding the remainder
of her hair in. 'I'm doing mine with grits and cheese.'

'That sounds delicious,' the mother said.

'I'm pleased to meet you, Mrs Sloane,' Lia said, slicing the
bacon up. 'My name's Lia. I'm seeing Erwin.'

'Nice to meet you,' said the mother, and they sat at the table,
both fiddling with the tablecloth, waiting for the grits to boil.

3

Ezra Bellamy Sloane sat in a bar, alone, and drank. He was,
he knew, a cliché. He stared at the waitress, too young for him,

watched her as she bent to pick up napkins that were thrown on the floor, leant over when she collected ashtrays from the tables. He smoked furiously just to make her come to his table more often, to give him a fresh receptacle. As the night went on he grew tired and hoarse and drunk, and the waitress ended her shift, replaced with another: less attractive, but still he watched. He complained to the owner of the bar – who listened to him for want of anything better to do, as it was a quiet night – that he was stuck with women his age, that the only women interested in him were old, wealthy (or in need of wealth), and that he knew them all too intimately.

'Never mix business with pleasure,' he slurred.

'Just be glad that you've got any women to be stuck with,' the man said. 'You want a young woman, you have to pay for it, you know?' He was talking about the demands of younger women, about sexual equality and women's lib; Ezra heard it as a suggestion that he turn to financial equity as a trade for sex. It would be the first time that he had even considered it, for some reason, and the thought, as he swanned through the streets to his hotel, thrilled him.

Ezra was the finest gynaecologist in all of New York City. He had trained in France, at the École Française de Gynécologie, and was widely regarded as one of its proudest students, and their first American graduate. His tutor and mentor over his six years at the institution, Professeur Laurent Hoop, said, at Ezra's graduation, that he was 'almost perfect, but, like a soufflé, needs the right amount of time to rise to the optimum height'. (The audience all applauded this, and this made Ezra's father, Quaid, especially proud: he came from a long line of groundbreakers. His great-great-great-great-great-great grand-father had been one of the first people to step foot on American soil – they still had the compact from the Mayflower, in a box in his father's office.) As soon as he returned to America he borrowed the money to start his own practice, and a year later met his future wife, Evelyn (née Beaucomb). She was the daughter of another of his patients, and of his own GP, sent to him for a routine check-up. As she lay on the table, he sighed, and told her to get dressed. 'I cannot examine you,' he said, 'because I find you too attractive, and it would ruin my professional conduct.' She had never heard anything sweeter. They began dating, just walks in the park at first, then moving onto dinners, movies. Their favourite restaurant was a small place on 2nd called Laguna, that would, thirty years later, be purchased by a man called Vito Di Bennato, and renamed Saint Christopher's. A week into their courtship Ezra announced his intentions to her father, Dr Lucas Beaucomb, and when Evelyn returned home that day, it was announced to her, in front of the whole family, that they were to be married. She would, in later years, regret the lack of pomp and circumstance behind the proposal, but on that day was just ecstatic that he wanted to marry her. They married within the month, at the Beaucomb family estate in New Hampshire, where they then spent their honeymoon, surrounded by Evelyn's family. He never strayed, and loved Evelyn – he told himself – as much every day as he did the day that they married.

Then, more than thirty years into his marriage and career, he stood in his office performing an oophorectomy and felt himself stir in his trousers. He marked it down to the temperature, a change in the weather. The next patient, a tubal ligation, instigated the same reaction. That night he dreamt of his assistant, Wendy, in stockings, her feet in the stirrups that he kept in the offices. A week later he told his family that he was leaving, and instigated a divorce.

Post-separation, Ezra's opinions on virility shifted dramatically. Whereas his sex life with his wife had been all but non-existent since Maynard's birth – aside from the occasional roll on a birthday, if there was alcohol involved, his sexlife post-marriage was completely different. The power that he felt when he had a woman on his table was extreme, and his confidence grew. The first time he made advances on a client was with June Rapplebaum. She lay on the table, going through the menopause, and he reassured her that everything was proceeding normally. It wasn't until she was dressing behind the screen – made with an Asian print, because Ezra thought that it would make the women more comfortable – that he made his move.

'May I call you June, Mrs Rapplebaum?' he asked, and she told him that was fine. They went out for dinner and dancing – he hadn't been dancing in years, he told her as he swung her around – and then went to her apartment, inherited from her own messy divorce, where he made love to her on her water-bed. He found himself adept. His reputation spread.

Annie Miller (of the Miller dynasty) was next, accompanying him to a National Gynaecological Society dinner where Ezra was the guest of honour. They had sex in the back of her car. After her, Chase Ripley, local librarian: sex between the biology and engineering sections after hours; Henrietta Morecambe, actress: sex in her dressing room; Laura Lucenti, reporter: actually had sex with him in his offices, on his gynaecological slate, fulfilling one of his fantasies. There were more. It helped that he was good looking, not conventionally, but he had a striking quality to him that women couldn't put their finger on, something mysterious.

'You seem like such a good man,' Chase Ripley told him post-coitally, 'and I can only imagine what your eyes have seen.' The things his eyes had actually seen, Ezra thought, were: New York (which, whilst admittedly well-regarded, was somewhat ordinary and to-do when you lived there); New Jersey (far less impressive, being New York's grey and uncomfortable tumour of a cousin); Florida (pretty in the *summer, but he visited in February); his family (impressive to nobody but themselves); and over fifteen hundred vaginas (an impressive number, but they all looked much the same, unless the toils of multiple births had taken their toll). He never saw Chase again, because he didn't call her. There were, he reasoned, too many women in the world. From that point, he went off the rails, more. He travelled to parts of the city that he had never been to before to find drinking holes.*

He took to drinking seriously.

'She's new,' the Madam standing at the desk told Ezra, 'fresh off the boat.' Her voice was coarse enough to make Ezra question her gender. 'She's good to go.' She patted him on the behind as he went through to the waiting room. The room itself was red – the colour of a womb, Ezra thought – and warm, with soft leather chairs around the edge and a fish tank embedded in one of the walls, sunken, cheaply installed and back-lit. He started at the fish – big ones, koi carp – and waited. He was pulling faces at the tank when he heard a voice from behind.

'Mr Sloane?' Her pronunciation was dreadful, even for delivering that solitary line, but she looked astonishing. She was petite, brunette, dark skinned (Spanish, Ezra guessed), her nails long and garishly painted, and she was young: early twenties, probably.

'I'm Ezra,' he said, and he stepped forward, shook her hand. 'You can call me Ezra. Mr Sloane was my father.'

'Eh-sra,' she said, rolling it around her mouth, the combination of syllables entirely foreign to her.

'And you are?'

'I Aurelia,' she said. 'You come with me now, Eh-sra.' She led him up some stairs to a bedroom, or what was probably the set of a bedroom, barely furnished, nothing practical in it, no clothes or real lighting, just soft pink bulbs in the various fixtures. 'Lie down, Eh-sra,' she said, so he did.

That night, on the way home – or, rather, back to the hotel that he referred to as his home but actually felt anything but – Ezra found himself confusedly wandering down the street that he used to live on. He sat across the road and he watched his old residence. The curtains didn't twitch, nobody came out, nobody saw him, but he sat there and watched it nonetheless. He missed the house. He missed his family. He missed it all, his life as it was, and yet, couldn't stop thinking about the next few days, and seeing Aurelia again. He called his assistant and told her that he was feeling ill.

'Clear the next few days,' he said, 'rearrange the appointments. We'll reconvene on Monday.' As soon as he hung up he phoned the brothel, and made a block-booking.

4

After Lia met the mother, the atmosphere in the house began to change. For a start, the previously hidden matriarch decided that she wanted to get out more. She started to make herself more presentable, appearing downstairs more often, her bald head wrapped in a headscarf. A few days later she called Lia to her room and asked for help and advice, as she wanted to start wearing a wig. Lia fetched a selection from a local department store and tried them on, with the mother eventually settling on a brunette one, shoulder length, that wasn't dissimilar to Lia's own hair. They spent their days talking, waiting for the men to come home. They discussed Lia's father's restaurant (which Lia decided to give to her uncle, so that he could make a go of it, as long as he renamed it Vito's, in tribute), and they spoke about Erwin, how they both hated his cooking but couldn't tell him, and they spoke about the future, and what they both wanted. The mother, in particular, was shocked to find that she did still want things: she wanted her life back; she wanted to feel strong again; she wanted some excitement. Neither of them questioned the speed that Lia and Erwin's relationship had seemingly developed; instead, they acted like Lia had always been there. (One day, Lia told the mother, out of the blue, that she was with Erwin because he made her feel safe. 'He feels like he'll always be here,' she said. The mother nodded, knowing that feeling well.)

Maynard had an entirely different reaction to Lia's being there, however. The reception that she gave to his piano playing spurred his creative instincts, made him wish that he was indulging that side of his personality instead of going to the grind of the law offices every day. When the weekend arrived he spent his free time playing, or talking about, his music, the piece that he was writing. The mother and Lia were interested, but Erwin had heard this all before. When Monday rolled around he found himself back in his office, trying to work, and he went by, day after day, wishing that he wasn't.

He discussed the problem with Lia and his mother, who both sympathised.

'I hated waitressing,' Lia said. 'I used to love everything else about the restaurant, but I hated clearing plates. One day I would run a restaurant again, only do the parts that I enjoy.'

'What point is there in doing anything else?' asked the mother.

'Life's too short, Maynard,' Lia said, and then asked him to play his (still unfinished) piece for her again. He did, and she clapped when he finished, or reached the current end, then went to make lunch. Maynard sat still, and tried to burn her outline into the shadows on the wall with his stare. The following morning he handed in his notice at the law firm, and spent the afternoon in a piano shop playing his piece on instruments that were far out of his price range, but that made it sound exceptional.

Ezra Sloane was a man of regrets. He regretted his career, that he maybe didn't choose something that he wanted. He regretted those women that had come into his life and he had failed to woo, or that he had wooed and then lost. He regretted his relationship with his father, Quaid, because Quaid had spent much of Ezra's life in hospital; and he regretted the way that he had left his wife and sons, regretted that he couldn't have dealt with the situation better. (Ezra had woken up one morning, felt unhappy, thought about his attractions to the women in his surgery, stared at his wife's face, her wrinkles, her body that he knew too well, and immediately packed. 'It's for the best,' he told his family as he dragged his suitcase. 'I'll send for the house stirrups.')

He regretted having cut himself off from them, and that they, subsequently, had been forced to do the same to him. He regretted almost his entire life, and he wished that he could live it all over again. He told all of this to Aurelia as they lay in her bed, waiting for the slot that he booked with her to expire. He block-booked her for four hours at a time – always a morning – and managed to spend nearly thirty minutes of that time having physical relations (in three individual sessions). The rest was spent with him talking at her, and her nodding, pretending – he assumed – that she understood what he was saying. He booked her most days, whittling away chunks from his bank account (which was already dwindling thanks to the constant payments that he had to make to his wife and children), but he didn't care. This was, he decided, love.

'You're the only part of my life that I don't regret,' Erwin told her. He spent hours reeling off tales about the other women that he had been with, comparing them to Aurelia, and complimenting her on her youthful beauty. 'Compared to them, you are a precious rose,' he swooned, 'your hands petals, your face, a bud, a closed-up bud, still waiting for sunlight.' She didn't understand his compliments either, but she smiled nonetheless. A few days into paying for Aurelia's services he plucked up the courage to ask her if they could go on a proper date. 'You know, outside,' he shouted, doing the universal actions for walking, with his fingers.

'Eh-sra,' she said, 'if like. If money.' He asked her when they could go on this date, and she told him. '*Terça-feira*,' she said, but it took her pulling out a diary filled with men's names and appointment times for him to work out that she meant Tuesday.

After his dates with Aurelia, everything felt dull to Ezra. Back at work, he tried to get himself excited at the thought of his assistant, Wendy, but found it impossible. He stared at her as she brought him his lunch – cheese and pastrami sandwiches – and wondered how he ever found her anything more than a pretty variation on the average. When they were finished eating – they always took lunch together, to break up the day – he sat behind the door to his office and wept, thinking about how much he stood to lose if things didn't work out with Aurelia.

For years, his life had been a constant pattern. He had gone left when he was meant to go left, and right when right, and since deviating he found himself thinking thoughts that he had never even contemplated. Over the duration of their (admittedly unconventional) relationship he spent seven thousand dollars on Aurelia, buying either time with her, or gifts. He quickly became attached, purchasing underwear, teddy bears, giving her a picture of him in a frame. (She kept the picture in a drawer in her fake bedroom until he came around, when she put it on the dresser.) Every day when they were done he left her payment on the bedside cabinet, on what he referred to as 'my side', even though she shared that bed with any number of other men during the same time frame (including Erwin, who, coincidentally, thought of the same side of the bed as his own as well). Ezra asked her to try positions with him, things that he had done with the other women that he had slept with (but never with his wife). He asked her to say things, training her lips to form the words, though she drew the line at the pitiable declarations of love he tried to draw her into. He moved slower with her, the sex being less frantic than with some of his other lovers.

'You wear me out!' he told her, post-coitally.

'*Que?*' she asked, and they both laughed, neither knowing why, and he would kiss her wherever she let him, and leave.

5

Internally, Erwin was a disaster. He had woken for work in the early hours, as usual. He had gotten up from the floor and climbed into his bed with Lia, put his arms around her freezing cold body, rubbed her back, moved his hands to her chest, accidentally (on purpose), and he had kissed her. She had kissed him back, less passionately, and then, just as things were heading towards a place that he saw as an inevitability (but that they had not yet reached), she sighed and turned over.

'I have to sleep,' she said. He left the room, frustrated and irritated. He knew that he should be patient – she was still getting past her father's death, and had not even buried him, yet (mostly due to her own reluctance to visit the coroner, release the body, and make the necessary preparations) – but he found his passions stronger than any patience that he could muster. At work, his colleagues noticed his frustrations.

'You seem preoccupied,' one said, 'like something's troubling you. You're not yourself.' They were right. He had thought that the relationship would be exciting, but it slowed his life to a crawl. After the rebuttal of that morning he spent the day in a fug, it reaching a climax when he lost the plans for an air-conditioning system – misplaced, a common accident – and punched a wall, cracking the skin on his knuckles, peeling it back nearly to the bone. When lunchtime arrived, he decided that he had to leave work early.

'I feel sick,' he told his boss, and he was excused, illness not mixing with high-pressure equipment on building sites. But he decided to not go home, instead heading downtown. There he found a bar and drank, picking at the scab forming on his hand. After telephoning home to slurringly tell Lia that he was working late, he wandered to a brothel that he had been told about by one of the bar's patrons. The receptionist welcomed him in, confused him with her gender, and then showed him into a room, where Erwin stared at fish – he didn't know what sort of fish they were – until he heard a voice from behind him.

'Mr Sloane?' Aurelia said, and he shook her hand, clumsily.

'Please, call me Erwin. Mr Sloane is my father.'

'Ehr-win,' she said, 'I Aurelia,' and she took his hand and led him to her stage-bedroom.

He learned a lot about her, talking as they got dressed when they were done, struggling through the language barrier, piecing together what couldn't be communicated. She was from South America (he knew this from the way that she pointed downwards, and made car noises when he asked her how she arrived in America); she enjoyed drinking red wine (which stained her teeth almost immediately, so cheap was the bottle that she fetched from the reception after they had finished); and she was religious (which he knew from the way that she called out the name of the Virgin Mother when she was really enjoying the sex, and the way that she focused her eyes on the crucifix that she kept on the bedside table the entire time he was on top of her). She had thin blonde hairs on her arms and legs, not dark as most Latinos did (in Erwin's experience), and she had the tiniest corners of hair above her lip that he could feel as he kissed her. She didn't let him kiss her directly on the lips – it had to be slightly above, on the part that bridged towards her nose, or on the side – and she wouldn't kiss him back. It wasn't, Erwin felt, an ideal arrangement, but the physical contact, he noted, was better – warmer – than he got from Lia. That night he slept on the floor and didn't even think about the woman in the bed next to him; instead he dreamt of his foreigner, and pressed himself against the floor as if she might suddenly appear underneath him. He woke up sweating.

The following morning he left as always, first thing, but ran to a payphone and called his boss.

'I'm still sick,' he said, and then he caught a cab to Brooklyn. He ate breakfast in a diner, thinking about Aurelia's nipples as he punctured the yolks of his eggs, and when mid-morning rolled around, paid his bill and walked towards the brothel. He saw a flower seller on the side of the road – and thought for a brief second about the flowers that he had given Lia on their first date, an act that he had never repeated – and ran over, exchanged money for a bouquet of roses. He was putting his wallet away when, out of nowhere, he felt himself ricochet off the side of a building, onto the floor, landing face up in a hole, covered in blood, the sky all white apart from the smoke that poured across the sky, as his vision faded to black.

When he awoke the scene was chaos, ambulances and police

vehicles and dust in the air. Erwin scrambled to his feet and looked around to see if there was anything that he could do, but they had the major work entirely under hand. He helped a man catch his breath; he pulled a cat free of the wreckage; he opened a bottle of water for an elderly lady who was gawping at the scene. The police eventually told him to clear the area and go home, if he didn't require medical attention. He agreed, but ran instead to Aurelia, taking the stumps of the roses that he had intended as a prelude to the intercourse, and preparing a story of his heroics to wow her with.

On the day of the bomb Ezra had Aurelia's morning booked out, his first work-related appointment of the day being after lunch. They went for a brief walk through the neighbourhood, and then he paid for hot dogs, then they went back to her room, where they had sex. From the start it felt different. He began on top, as always, but found that he was having trouble with the pace that he set, going even slower than usual, so they swapped, and she moved on him, but he had to keep moving her hands because they were pressing on his chest, which was, for some reason, hurting him. At one point he was sure that he almost passed out, so she finished him – something that she had never had to do before, leaving him gasping, his ears blocked as the blood rushed around his body – and he dressed.

'Can you fetch me some water?' he asked her, and she did. He drank it down in one, but it tasted acrid and almost bitter, metallic. 'I have to go,' he said. There was no attempt at a goodbye kiss from his end, and he forgot to put her money down, so she reminded him as he was leaving. As he took his wallet out he fumbled it, his left arm tingling, and then, as he walked down the street he felt his arm go numb, and his vision blurred. He stopped a man by a payphone and asked him to call for an ambulance. 'I think there's something very wrong,' he muttered, remembering his days of pre-med, remembering that these were all the signs of an impending heart attack. And then the bomb exploded, and so, too, did Ezra Sloane's heart.

He lay on the pavement and stared straight ahead, seeing his son sprawled out on the other side of the explosion. Erwin didn't see him, so Ezra tried to call out, to tell him that he was there, to tell him all of the things that he confessed to Aurelia. He wanted, he would say, to start again, to make up for it all. He would tell him that he had been a fool. He wanted to tell him, one more time, how proud of him he was. Ezra tried to say all of these things but couldn't, and then he died, surrounded by rubble and ambulances and screaming, and his son stumbling off to lie to their mutual lover about how great and in control he had been at a time of great chaos and tragedy.

Aurelia listened to Erwin's story about the blast, and then rewarded him with a slight discount. As he was walking home Erwin stopped at a jeweller's shop, then made his way back just in time for dinner. After listening to him tell the story – censored for the parts about Aurelia, and riddled with lies for the rest – Maynard and the mother left the room for bed, congratulating him on his day. Erwin got up from the table and knelt down, the box in his hand. He directed it towards Lia.

'Marry me?' he asked.

'Yes,' she replied, because she didn't know what else to say, and because she felt so lonely, and they went upstairs where, for the first time since they had started seeing each other, they made love, only neither of them really moved, and it was as silent as the rest of the house, Lia thinking of the darkness, Erwin thinking of Aurelia, and of bombs. When they were done Erwin went down to his make-shift bed on the floor and stared through the darkness at the fresh pile of magazines and newspapers building up in the corner of the room that he had failed to read in recent weeks, and wondered where his time – his life – was heading.

6

The next day, Lia attended the funeral of her own father. When she dressed in black that morning, Erwin didn't notice. The funeral itself went as these things should, with everybody weeping for Vito, and telling nice stories of their memories, and telling Lia that her parents, both of them, God rest their souls, would be very proud of her. She took off the engagement ring before she got to the cemetery.

While Lia was out, Maynard answered the door to a sombre policeman who clutched his hat to his chest as he delivered the news that Ezra's body – the body – was waiting to be identified at the hospital morgue. Erwin and Maynard spent most of the day sitting with their mother in the living room, listening to the wireless, not really caring what programme was on. After a while Maynard went and played his piano, making it a few more bars into his piece. Lia got home just as it was getting dark, and he was winding down. She looked in on her fiancé and his mother in the living room, both asleep, heads tilted back, lightly snoring. Maynard was playing so softly it was barely audible.

'What's going on?' asked Lia, so Maynard told her, about the policeman's call, about the body that they had found, how it was apparently barely recognisable due to the blast.

'We have to identify him tomorrow,' he told her, and Lia started to cry, enormous sobs, her shoulders rocking, her face streaming. Maynard held her, his shoulder being drenched as he did. He didn't mind. Through the sobs she stammered:

'You think it's a good idea, don't you? That we get married, Erwin and I?' She wiped her eyes on his shoulder, curiously unsure exactly as to why she was asking Maynard for his permission.

'Do you want to marry him?' Maynard asked, and Lia shrugged.

'He seems like a good man.'

'He is.' Maynard shut the lid of the piano and went to the kitchen, running the tap fiercely into the kettle. Lia sat on the stool by herself, trying to work out why she even asked him in the first place.

The coroner was a dour man, tired and old and unhappy with his job. Maynard could tell this within seconds of meeting him – it was in his handshake, his slow speech, the way that his hair was hurriedly neat, glossed down with still-visible pomade – so neither brother tried to force small talk when they arrived. Instead the coroner led them to a back room and showed them Ezra's body. It was already lying on a table, covered with a sheet that the coroner pulled backwards, a magician drawing a curtain, and they saw their father for the first time since he left them.

'If there's anything you'd like to say to him, now's the time,' the coroner recited. 'I'll leave you three alone.' He shut the door behind him, and Erwin and Maynard stood there staring at what was left of a face that looked like their own might in the future – Erwin with his father's jaw and nose, and high brow, Maynard his cheeks and lips, and his deep-sunken eyes; their father filling in the gaps between their own looks – and it stared back at them even with its eyes closed, a portent, maybe, of what could come.

When they got home their mother was waiting in the hall,

surrounded by boxes. She was dressed smartly, her wig on, make-up applied. Behind her, sitting on the piano stool, was Lia.

'You father has had all of his possessions returned here,' she said, 'because this was the address that he gave to the hotel that he was staying at.' She opened a box, looked inside, dismissed it. 'I was going to throw this all away, but Lia thought you might want some of it.'

'I thought we could go through it,' Lia said. They dragged the boxes into the living room, stacking them against one wall, next to their father's shelves of medical journals, and started opening them, one at a time.

'We'll throw the clothes,' Maynard decreed, 'as they won't fit us. We'll give them to charity.' (Lia, looking at the clothes, noticed that they would fit the brothers perfectly, but decided to not say anything.) Books, it was decided, would go onto any spare shelf space (with duplicates going to the city library) and medical equipment could be sold, or donated to hospitals. 'Anything personal, we should deal with that case-by-case.'

They had been going for hours – at that point, knee-deep in old trinkets, faded photographs, illegible (unfilled) prescriptions, painful-looking medical instruments – when Maynard found the chest. It was nondescript but locked, so he had to crowbar it open, snapping some of the wood around the lip. Inside was a mass of papers, of print and handwriting, maps, drawings, letters and journals.

'This is incredible,' he said to Erwin, trying to get his brother to ask him what was incredible, but Erwin just kept filing books on the shelves and discarding hundreds of silk ties: gifts given at every opportunity to their father for want of anything else to gift. 'There's letters here from our grandfather, it looks like, and his father. Further back, as well.' Erwin still wasn't interested. 'Some of these aren't even in English,' Maynard told him, and Erwin nodded. He left the room soon afterwards and went to the bathroom where he thought of Aurelia, wondering when he might get to see her again, trying to not catch his own eye in the mirror.

Downstairs, Lia was having doubts that she had never – when she was a child, spending hours dreaming of her wedding day, picturing it, picturing her future husband – ever imagined. She thought of Erwin, of his current mood, of how little she actually knew him, and she wondered if she was making the right decision. Then she remembered her father, dead, and how alone she was, and she sighed and pressed the keys on Maynard's piano in a vague approximation of his song.

That night, after a dinner of left-over cold meats – Erwin was in no mood to cook a stew, much to Lia's relief – they all went to bed as normal. In their room, Erwin wept, and Lia expected herself to as well, but she didn't. Instead they had sex again, their hands running over as much of each other's bodies as they could manage comfortably, as far as reach and Lia's slight modesty would allow. The bed shifted across the floor under their collective weight, but they didn't notice until they were finished, the bed sighing – groaning – as Erwin disembarked. That night it was his turn to lie awake, listening to Lia sleep, glancing up at her, at the flutter of her eyelids. After a while he saw light from the hallway, seeping in through the gap under his bedroom door. It was coming from Maynard's room, so Erwin crept out and down the hall. The room, usually cluttered, was a disaster; torn apart almost, every surface covered in papers and photographs, drawings, etchings, hand-scrawled letters.

'This is our family,' Maynard told him, excitedly, 'this is what's left of them, all of them.' Erwin leafed through some of the letters, utterly illegible, due to either the handwriting or the language that they used.

'Where's it all from?'

'I assume it's passed down,' Maynard said. Erwin watched as Maynard put papers in piles as he came across them. 'Generation to generation, as they say.'

'I miss him, you know,' Erwin said, and then he started crying. Maynard dropped everything, put his arms around his brother and held him, his shirt being doused for the second time that day.

They sat on Maynard's floor until it was nearly light, Maynard reading as much of the papers as he could understand, Erwin helping him by sorting them into a chronological order, if he could find one. When the first one was done – for a man called Bellamy Sloane, their earliest easily-readable ancestor (there was one that preceded him, but his story was written in Spanish) – Maynard read it in silence, Erwin watching his lips move as they ran over the words. When he was finished he sighed, waking Erwin from his near-sleep. Erwin asked him what was wrong, and Maynard told him the story, pieced together from the letters and journals that he had found.

When Bellamy Sloane heard about a trip to what was being termed 'The New World', a trip that needed people to man a ship called The Mayflower, *he immediately offered his services. He needed employment – his mother had recently passed away, and his father had never been known (as, by all accounts, his mother had been that sort of woman in her youth) – and his desire to leave Billericay – a small town with few opportunities for a youth as intelligent as he felt he was – was great. There were places for staff on the boats, with the promise of a new life when they reached the other side, and the right to claim land of their own. They were to travel to Virginia, newly settled by some of their countrymen, and help them establish a more powerful colony there. There were rumours of natives, savages* who could not be reasoned with, so the travellers were packing weapons, flintlocks and muskets, just in case. Bellamy married his wife, Letys, a week before the trip, and they set off. Nobody seemed sure of how long the trip would take. They left Plymouth on September 6th, and finally landed on November 11th, just inside the hook tip of Cape Cod – and some way off from their original destination – and when they landed searched for a name to claim the land as their own.

'Let's call it Plymouth!' the wealthier men decreed (thus beginning a tradition of naming everything after the things that they tried to leave behind; travelling further than almost anybody else, and yet not actually going anywhere). They established camp that evening, asking Bellamy to head out with a party of fellow workers and kill something fresh for their dinner. 'We must eat from the land now!' they shouted. Bellamy killed a boar, and that evening they ate their first proper meal – one that hadn't been buried in salt – in months. When they awoke the next morning they saw the native people standing at the edge of their camp. 'Get your gun,' Bellamy was told.

As it happened, the natives were friendly. Bellamy spoke to them gently, brokering a tepid peace, showing them tricks and explaining who they were. He used cinder to make fire where they were rubbing sticks and stones; showed them the effects of gunpowder on local animals; cooked them meals using some of the seasoning that they brought on the ship. 'Can you believe it?' he asked Letys one evening, 'they have no idea that you can eat eggs!' (They did, of course, but they were being polite.)

The male immigrants began treating the land as if it were theirs. 'We had thought that we would be alone,' said one.

'The natives will get restless,' claimed another, 'the savage always wants what he cannot have.'

'Have you seen the way that they stare at our women?' asked a third, which they hadn't – because the women were not being stared at – but it planted an idea. The gossip – about the natives being evil, deadly, rapists, even witches – spread throughout the camp. Bellamy's strong sense of moral propriety – or maybe his possessiveness – turned his thoughts to protection, so he went to the elders.

'We have the guns,' he said. From then on, the 'Indians' were not allowed into the camp of the 'civilised' people when there were no men around – or, more specifically, when there was nobody there who knew how to fire a gun, and wasn't scared of killing another living person. They were not allowed to eat together, or to share any of the food, and some of the livestock was corralled from the land into pens, to draw lines between the two peoples. A couple of weeks in, two of the natives were shot for 'staring lustily at the wives of certain of the men'. This was the breaking point. Hastily built walls were erected to keep the natives out, and to keep the white womenfolk in. The men went out on to find local animals that could be killed or reared. They pushed their boundaries further every day, knowing that the natives had nothing to equal their weaponry, or their resolve. They feared no reprieve.

Eventually they had basic housing constructed, farming sheds made, crops planted. The first children were born, and lists of laws and rules were drawn up to be followed. Bellamy and Letys got on with their lives, pushing their way up the (extremely limited) social ladder, expecting their first child, and enjoying the new, quiet normality of their new life.

Soon enough, the settlers took to employing the natives for work – mostly cleaning, but also cooking, and, on occasion, sex. Bellamy and Letys eventually had enough chickens that they were able to pay for a woman to come in and clean their dirty clothes whilst Letys, in her pregnant enormity, stayed splayed on their bed. Her name was unpronounceable to him, so he just grunted at her, instead. [Unpronounceable Name] would come in the morning and take their clothes to the river, wash them, then return and cook them a broth from animal bones and potatoes. She would watch them as they ate their lunch, smiling her toothless smile, and then Bellamy would escort her out of the compound. There, in the outside world, hidden behind a cluster of trees, he would have sex with her, and when it was finished he would pay her in eggs. As he lay in bed at night next to his wife and unborn child, he wondered if it was possible to be in love with a woman that he couldn't even communicate with.

Bellamy's relationship with [Unpronounceable Name] began to preoccupy his days. He didn't know why he thought about her as much as he did; after all, he reassured himself, in Letys he had found a reasonably bright and moderately attractive wife willing to dote on him and bear his child. With [Unpronounceable Name] he had found somebody who, in theory, he was attracted to for no reason other than the physical; the roundness of her hips, the darkness of her hair and skin, the strict tautness of her stomach. When he made love with Letys she complained that it hurt, and just lay back and waited for him, stale and dull. [Unpronounceable Name] made noises, bucked, and spoke in stilted circular patterns, repeating herself in an attempt to make him understand her, always to no avail. As he slept, this dark-skinned, toothless woman was the subject of his most desperate fantasies.

A month later, Letys felt an ache.

'I think it's coming!' she howled, so Bellamy went out and had sex with his native against their fence. When it was done he told her to leave forever.

'This has to end now,' he told her, 'for I have a child coming, and responsibilities.' She didn't understand, so he slapped her face, hard enough to break the skin, to bruise her eye, and she ran. Back at his new home his wife was breathing deeply, surrounded by some of the other women, there to help her.

'Stand back!' they instructed Bellamy, so he did, walking around the rim of the camp. In the distance he could see the natives assembled, where [Unpronounceable Name]'s lover had examined her cut, her bruise, and was coming to get Bellamy with ten of his men. He ran towards the camp, and Bellamy saw [Unpronounceable Name] clutching her cheek, and knew what was happening.

'They are coming!' he shouted. 'They want to take back their land!' The settlers rallied around, grabbing guns. 'They want our wives, our children!' shouted Bellamy, louder this time, and the men around him roared their disapproval. This was to be war. They fired their rifles, and tore through the advancing Indians, picking the stragglers and injured off with their flintlocks and their swords as they tried to crawl away. Bellamy headed towards [Unpronounceable Name], who crouched cowering, nursing a native man's ruined and bloody body. She shook as she wept.

'Bellamy,' shouted one of the other settlers, 'is she not your worker?' Bellamy didn't answer; instead, he raised his gun and shot her in the chest.

That evening, his wife gave birth to a son. 'We'll name him Plymouth,' Bellamy decided, 'after Plymouth.'

When Maynard had finished reading neither brother said a word, just turned over and lay on their backs, staring at the ceiling. They slept soon after that, the light still on, both thinking about their father: Maynard was grateful that he had found this way of seeing into their past, a way that he could almost connect with his father even though he was gone. Erwin was grateful that he could start the next day afresh, with the worst of it over. He dreamt of Aurelia's dark skin, and when he woke up crept to the pile of photographs that Maynard had sorted through. There, buried halfway down, was a picture of them all as a family, the Sloane boys as children, their parents looking happy, holding each other. Erwin took the picture and folded it into his wallet, then crept back to his bedroom, putting himself onto the floor at the side of the bed before Lia ever realised that he had gone anywhere.

A new day meant that Erwin was back at work, though he cried off again at lunch, telling his boss that he couldn't stop thinking about his father, and he couldn't concentrate on his work (which was, for once, absolutely true). He left and went to Aurelia's brothel, where he had to wait for her to finish with another customer (a bloated whale of a man, whose groin-fat inflated his trousers to near comedic proportions, and made Erwin feel slightly ill when he saw her bid him farewell in the doorway, a blown kiss and a smile just like the ones that she gave him).

'I wash now,' she said, and then disappeared, leaving him there with the fish for a few minutes. They gawped at Erwin through the glass. When Aurelia reappeared she was in a new negligee, bright red, cheap lace like a doily along the top, attached by puckered seams to the even cheaper silk. 'You come now,' she said. They went into her room, stripped each other perfunctorily, and then Erwin climbed on top of her. It was basic and blunt, and when he was done he started to get dressed. She reached over and rubbed his back. 'You are not here?'

'I'm distracted,' he said, qualifying what she meant. 'My father died.'

'You father?' She pointed to her belly.

He shook his head. 'No, my father. My *padre*.'

'*¿Su padre?*'

'Yes,' he said. 'He's dead. *Morte*. He had a heart attack.' He was, he realised, crying, and she held him (because, he supposed, it was all that she knew how to do). 'I never said goodbye,' he sobbed, and then pulled the family portrait from his pocket. Aurelia leant over and peered at the picture.

'He much like you,' she said first, it taking her a second to register who the man was. Her memories of what people look like were often tempered by the red lights, by the angles from which she spent most of her time viewing them from, by her trying to maintain as little eye contact with her clients as possible. Then it hit her – that the man in the picture was Ezra – and she felt the breath punched out of her, her gut closing in on itself in a fist. 'He is dead?' she asked, and Erwin nodded. 'What was his name?' She trembled as she asked it; Erwin mistook it for her voice's natural vibrato.

'Ezra.'

'Eh-sra,' she nearly repeated.

'Anyway.' He wiped his eyes with tissues from the table on the side of the bed that he had shared, unknowingly, with his father, and put the picture back in his wallet. 'I should go. Get back to my family.' He left her still sitting on the bed, and when her boss came in to tell her that her next client had arrived Aurelia barely reacted.

Ezra, had he been alive, would have told his family that they had done everything wrong with regard to his funeral. He would have chosen a burial service, for starters, whereas they went with a basic blessing preceding a cremation. Post-service they opened their house to anybody who wanted to come for the wake, having put an announcement in the obituaries section of the newspaper listing the date and time – and they put out enough food and drink to feed many of the borough's homeless population. Ezra had always felt that wakes were crass. The wake wasn't for Ezra, however; really, it was for his erstwhile wife. She seemed, ostensibly, to be absolutely fine. She had mourned when she lost her husband for the first time, and had had no contact with him since the subtle delivery of divorce papers that occurred six months previously – when Ezra had arrived at the doorstep and left the envelope on the front mat, running off before anybody could see him, not realising that Evelyn had spied him through the living room windows. By the time of his death she felt comfortable with his absence (having been through every stage of grief already, and managed to arrive on the other side) and so drank whiskey with his business associates, flirted with his old college room-mates, lounged on the sofa accepting gifts of commiseration from various medical instrument suppliers that Ezra used to have dealings with. The brothers did their best, or the best that they were able at the time; Maynard played the piano, and Erwin spoke to people that he knew, being polite, but willing them to move along and leave the house, thinking of Aurelia the entire time. (Everything on the buffet table reminded him of her: the prawns reminded of the skin on her toes; the quiche her cheeks, her yellow skin caked in blusher; the red wine that stained the teeth of everyone at the party letting him see her mouth wherever he turned.) Lia served food, walking around with a tray.

'Stick with what you know, I guess,' she said to Maynard on her third pass around the party. He played her some jaunty music to accompany her passing by, and then returned to his piece (which, the guests all agreed, was both wonderful and haunting and reminded them of everything yet sounded like nothing). Erwin held a corner of the room and took the brunt of the platitudes.

'He was a wonderful man,' agreed Joshua Mandlebraum and Frank Waits, standing in the corner, waiting to talk to the mother. Erwin had to bite his tongue to stop himself from correcting them. The women in attendance, for their part, seemed to know nobody else there, hovering around the drinks and doorways like dust-mites. The mother watched them from her seat and made sure to laugh extra loudly at whoever was charming her, to make sure that the gaggle saw her enjoying herself, emotionally done with Ezra Sloane.

'I don't care how they knew him; if they knew him that way, intimately, or if they were just acquaintances, clients,' Evelyn told Lia as they fetched a load of glasses from the kitchen. 'I don't care. I was there before them.'

When everybody had left, the mother was first to bed – Ezra having to help her upstairs as she swayed – the after-effects of the alcohol – and Maynard and Lia cleaned glasses. When he came downstairs Erwin opened a bottle of whiskey, and they all drank from it, taking swigs, not saying a word as they passed the bottle around, before passing out, one by one, like dominoes. Erwin woke up hours later, took himself to bed, stumbling up the stairs, banging the doors, feeling sick. When Maynard woke he had slumped across the sofa towards Lia, and was resting his head on her shoulder. He eased himself away from her, covered her in a blanket, and went upstairs. An hour later Lia opened her eyes, found herself alone, and retreated to the bedroom that she shared with her soon-to-be-husband. Erwin had taken the bed. She lay on the rug that he had been keeping on the floor, but couldn't get herself comfortable, so just spent the night lying there, staring at the light bleeding through the cracks in the door from the hallway, light that was coming from Maynard's room.

7

Maynard felt a hibernation growing inside himself. He had watched as his brother and Lia seemed to get closer, and he felt jealous – though if it was of the relationship or of Lia, he couldn't say, or didn't know. The feelings were exacerbated when he saw how unhappy his brother was at their father's wake, with none of that unhappiness appearing to come from the mourning that they were going through. He saw Erwin, and saw how he was with Lia, and he wondered why he couldn't just be a bit happier.

The day after the wake Maynard rose early, having barely slept, and he remembered the smell of Lia's hair – like fruit and red wine – and finished the clearing up that they had started the night before. The rest of the house was asleep so he made himself breakfast, worked at his piano, wrote a (clumsy but heart-felt) poem, and then was just starting to prepare lunch when he heard a soft rapping on the front door. He answered it to a girl, short and blonde and, he thought, very pretty indeed.

'Hi,' she held out her hand. 'I'm Wendy Bathulur; I was Ezra's assistant.' Maynard shook her hand. 'I'm here for the wake.' After Maynard had explained to her that she had missed it – she cursed when he told her – he offered to make her something for lunch.

'I've got stuff in,' he said, so they went into the kitchen where he put together the sandwiches that were already on the menu. (He made them slowly, and with far more attention, and put garnish on the side of the plates when he was done.) They spent their mealtime talking about Ezra – Wendy talking, Maynard listening, nodding. After lunch they decided to go for a walk around the park, then went for a drink at a bar on 5th, for dinner at a tourist-heavy place in the theatre district, then decided on the spur of the moment to catch a performance of a new musical just off Times Square. Wendy smoked constantly, obnoxiously pot-pourri perfumed cigarettes whose packets proudly announced that they were imported from France. When the day was done Maynard kissed her, pressed her up against a lamppost, and she invited herself back to the Sloane house, where they snuck upstairs together, avoiding the creaky floorboards, shutting the doors softly. His family sat in the living room as they snuck in, listening to their giggles. Erwin seethed; the mother sighed, happy for her son (though had she known that it was Wendy he was with, she would have been less happy, as she always believed that the assistant was the woman that Ezra left her for); Lia bit her nails. That night Maynard only thought of his brother's fiancée once while he and Wendy made love, and when they had finished they slept together in his single bed, curled up next to each other.

'This is nice,' Maynard said before they fell asleep.

In the middle of the night Maynard awoke, thirsty, so he clambered out of the bed (where Wendy was sleeping soundly) and headed downstairs. He had just finished pouring from the pitcher that they kept in the refrigerator when he was met in the dark by Lia, their bodies bumping each other, putting them in an embrace in the pitch darkness. They kissed without saying a word, neither one absolutely positive that they weren't kissing their actual partners, and yet not stopping to ask or check. When they broke off from the kiss Lia ran back upstairs, unsurprised to find Erwin still there. Maynard waited at the sink, finished his glass of water, and wondered why the woman that he kissed didn't taste of cloves and French tobacco and rose petals.

Early the following morning Wendy and Maynard sat on the end of his bed and debated whether to tell the rest of the family about their relationship. Wendy's argument was strong: their love was great, and they would want to show it in public as often as possible. (Wendy was a great romantic, if not slightly premature.) Maynard's argument won out in the end, however; being that his mother believed Wendy to have had an affair with his father, and given that his father had been in the ground – or, in an urn, mounted on a stumpy plinth – for only two days, he felt it tasteless. Wendy kissed him, a full, lingering kiss and left the house. Maynard tasted the tobacco again, and lay on his bed for what seemed like hours, listening to her heels on the street as she walked halfway across the city to her apartment. Eventually the rest of the house woke up, so Maynard made breakfast. Lia and Erwin were already downstairs; Maynard listened as Lia asked if she and Erwin might go for a walk in the park, or perhaps to eat a meal together in a restaurant. Erwin grunted and shook his head.

'You can't just take a day off when you feel like it, not in my business,' he said. He slammed the door on his way out, and Lia stormed upstairs. Maynard put down his spatula and went to follow his brother, to calm him down, but their mother, sitting at the kitchen table, almost completely back to her old self – the woman that she was before the divorce – told Maynard to leave him be.

'It's all to do with your father,' she said. 'Erwin needs to work things through. You worry about him too much; you forget to worry about yourself.' She was drinking coffee – which Maynard knew she never drank – and her wig was different, more styled. Maynard sat down in agreement.

'Your hair looks nice, by the by.'

'I'm thinking of changing it!' she said. 'Maybe buying something in red, maybe, or a black. I've never thought of myself as the sort of person who could have black hair, but maybe I am.'

'What's prompted this?' Maynard asked.

'Nothing,' the mother said, going back to her coffee, and reading the newspaper. A few minutes later Lia came downstairs to eat her breakfast with them, and she smiled through it, trying to keep as good a humour going as she could manage.

Maynard's hand brushed against Lia's as they washed up the dirty breakfast dishes. She smiled at him as she left to get herself ready for the day (as she was taking the mother shopping). Maynard wondered how long he had to wait before he could go to his piano, so that it didn't seem too obvious. Lia went back upstairs to do her make-up, and had to apply it three times as her tears kept getting in the way.

'I'm so lonely,' she sobbed to herself, thinking about how much she missed her father, and how Erwin was the only replacement she had in her life.

That afternoon, Erwin stood in the waiting room with the fish, waiting for Aurelia. The madam told him that she had left, and they didn't have an address for her.

'We can give you someone else?' she said, so Erwin nodded. In the room – the same room that he once shared with Aurelia (and his father, and hundreds of other men) – he tried to act just as he had before but this girl – from Eastern Europe, and full of what many would call Slavic charm – didn't do anything for him.

'Do you mind if we don't?' he asked her.

'*Nyet*,' she replied.

8

The months went quickly. Maynard spent more time with Wendy, eventually bringing her to meet the family – the mother didn't react at all, and he wondered if he was ever really concerned that she would – and dragging their relationship into the open. He quit his job in the most inconspicuous of ways; one morning he announced that he had been let go, so would be pursuing other, more creative endeavours. In reality he just hadn't gone into work in weeks, and had been fired, but Maynard blamed it on cutbacks, and nobody questioned him. Lia and Erwin, at Lia's constant prompting (for want of something to do; primarily to stop her thinking about how shabby her life had become), began to plan their wedding, working with the mother to realise all the details. Lia had ways that she thought the day would go, and Erwin didn't care. For his part, he dove into the role of being the family's primary breadwinner, working harder and for longer hours. He began seeing a selection of women, all of them paid for. When Erwin and Lia bickered as they all ate dinner – something that they did regularly – Wendy and Maynard gripped each other's hands, because they knew that they would never bicker like that (as Wendy loved Maynard so much, and Maynard didn't want Lia to think that he was anything like his brother). Lia would stare at their clutched palms after Erwin had invariably stormed off, and think about the time that she was sure she kissed Maynard in the kitchen.

Their living situation started to annoy everyone. Wendy had all but moved in, only unlike Lia she had come without an invitation. She would meet with Maynard most evenings and then come back with him, eat dinner with the rest of them and then stay the night. They had sex with a frequency and volume that far defeated Erwin and Lia – who almost never did, apart from nights where one of them got over-emotional, and even then they didn't talk before or after, just using each other as vessels.

'I can't stand listening to this,' Lia would say sadly as they tried to sleep, her still on the bed, Erwin still on the floor. 'We should move, maybe.' Erwin would nod in the darkness, or pretend that he was asleep; either way, Lia felt that she wasn't getting anywhere with him, and wasn't sure that she even wanted to. 'Why are you so sad?' she would ask, and he would shrug, again, through the darkness.

In Maynard's bedroom, Wendy would chat post-coitally for hours. She had an inability to whisper so Maynard continually tried to calm her, to tell her to go to sleep.

'You'll wake the house!' he told her, and then held her in the darkness, the smell of her cigarettes in her hair reminding him constantly of who she wasn't.

'But think about when we leave here; we can get married, have children. You can teach piano somewhere, a school.' She sounded excited, so Maynard kissed her. As he tried to sleep he pictured it; that future, that new house, that family. He managed to see it all, with one vital exception; the wife was always Lia.

The tension in the house wasn't helped by the fact that Lia and Wendy refused to make any real attempts at friendship, relying instead on the early hostility that rivals cultivate. They skirted around each other when left alone, avoiding eye contact when possible, and each of them fought for the maximum approval of the mother.

'Can I knit you something, Evie?' one would ask, before the other offered 'something to eat?' or the promise of a 'shopping trip, to buy a new wig?' They waited on her hand and foot (something that she despised since getting her health back, but hadn't told them), constantly undermining each other; 'That knitwear is terribly ill-fitting,' or 'Oh! That bread had gone stale!' or 'That wig really seems like it isn't your colour.'

And so it went on. Erwin and Maynard didn't notice it, being caught in their own worlds. Erwin wondered how to go through with this marriage to a woman that he didn't really love, or how to get out of it. Maynard wondered how to work out who he loved in the first place.

One morning, a month before his wedding, Erwin awoke to the sounds of an argument downstairs. Lia had asked the mother for her opinion on the colour of the bridesmaid's dresses, and the mother had suggested that she ask Wendy, and Wendy had suggested a lilac, presumptively thinking about how good she looked in purple. Lia then suggested that it was a selfish decision designed to ruin her wedding, and Wendy took umbrage, insisting that she would never be so underhand. They were talking in raised voices, not quite shouting. Erwin stood in the hallway and listened to them argue for a while before he went into the bathroom that he had so proudly installed and locked the door. He pulled his pocket knife from his trousers and slit his throat as he stared at his face in the mirror, thinking how much he looked like his father. The blood splashed over his shoes, and then he fell, with a thud, to the hard floor. As he lay there he remembered the last time that he had spoken to Ezra.

Ezra had visited Erwin one night, drunk on scotch and beers. He sat on the end of the bed and sighed, and Erwin asked what was wrong. Ezra shook his head. Erwin asked what his plans were for the next few days. He wanted to take his father to show him the building that he had been working on, an incredible glass thing near the World Trade Center, and that weekend would be the perfect opportunity. Ezra made his apologies, claiming that he had too much work. (He was, in fact, just aware that he was about to leave them all.) 'I can't come, and I'm sorry,' he had said, 'but I'm so proud of you, son.' Erwin had stared at his face for longer than he ought, knowing that something was up, but desperately happy with the burning sense of paternal approval that he had just gained.

Erwin thought of that as he felt the warm blood pump from

his neck, washing up around his cheeks, soaking his hair, lining his lips like cheap red wine.

9

Erwin Sloane was, as best Maynard could tell, as good as dead. Maynard had heard the thud, and run upstairs to discover the fluttering, twitching body on the floor. The ambulance was there within minutes.

'He won't stop bleeding!' Maynard shrieked as they ran up the stairs, loaded his brother onto a stretcher. 'His body is cold!' They invited Maynard to ride with them to the hospital; he sat back, terrified, as they worked on Erwin as they drove.

'We need blood!' was the last thing Maynard heard from the doctors as they ran down the halls of the hospital, leaving him at the flapping entrance doors to the waiting room. The people around him stared at the shock of blood down his shirt and cream trousers.

'He lost a lot of blood,' the doctor told Maynard. 'I've never seen anybody survive losing that much. He was the colour of the sheets.' When the doctor had gone Maynard stood there and wondered if hospital bedding was white or blue, and if it mattered either way.

When he was finally allowed in, Erwin couldn't speak, or even grunt, and his eyes stayed shut. The doctors told Maynard that Erwin had nicked the vocal cords, and might have trouble speaking when he woke up. They didn't know when that would be. (Maynard started thinking up a series of catch-all answer cards that he could create for his brother, allowing him to carry them around when he got out of here. Some of the answers included, 'Yes,' 'No,' and, 'Give me some time to think on that one. I'll get back to you.') He sat and spoke to Erwin for hours, well past standard visiting hours, right into the night-time and beyond.

'I love you, Erwin,' he said, something that was rarely spoken, and then he read him another story from their father's chest, whether Erwin was listening or not.

Plymouth Sloane, named after both the place where he lived and the place that his parents had come from, had always had trouble sleeping. His mother, Letys, would come to his room at night when he was a child and reassure him that the noises that he heard, that kept him awake, were not real; that they were just a part of his dreams. But in the morning, his father, Bellamy, would tell him that she was lying.

'She's trying to protect you. There are things out there that can kill you, son; things that will kill you. That's what makes the noise.' The seven-year-old boy would then have trouble sleeping the following night, pulling his bed-sheets higher, and squeezing his eyes shut. The noise continued unabated. Some nights, despite knowing that it had to be the wind and the river, a combination of the two, even Bellamy wondered where it came from.

Plymouth's parents were perpetually busy. Bellamy super-vised building work as they assembled the beginnings of new towns further inland, with more settlers arriving almost weekly, and Letys worked for the committee that registered the new arrivals, determining where they were able to work – and live – when they landed, depending on their skills and talents and wealth. As soon as Plymouth was old enough he took a job with a trapper, learning how to catch animals and prepare their skins and meats for sale. Plymouth's first role was to clean the skins in the river and cut the flesh from the inside of the hide. When it was done he dried the skin over a flame. Even as he grew older he worried about the noises at night, always wondering if they were wolves, or natives, or that intangible something worse that he could never put his finger on. Whilst he slept, or tried to, his parents had conversations about him, where they wondered why he hadn't yet started seeing the local girls.

'Some are late starters,' argued Letys, but Bellamy worried.

'I think that you should talk to him,' he said, and that was that. (That night Bellamy dreamt of the native woman that he used to love, and heard the wind/river as her dying screams.)

The next day, as Plymouth was cleaning the skin of a buffalo, black and coarse, like stubble, his mother appeared as ordered. She sat on a log behind her son and asked him about the process. He ran through it; how he washed the skin first, then pulled the longer in-growing hairs, then the flesh, and how he then made fists in the skin from the outside, allowing him to scrub the inside properly, tearing off the small white chunks of fat that were left.

'Does this make you happy?' Letys asked.

'Sometimes,' he replied.

'What about a woman? Would that make you happy?' she asked, and he shook his head.

'I don't have the time,' he replied.

'Plymouth,' said his mother as she gathered up her dress to step over the log and head back to the town, 'that is all that any of us truly have.' That evening, whilst he slept, he dreamt of women as tall as ships, with teeth as large as knives swooping in towards him from their hiding place on the moon. He woke up, sweating and erect, and stood outside their house listening to the noise for as long as he could stomach it.

From that day onwards his parents had a plan. They organised dinner parties with their friends, all of whom seemed to have daughters of the right age. They would sit around the table eating whatever meat Plymouth had brought home from work (and this would be referenced repeatedly, the manly way *in which the food was provided for the table), and talk would invariably wind its way around to marriage.*

'Oh, well,' indicating the daughter, usually seated next to Plymouth, and usually too shy to remove her bonnet until her mother instructed her, 'she hasn't been allowed to court, yet. We think she's just coming to the right age,' they would say, at which point Bellamy would grab the thread and unravel it.

'Plymouth hasn't had the time, have you son?' He would do something fatherly then, like placing his hand on Plymouth's shoulder. 'He's been working to establish his career. Maybe you two should spend some time getting to know each other?' The parents would then all retire to a different room, leaving Plymouth and the girl to sit and talk. It would usually be minutes before either of them said a word, and then they would discuss their mutual acquaintances, and then Plymouth would ask if she had ever listened – really listened – to the river and the wind, and they would sit on the porch and do just as he promised: listen. (She would be expecting him to make a romantic advance as they sat there on the bench, but he was too intent on catching whatever sounds bounced off the trees.) The parents would find them sitting there, and they would leave, dismayed, and then discuss the rejection with their daughter as they walked home, invariably coming to the conclusion that Plymouth was 'stunted, or underdeveloped'. (He was neither.) The next day, Letys would visit Plymouth again at the river and quiz him about the evening previous.

'What was wrong with this one?' she asked him once, talking about the girl that had visited the previous evening, Jane Plaskett, a busty girl whose parents were some of the richest farmers in the area.

'Nothing,' Plymouth told her, 'she just wasn't for me.'

'How do you know what is for you,' asked the mother, standing next to him in the shallow water as he plucked a thick

bush of hairs from the underside of the hide with his teeth, 'if you won't try?' He shrugged. 'Plymouth Sloane,' she said, 'it won't be long before you have to take a wife. Make a choice, before people start to wonder how much you really do care about your community. We've asked Jane and her family back tonight. Try harder this time.' When she had gone Plymouth raised the hide to his face to cover the tears that had unexpectedly started pouring down his face.

That evening they ate boar. As always, the youngsters were left after dinner, and Plymouth took Jane to the bench. There, amongst the wind and the river, he moved closer to her and took her hand, and she smiled at him, nearly as shy as he was. He didn't smile back, as he was concentrating so hard on the sounds of nature. Their courtship continued for the next few weeks with no forward movement of physical intimacy. Jane was happy to sit with him and listen – she was dull in her own pursuits, so went along with whatever he wanted – but after weeks without a kiss she started to worry, and spoke to her mother who, in turn, went to Letys. Letys then went to the river, as had become a routine.

'Why haven't you kissed her?' she asked, and Plymouth told her that he didn't know if he wanted to. 'Well,' Letys said, 'she wants you to. She wants you, Plymouth, so take her.' She left him skinning a ferret; barely enough to cover one eye's worth of tears as he clutched it to his face.

That evening Plymouth led Jane into the woods. There, surrounded by the wind and the roar of the river that he so loved and was so scared of, he kissed her, and didn't stop. Instinct kicked in. When it was finished Jane ran home, and within the hour her parents were at his house, demanding marriage. 'She could be pregnant!' they shouted. They married a week later, and at the party, he sloped upstairs.

'Where's the groom?' the attendees shouted. 'Where's

Plymouth?' Bellamy searched for him throughout the house, finally finding him in his bedroom. The door wouldn't open, so he peered in through the crack. Plymouth was standing on his chair, rope around his neck, the door blocked by his bed. And then he stepped off, the sound of the wind and the river rushing into the room as the blood rushed from his head, before drifting off to absolute darkness. Bellamy howled. Eight months later Jane gave birth to a son, and named him Roscoe.

Erwin didn't say a word, and when Maynard had finished reading it was dark outside, so he let his brother sleep. At home, Maynard lay in his bed next to Wendy.

'I wish I knew why he did it,' he told her.

'He never seemed very happy,' Wendy said, 'he always seemed like there was something on his mind.'

'Only since my father left,' Maynard told her. 'He's only been that way since then.' As they tried to sleep Maynard found himself distracted. He could hear Lia downstairs in the kitchen, sobbing. He thought about going downstairs to console her, play the piano, do anything that he could to make her feel better, but he fell asleep before he could decide if it was appropriate or not.

The next day Maynard went back to the hospital early. Lia had decided to stay at home until Erwin woke up – she was worried that she was to blame for his attempt on his life, and didn't want to upset him if he didn't want her there – so Maynard took the message from her, and the next story fr their father's chest. When he arrived Erwin's room was em

'Where has he been moved to?' Maynard asked the on duty, and she asked what he meant. 'My brother, fourteen. He's gone.'

'I've just come on shift,' she said, 'so I'l

Maynard watched her approach a group of doctors at the end of the hall. He saw one of them mouth the word 'died', clear and distinct, the syllable moving from the teeth to the lips, hard at both ends. The nurse walked back over and asked Maynard if he'd go with her to a private room. There he asked her if he could see Erwin's body, and the nurse shook her head. 'I'm sorry,' she told him, 'but the body was destroyed. For hygiene reasons.' Maynard asked her why and she said that she didn't know, but she'd look into it, and she left him alone. He kicked a chair out of anger, but they were built sturdily, to take it.

The doctor who declared Erwin dead went down the stairs at the back towards the morgue, then turned left, through the fire escape doors at the end of the corridor. There, in the paper gown that he had been wearing, was Erwin.

'It's done,' the doctor said, and handed Erwin a bag of medicines and his blood-soaked clothes. Erwin nodded, gave the doctor the wallet from his trousers and thanked him, then staggered off, away from the hospital.

Upstairs, Maynard sat all night on the plastic chairs that lined the walls of the waiting room. When the next morning rolled around he could barely move. As he pulled himself to his feet, knowing that he had to walk home to tell the mother – to tell Lia – what had happened, he wondered how any of them could come back from this.

At the same time, the mother answered the front door to the postman, and a letter from the hospital, her name and the details crudely typed onto a generic formatted letter. She paused to think about the china that she only seemed to bring out when somebody died, and then went out to visit the undertaker. She forgot to tell Lia about the letter; she was still ng in Erwin's bed, worrying about what she was going to when she next saw her fiancé, and how she was going to

60

ask him if he tried to kill himself because of her.

When she finally dressed and went downstairs Maynard was just coming in. She greeted him as she always did, with a wave and a smile, and he told her to sit down. He told her what had happened – or, at least, what he thought had happened – and she just sat there, wringing the tablecloth in her hands. Maynard fetched whiskey from the living room, and they both drank their fill on empty stomachs, neither of them speaking. Eventually, Maynard (slightly slurringly) broke the silence.

'If you need anything,' he started, but didn't get to finish the sentence as she leant in and kissed him. There was no pretending that they were kissing anybody else in the daylight of the kitchen, and neither of them cared. They kissed across the tablecloth, and then he led her upstairs to his bedroom. In Maynard's bed Lia noticed her engagement ring was still on her finger, and took it off, leaving it in his bedside drawer in case he saw it and felt guilty, and stopped.

The next few days were awful for both of them. Instantly filled with regrets – not at what they did, but more the circumstances in which they did it. The mother was the only one pretending to be in control. Lia and Wendy kept telling her how well she was holding up, but Maynard could see the cracks. He saw her hands shake when she held glasses; saw her eyes water when Erwin's name was mentioned; saw her scratch at her head through her wig, pulling hairs out from underneath it where they itched her. She refused to talk about Erwin, but that, Wendy reassured Maynard, was totally normal. You couldn't be expected to experience as much tragedy as she had suffered and not have to compartmentalise, she told him.

Maynard and Wendy spent their time enveloping each other; Lia assumed it was on Maynard's part a reaction to the infidelity that had been committed. Lia just watched, playing the part of the dutiful widow, wearing nothing but black. At night, she listened to Maynard and Wendy make love in his bedroom, and thought about what to put in a letter that she was planning to write; a letter that announced to her erstwhile and makeshift family her departure.

The funeral was held in a church, though without a body there wasn't much in the way of ceremony. Maynard made a speech, telling stories of what a happy child Erwin had been. Lia cried, the dutiful nearly-wife, and everybody consoled her with lies, saying the wrong thing. ('He loved you so, so much, you know,' was the most common platitude.) The mother sat silently and thought about how ruined – and ruinous – their lives had become. Wendy took Maynard's hand as they led the processional from the church.

'That was a beautiful speech,' she told him.

'It's a shame Erwin had to die for me to give it.' They walked in silence the rest of the way.

The wake featured most of the same characters as their father's had, apart from losing Ezra's women and gaining Erwin's burly workmates. It was a noticeably man-heavy affair, and they all stuck to their social groups, offering the mother their condolences in clusters. (One woman did come, but nobody saw her: Aurelia, who stood across the road and watched the house. She had read the announcement of Erwin's death in the newspaper, and wished to say goodbye to both Erwin and Ezra one last time. She had ceased whoring, having come to believe intercourse with her to be a curse that condemned her customers to death. She was thinking about a career in nursing.) The afternoon was winding down when Maynard saw his mother alone in the kitchen, standing by the sink. He could see in the light through the window that her whole body was shivering, almost vibrating, just as she used to when Ezra had first left. He approached her from behind, embraced her, and she rubbed his arm brusquely.

'Get back to the party,' she said.

'I'm worried about you.'

'I'm fine. Joshua Mandlebraum's looking for you, you know.'

'Okay.'

'You should go and talk to him.' The vibrations ran through her throat into her voice. 'Go.' She took his arm from being around her and shooed him off.

Joshua Mandlebraum – Josh, as he was known – and Ezra were the best of friends, knowing each other as both neighbours and school-friends, and not carrying any baggage into their friendship as a result. They were friends when they were just toddlers, they had raced each other up and down the street and looked at the stars and imagined what they might be when they grew up. They went to the same school and sat next to each other whilst they studied their five times tables. They played at lunch times, and they walked home together.

Soon, Ezra started to notice that Josh had a sister. Her name was Grace. He would knock on their front door and she would answer, and he would see her casually developing body through her soft cotton dresses. They would have flirted, if they had known what it was they were doing.

'You want Josh?' she would ask, and Ezra would nod furiously. He stammered when he saw her, so tried to not speak if he could help it. One such day he knocked and she answered. 'You want Josh? He's out the back.' Ezra walked through their lavish house – a demonstration of wealth over practicality, as marble busts of people they would never know stood at the foot of the stairs, and an ugly hairless dog that cost more than Ezra could imagine ran around yapping mindlessly – towards their garden. As he reached the window he saw his friend talking to

some younger girls. He looked at Grace and noted the bow in her hair, the new dress, and then saw a cake on a table, and realised that it was her birthday.

'Happy birthday, Grace,' he stammered, and she thanked him and leant over and kissed him on his cheek, a lingering kiss that pulled at his cheek's soft hairs, not yet stubble.

'Come outside,' she said to him as she opened the doors and guided him to the buffet. Across the yard full of blonde girls, Josh ignored him. 'It's meant to be my party, you know. I invited them all over, and they're ignoring me.' Grace reached across Ezra and took a piece of cheese skewered to some apple. 'From the way that he acts anyone would think he was the important one here.' Ezra noticed her hair falling over her face as she leant over to pick up a slice of quiche, and decided to make an invitation of his own.

'Do you want to throw a ball around some?'

Grace proved herself somewhat proficient at catching (mainly because Ezra threw terribly easy balls at her to bolster her confidence, and make the game last longer), and they spent the best part of the next hour just hurling the ball from one side of the street to the other. They found it hard to know what to say to each other, so the distance made this easier; they could only shout, and it meant that they could speak more slowly, more assuredly. Ezra was always thinking three lines of dialogue ahead. After they were done with their throwing they walked down to a local diner and bought ice creams, which they ate as they sat on the front steps of Ezra's house. Again, the food was useful, as they had time to plan the conversation in between bites. When they were done with that it was getting dark.

'I should get back to my party. My parents'll be wondering where I am.' Grace leant over and kissed him, this time closer to his mouth, so much that their lips touched at the corners, and Ezra felt his mouth open a little as he breathed, as the kiss *lasted for seconds. And then she was gone, and he stood on the sidewalk and felt like he was going to vomit.*

That evening, Ezra discovered onanism.

The next day Ezra went round to see Grace by way of seeing Josh. Josh suggested that they went to Central Park and threw the baseball around. Ezra agreed, and invited Grace without asking Josh's permission. As they threw the ball Josh seethed, and, despite the throwing game being a free for all, he barely touched the ball as Grace and Ezra threw it between themselves. After dinner that evening Ezra and Grace snuck out of their houses to meet in the middle of the road, where they properly kissed for the first time, clumsy and confused but perfect all the same. A week later, as with all the best loves, they were wrenched apart: Grace and Josh's parents told them that they were moving away from New York. They barely had time to tell Ezra before they were packing up their things and leaving for the train.

'I'll miss you every day,' said Ezra as they boarded at the station, but neither Grace nor Josh knew which one of them he was talking to. Many years later, after university, Joshua returned to the city and looked up his old friend. When Ezra — having only just started his practice and having not yet met his future wife — asked after Grace, Joshua told him that she was married. It was a lie, but Ezra never found out.

Joshua Mandlebraum's handshake was almost, Maynard discovered, violent.

'My brother was always fond of you,' Maynard told him as his arm flew up and down.

'And I of him, he was a good boy. He'll be missed.' They stood in silence, watching another young black family move in across the street, their furniture being carried by their family and friends into the house, everything that they struggled to get up the steps fresh, new, still wrapped in the plastic sheeting. They laughed as they heaved it through the door.

'The neighbourhood is going to pieces,' Mandlebraum said. 'I'd get out whilst you still can.'

'They're not hurting anyone,' Maynard told him, and the old man shook his head.

'Yet,' he said, 'they're not hurting anybody yet.'

'I can't uproot mother.'

'She'll appreciate it, in the long run.' He took out a cigarillo case, gingerly lifted one to his lips. 'Do you smoke?'

'Sometimes,' Maynard said, but didn't take one. He couldn't see Wendy anywhere, but wanted her to save him from the conversation. 'My father told me I shouldn't.'

'Your father was a wise man, and he smoked.' Mandlebraum smiled at Maynard. 'He would want you to move, you know. I was his oldest friend, I know these things.' He looked back at the family, now creased over with laughter as they struggled with a refrigerator up the stairs outside the house. 'The pigeons are acting like they're doves, Maynard. We're leaving, and you would be wise to do the same.' He handed Maynard a business card. 'He's a realtor. You call him.' Maynard pocketed the card and smiled at Mandlebraum, but he really didn't want to.

After the wake ended and the last guest left, the inhabitants of the Sloane house sloped off to bed without another word. The mother's wig looked haggard, and she shook as she undressed before bed, and shook as she took some of her sleeping pills, and shook as she lay waiting for sleep. Lia found herself unable to sleep in her dead fiancé's bed, and couldn't bear the thought of trying his floor-groove again, so took herself back downstairs to the hard leather sofa. Maynard lay with Wendy and thought about Lia, about what would happen if he tried to kiss her again. When he fell asleep he dreamt of Erwin in the bathroom slicing across his neck, then squeezing the hole shut before slicing it apart all over again, the blood running over his fingers as he tried to hold himself in place. In the dream, Maynard was downstairs, playing the piano.

10

Maynard watched it all fall apart over the following few weeks. Lia distanced herself from him, and wouldn't tell him why. They would meet in the kitchen and make food and not talk, and he would ask a question – about anything, the weather, maybe – and she would brush it off, waving her hand, ignoring him, busying with something else.

'What about what happened, between us?' he managed once, sandwiching her between the kitchen and the living room, and speaking in as quiet a voice as he could muster. 'Can we not talk about it?'

'We did something awful,' she said, and that was that. She had started to feel sick, both physically and emotionally, and couldn't bear to have Maynard pester her when Wendy wasn't around. He was tormented, and not sleeping, wanting to end everything with Wendy but having no excuse to do so. He still liked her, maybe even loved her, he reasoned, but his feelings for Lia were different, and ran stronger. She was all that he thought of when he cried for Erwin, and not from some fraternal duty. And the mother, for her part, had done what Maynard was most afraid of, months and months of good work undone in a heartbeat (or in the perceived lack of one).

'If Erwin were alive, he wouldn't have been able to bear what this has done to mother,' Maynard said to Wendy one morning. After three days of attempting to stay herself after Erwin's funeral she stopped wearing the wig, and two days after that didn't even bother to get dressed. From that point she stopped eating again, and she spoke less, more softly, and wouldn't instigate conversation. Maynard began to fear waking her up again. Wendy did basic medical diagnoses on her, and declared her depressed. ('I know that,' thought Maynard, but he didn't say anything.)

'They have a drug for that, now,' Wendy said, and came home one day with a jar full of bright blue pills stolen from her new workplace – a clinic in Brooklyn. 'Give her two of these,' she told Maynard, so he did, helping her take them in the mornings. The mother grew thinner every day and stopped making eye contact, and Maynard's worries grew. 'You have to let her be,' Wendy told him one day, stroking his hair to calm him. (Wendy didn't realise that Maynard was drifting from her, however. She wrote in her diary that 'Maynard is the man that I am going to marry,' and she totally believed it. She even found Lia's engagement ring in Maynard's bedside table one day, and assumed that it was to be given to her at some point, so didn't say a word about it to him. Lia, for her part, quite forgot that it was there, or had ever even really existed.) Maynard gave Evelyn the pills when she woke up, before food, as the bottle told him. She didn't even ask what they were. They didn't seen to make a difference. Maynard held her, and fed her, and told her that he loved her but it didn't revive her. She heard the words but didn't react, instead moving them inside her head where she dreamt of the time before the deaths, before her abandonment, when she and Ezra were happy and married still, with her sons around her, their lives ahead of them. She heard the declarations of love inside that dream, and smiled inside.

Maynard didn't hear his mother when she had her stroke. He didn't hear her choke, or splutter, and he didn't hear her yell because she couldn't. He didn't know a thing about it until he took her a bowl of soup, called for her to wake up, but she didn't; just as had happened so many times before, only this time it was for real. He dropped the tray, grabbed her body, saw her eyes roll backwards, and then shouted desperately for Lia to phone an ambulance. He sat in the bedroom holding her – the second of his relatives to die on his watch (or so he thought) and he howled.

The rules that they had to follow in order to bring Evelyn home from the hospital were hard to remember, given to Maynard on a piece of paper, numbered, and filled with jargon. The ambulance drove them to the front door and carried the mother upstairs, her face sloped and drawn. Maynard watched her swat at the men as they lay her on the bed.

'She'll sleep now,' Maynard was told. She was worse than they had hoped. When Maynard had been told that that it was a stroke he had read about the attack in the medical books, and decided that she would be fine, that it would impact her lifestyle a minimal amount. He had pictured her coming home in a cab, walking with a slight limp, having troubles at dinner time holding her knife, or maybe her fork (probably only one or the other, depending on the side), maybe slurring a little. The reality was far worse; she lay propped up in the bed because she could barely move, unable to speak, her pillow rapidly covered in drool. ('It could take years of therapy,' the doctor told Maynard, 'and even then, there are no guarantees.') Her eyes scanned the room, but they didn't seem to recognise anything. Maynard couldn't even be sure that she recognised him, but she cried when he told her that he loved her, which he took for a good sign. Wendy avoided the mother's bedroom altogether; Lia took her drinks, but didn't stay sitting with her, as she found her eyes terrifying, the way that they looked past you, through you. It didn't matter. This was, Maynard reasoned, a family matter, and he would deal with his mother himself, and he spent all his time doing so. The dust settled in on his piano.

Maynard was responsible for giving his mother three tablets thrice daily. She couldn't swallow them, her throat seemingly unable to perform the action needed to take tablets of that size, and they took far too long to dissolve in glasses of water, so Maynard devised a new way of delivering them into her system; he crushed them into a handkerchief with a pestle, all three in one go, and then held the powder up to his mother's mouth so that she inhaled them as dust. He then poured water into her mouth to wash the remnants away from her throat. The process made her cough violently for ten minutes, but, Maynard reasoned, at least he was giving her the medicine as instructed. He held the handkerchief to her mouth three times a day, and three times a day she partially choked as he tried to save her life. He looked in her eyes every time he finished, and just couldn't get over how sad she looked, every single time.

One morning Maynard looked in and the mother was awake.

'How are you feeling?' he asked. She nodded.

'I'm feeling a bit better,' she croaked. (She didn't look it, but he smiled, nonetheless.) 'Can I have my tablets?' By the time Maynard had fetched them, along with a fresh glass of water, she had passed out again. He spent the rest of the day wondering if that conversation had even actually happened...

It would have been all too easy for Maynard to make the simple mistake that killed his mother. His story was sound; he had crushed the tablets into their fine granules as he always did (and they were no less or more crushed than any other day) and he had poured the contents into the handkerchief, the same handkerchief that he used every other day. He had then, as normal, gently placed the handkerchief over his mother's mouth and briefly pressed down on it to create the illusion of a lack of air for his mother. She had then, as with every morning, attempted a sharp intake of breath to take the powders inside her lungs, where they would slowly absorb into her bloodstream. There was nothing untoward in the powders, nothing abnormal. They asked why there was wetness over his mother's face and pillow.

'I cried when I found her,' Maynard told the police who came to interview him and collect the body. They asked why the powder was still lining her mouth, why Maynard had not attempted to wash it away as he did every other morning. 'I was shocked by her coughing and I didn't even think about it.' But when they asked him why his mother's face was pink and bruised where he had pressed his hand down hard upon her mouth, Maynard simply cried, and had no answer. (Upon discovering that she was dead, Maynard had spent ten minutes at the piano before calling for an ambulance. The house was otherwise empty, Wendy being at work and Lia out planning for her own departure, looking at ticket prices and places to travel to, not having told anybody of her intentions. Maynard sat with his fingers on the start keys, wondering if he could play his piece now, and maybe even finish it, but he couldn't. He had thought that the piece was about pain, about sorrow, about release; maybe, he realised, he was wrong.)

The police asked Maynard to accompany them to the station, to answer some questions. He sat in the waiting room to be processed, having left a note for Lia about where he was (and asking her to tell Wendy), and he read another story from his family history box as he waited for the detectives. It was the last thing that he would do before he was formally charged with the murder of Evelyn Sloane.

After the funeral of his mother, Roscoe Sloane discovered that it was assumed he would take over the care of his twin brother Buckley. Roscoe was an architect: he designed houses, and almost everybody in the area went to him. He had built the house that his mother had lived in – the same house that she died in – and it was a house that he now inherited, along with Buckley. Buckley had been born sideways, went the family myth. 'He sees things from a different angle,' was the punch line. Buckley rarely spoke, and when he did it never really counted as part of the conversation. Prior to her death, caring for him was their mother's full-time job; after it, that responsibility fell to Roscoe.

For the first three weeks after her death Buckley did little but pine. He would sit by the window, as she used to, and listen to the sound of the wind and the river. Roscoe put his mourning aside, taking any job that he was given (and he was given a lot over the first couple of weeks, many of them borne from sympathy or pity, as people searched for holes in their roofs that needed patching, or guttering that needed replacing). The towns were becoming more crowded, and need for his services had never been stronger. After each job, he and his men would end up drinking in local bars, and after a few rounds talk would turn, invariably, to Roscoe's private life.

'No woman yet?' they would ask, and he would smile.

'Not yet,' he would reply.

'Maybe you like it the other way?' they teased, and he told them that he liked women just fine, but had too much else to worry about.

'I have Buckley to care for,' he said, and they let it drop then. ('You can't tease the boy over a retard,' his hod-carrier remarked.) When he finished drinking he would stumble home, genuinely believing that his excuse was the absolute truth, and not realising how similar to his father he was.

Roscoe's life became more hectic than he ever dreamt. More people moved in, either from overseas or heading back from the west (where the French, rumour had it, were causing trouble with the settlers). Buckley became more demanding, as he missed his mother more. Roscoe found that the time he spent drinking with his friends grew thinner, and his time spent watching his brother sleep swelled. Then, on the night of his thirty-first birthday, he asked a neighbour, Mrs Catscombe, to watch Buckley.

'I'd like some liquor tonight,' he told her, and she wished him well.

'You deserve it,' she said. He drank and drank, and as the evening was winding down his friends gathered together in the centre of the room.

'We've got a present for you, Roscoe; one that you have gone far too long without!' They parted, and through the gap Roscoe saw the most extraordinary woman he had ever seen. She was a wave of red, a long dress, auburn hair, looking for all the world like a princess, the only thing that belied her being the dust that kicked up from the floor around her bare feet and ankles. She took Roscoe by the hand and led him upstairs. When he woke she was gone, and he was alone.

The following evening, after work, and after Buckley had fallen asleep, Roscoe left for the bar. He greeted the barman, who grinned.

'You looking for Alison?' he asked. Roscoe asked how he knew. 'Son, they all come in after her,' was the (not entirely satisfactory) answer. 'She's upstairs.' Roscoe went up and found himself in a hallway that he didn't pay attention to on his first visit, adorned with primitive decorations – skins, a flag – with moans coming from each of the rooms. Then, from the furthest door came a man, clutching his hat to his chest and laughing, buttoning up his trousers. Alison stepped out from that doorway and watched the customer walk off. She smiled at Roscoe, and he noticed the gap between her teeth, big enough to press her tongue through, which she did as she saw him, a tiny blot of pink flesh through the white.

'What can I be doing for you, Mister Sloane?' She pushed her chest forward, her breasts trapped against the fabric of her corset, a hint of her large nipples at the dress-line.

'This is where you work?' he asked, aware as soon as he said it that it was a stupid question. She smiled.

'It is,' she said. 'Am I to be put to my business now?' She rocked backwards with laughter, deep and guttural, like a man's. 'Or do you just want to talk?' He didn't. When he woke up she was gone again, so he left tokens on her dresser before heading to work.

Roscoe's life began to change further, two factors working alongside each other; he ate into his savings to give himself more time with Alison, and Buckley was left to his own devices more and more, neglected most evenings. Those same people who smiled after Roscoe's first night with the whore now scowled, knowing where he spent all of his time (and money). Roscoe's routine with Alison had become more natural, more casual. She had curbed herself from seeing too many other clients, and they spoke more about general topics, drank wine together, and occasionally ate meals. He started waking up with her next to him and on one instance she visited him at home when Buckley was running a fever, and slept with Roscoe in his bed. They began to kiss each other goodbye, and Roscoe thought of her rosy face during everything that he did. In their third month of seeing each other he stopped the (what had become token) payments for her services, replacing them with gifts, bringing her expensive foodstuffs or dresses. Then, one day, Alison found herself thrown out of the bar.

'I'm not bringing my wage,' she said, 'so I thought that I could move in with you.' Roscoe was ecstatic. A month after she moved in Roscoe went down on one knee, his mother's wedding ring in hand.

'Marry me,' he asked.

'As long as you get rid of your brother,' she said.

She hated Buckley. He was needy, which was to be expected, but wouldn't leave them alone when they were in the house. And when Roscoe was at work he expected Alison to spend time with his brother – 'He will finally have some company in the daytimes!' was his excited cry when she moved in – and she hated cleaning up after him, cooking his meals and changing him when he dirtied himself. To make up for it Roscoe still showered her with presents, but nothing, she told him when he proposed, would be enough to spend any more time staring at his desperate, insistent face.

And Roscoe, though it should have been an easy decision, was torn. Whilst Buckley was his brother, and he did love him, he was a burden. He was a burden to them, and he had been a burden to their mother, and he would be a burden to anybody else along the road. His heart, however, told him to stick by his brother; Alison ruled his other organs.

'I'll give you a week to decide,' she told him, and that was that.

On the first day Alison woke Roscoe with sex, and then left him to have breakfast with his brother. They played all day, and then Alison returned with a new dress, cooked dinner, and then they had sex again. When they went to bed Buckley wanted to play more, so they argued about him for hours, Roscoe raising his hand to strike one of them, but he wasn't sure which.

On the second day Roscoe returned from work to a dinner and a naked Alison, and Buckley with a painting that he had drawn of the three of them holding hands.

On the third day they all went for a walk after work, and

Buckley played in the stream and got filthy, and Alison complained the entire time that her feet hurt.

On the fourth day Buckley was moody and threw his food, and Alison sobbed as she cleaned it up from the floor. Roscoe woke in a fit at four in the morning, having nightmares about his decision.

On the fifth day Roscoe got drunk with his friends and cried. Their advice was to 'choose the pussy, as the retard won't live long anyhow.' When they went to bed he heard Buckley crying for attention, as Roscoe had worked long hours that day, and Alison soothed him as he relaxed with her hands and her mouth.

On the sixth day Roscoe woke up knowing the answer, and told Alison to pack her bags. 'You're throwing me out?' she asked, and he cried. 'No,' he said, 'we're running away.'

The next day he cooked breakfast for Buckley, and kissed him goodbye as usual.

'I love you,' he said, and then told him that they were going to shops. Alison and Roscoe rode all day, and arrived at their destination just after sunset. Roscoe couldn't stop crying, so Alison pleaded with him.

'You're with me, and I love you with all that I am, all that I have!' she told him, almost grovelling, but he decided to go back. It was morning by the time he got there, and he could hear his brother's crying from outside. Buckley was sitting on Roscoe's bed, and he was overjoyed to see him. As Roscoe took in the devastation that Buckley had created – the house overturned and disgraced by a grown man who couldn't feed or wash or even dress himself – Buckley embraced him. They held each other, both in tears, and then with one swift crick of Roscoe's arms, Buckley's eyes rolled back in his lolling head. Roscoe clutched him to his chest until the convulsions passed, then left his brother's body on the floor of the bedroom.

He sat against the back wall of the house all day so that

nobody saw him, waiting for the darkness. As soon as night fell he piled kindling against that wall and lit it, riding away and trying to control his overwhelming urge to go back and hold his brother's body as the flames ate them both up.

Alison and Roscoe began to talk less. They married three months later, at her insistence, and, two years after that, after they had almost completely ceased any sort of physical relationship, got drunk and conceived a child. It was a boy, and Roscoe wanted to call it Buckley but Alison won out, and they named it Godwin, after her father. Six months later Roscoe caught a disease from a prostitute, and it turned into a fever. He died, thinking about how it was almost a small mercy.

Part Two

Black sheep boy,
blue eyed charmer,
head hanging with horns from your father,
oh, in a cold little mirror you were grown,
by a black little wind you were blown,
alone, alone, alone.

Okkervil River, *In a Radio Song*.

11

Maynard's note – left on her tablecloth – rocked Lia more than Erwin's death. ('Dear Lia, I have gone to the police station – and most likely, after that, to prison – as my mother has died. She was very ill. Lia, I will miss you tremendously, in a way that I cannot even begin to express. Love always, Maynard Sloane. PS – Please tell Wendy what's happened.') She gathered her things from Erwin's bedroom; her clothes, the few items of jewellery that she brought with her, some photographs of her family. The letter that she herself had been writing, addressed to the entire remaining Sloane family (before the mother died), she threw away.

'Who would I even give it to now?' she asked aloud. She debated taking pictures of the Sloanes from the living room and the mother's bedroom. There was one of the boys playing as children, and one of the mother and her sons. The picture was taken in front of the house, with a slightly blurred pink smear intruding on the frame – no doubt, she thought, the finger of Ezra, nudging his way in. Trying to ruin everything, Lia thought, even though you can't actually see him.

She lugged her bag to the foot of the stairs, and then went back to Maynard's room, and lay on his bed, gathering her thoughts. She was drifting to sleep – rare for her, to sleep in the daytime – when the front door sounded, three solid raps.

'Who is it?' she called from the foot of the stairs, nervous about answering – this was, after all, not even her house to begin with.

'It's Joshua Mandlebraum; we met at the funeral.' the voice came back through the letterbox, a glimpse of an eye peering in. (Lia nearly asked which funeral, a depressing thought.) 'I came to see that you were alright.'

'I heard about what happened to Maynard,' said Joshua, as Lia poured coffee. 'It's terrible. Did he really kill her?'

'I don't know.'

'Terrible business, either way. So much pain in this family.' He blew the steam from the top of the cup. 'Did Maynard tell you that we're leaving?'

'No,' Lia replied, 'where for?'

'Europe. We're not sure where we'll settle, yet. That's the joy of modern travel, I suppose.' He sipped, pulled a face, resumed his blowing. 'I recommended that he sell the house. Did he look into it, do you know?'

'He didn't say anything, not to me. Maybe to Wendy.' Mandlebraum nodded.

'No, that means he probably didn't. I didn't think that he would. It will still be here when he gets out – gets home – I suppose.'

'It'll be empty.'

'It's always been empty.' The coffee was still too hot, and the mug just sat there in his hand. 'What will you do?'

'I'm not sure. I have some money in the bank' (from the sale of her family home), 'and I've always wanted to travel, so

I might do that.' She watched the cogs turn in Mandlebraum's mind, followed by his hands slapping the table.

'Do you have experience with childcare?'

'Some,' Lia answered, 'I used to babysit a little, when I wasn't working in the restaurant.'

'Come with us, then! Save your money for when you return, and come with us. We wanted to hire a girl to look after the children, so better that you do it than we have a stranger!'

'Oh, I couldn't!' Lia said, but even she didn't think that she sounded convincing. In that second she pictured herself leaving this city, a city that kept nothing for her but some distant family members and memories that she would never extinguish.

'You could,' Mandlebraum said, and that seemed to be the end of the matter. 'It'll do you wonders! We leave for London within the week. All you have to do is make sure that you're packed, and we will take care of your ticket. Just say that you'll come.'

So, because it was easiest – just as it had been when Erwin asked her to move in, then to marry him – she said that she would.

12

Erwin's still-healing throat rendered his speech useless for his first few days on the street, which helped him to fit in, and yet made his life slightly harder than it ought. He wasn't far from the hospital when he had to rest, to gather his strength, and a man with skin so tanned that Erwin at first thought he was African but who was actually from South America then showed him what he could and couldn't eat from the dumpsters.

'This is fine,' the South American repeatedly cuckooed in his clumsy accent when he found something edible – half a blackened banana, a partially-eaten cob of corn – and then drew a line across his neck when something wasn't suitable – chicken bones and the like, mostly. The motion made Erwin feel ill every time. He could still taste the blood in the back of his throat and repeatedly had to spit it onto the floor (where it sat, blacker than it was red, thick, like chewing tobacco). 'This is fine,' the South American told Erwin, referring to a stale cheese, white and flaky, and smelling like deadwood. When Erwin had the strength he left the South American and made it across the bridge, to New Jersey. He caught a lift with a man in a truck, who dropped him off when he found himself too frustrated – or too bored – by Erwin's lack of conversation.

'I pick up hitchers to keep me company, son,' he said, 'and I can't be pitching in for no mute.' Erwin slept that night behind bushes at the side of the road. In New Jersey he found his first homeless village, a group of people living under the on-ramp to the George Washington Bridge, and they showed him more tricks – tips for staying dry, how to build a bin-fire, how to work out which water sources were safe to drink from – and they took him in as one of their own. After a month with them his voice started to come back, far harsher than it ever was before.

'You sound like a fucking killer!' was one of his new friends' declarations when he spoke for the first time, his voice like a mockery of a demon, maybe even the devil, low and rasping and torn apart even on single-syllable words. He would stand there and examine the scar as it healed, stretched across his neck like a noose, staring at his reflection in shards of broken mirrors. His attempt at suicide had been too wide and not deep enough and had healed pink and sore. His new homeless friends stared at it when they spoke to him, flicking between the scar and eye contact, and it throbbed when he swallowed like it was a vein.

'What does it feel like?' he was asked, and he felt it, pulled at the still-new skin.

'It feels new,' he growled. A few months after arriving – months in which his skill set had proven invaluable to his gang, building them better temporary shelters from grating and cheap roofing materials that they stole from a landfill – the police descended. They came in the night with dogs and torches and they screamed at the vagrants to move along, throwing their makeshift housing into the river. All the homeless scattered away from the camp, and none of them ran together. This part, Erwin thought, hadn't been explained to him; that when you moved on you were on your own again. It was something that he wasn't fond of.

He travelled north towards New England, and landed in a town called Killington in the middle of one of the worst winters since records began. He was forced to steal coats from a chalet in a newly-constructed ski resort, and wore three of them in layers when the snows got bad enough. He slept against the back walls of concrete buildings, their vents pumping out warm air, and in the days he would walk amongst the tourists, passing as one of them in the visibility-tainting and softly falling snow. He washed in the snow, rubbing the frozen water over any part of him that needed cleaning, and he had a constant cold, but stayed because he kept wandering across parties in the evenings. They would invite him in for the revelry, thinking him just another eager fan of skiing.

'Have you done Europe?' they would ask as he dunked bread in the fondue that all the parties seemed to have. 'France, Switzerland? The mountains there, let me tell you!'

'No, not done them yet,' he would answer, his mouth full of fondue cheese, his voice still so hard it could cut ice, 'but they're on the agenda.' They recommended places and he listened dutifully before he left, slightly drunk and warm from the inside out. When tourist season ended, Killington died. The snow became brown and clogged the drains on the sides of the road, and the buildings in the resorts turned their power off, so Erwin moved on again. By now, he felt like he was an old hand at this stuff.

He landed in Boston, and there learnt how to make himself more presentable. Bags full of clothes left outside charities were raided before the shops opened, and he soon had outfits – a jumper and jeans for casual days, a suit (with blood-stains embedded in the silk lining) for business, a pair of swimming trunks for use of the public municipal pools that he used as a way of bathing – and he trimmed the beard that he was growing with shards of glass, using them much as a barber would use a flat-blade razor, holding the hair taut and then running the sharp edge along it, slicing off swathes of the dark, brittle hair. (The beard was partly because of the practicalities of such a thing – it was hard to maintain a clean-shaven look, so a beard was the only way to go – but also because it hid the scar.) From there he set up in another camp, and was interviewed by a local news station on the plight of the homeless. He refused to give his name. His skin got darker as he spent time in the late-springtime sun, and, as soon as June arrived, he moved on again, intending to head west. He got caught up in a movement of people flowing towards New York State, to a music festival. He spent days there, dancing and talking to people so different to himself they were almost aliens. He was given drugs and he took them, and he lay in a field and spoke to himself, listening to his own voice, so strange and so cold. He missed his family, but knew that he could never go back. This was it, here, and he watched as a rock star played his guitar with his teeth, and set it alight. (A woman started to cry, and Erwin consoled her. 'You think this is good,' he said, 'you should hear my brother's symphony.')

One day he stood in a town, outside a shop, and stared at the new radio that they were crowning on a podium in their window. He thought about the one that he had built for Maynard and began to cry. Nobody noticed him, or, if they did, they pretended that they didn't.

Chicago was next. He took a tent that he'd aqcuired at the festival and set it up in a forest, along with other campers. Nobody questioned him, and nobody stopped to ask why he was there by himself. He woke up every day and breathed in the woodland air with the other people, and they all ate together occasionally, burning sausages over camping stoves. When they packed their car at the end of their holiday they asked him how long he was staying for.

'Until I leave,' he said with a smile. When winter fell again he headed south, where it got warmer, Missouri and Arkansas and Mississippi seeing him through. By the following spring he was heading further west, and feeling more comfortable with his new life with every passing day.

13

Maynard was, before he ended up there, petrified of prison.

There was a Sloane myth created about prison, devised by Ezra to scare his children into morally adjunct behaviour. 'I know the warden of Alcatraz,' he told them one day when he caught them burning ants in the garden under a bit of glass, 'and he could do me favours.' He waved this over their head until they knew better. 'I've spoken to him, Maynard,' he would say when Maynard broke something semi-valuable, 'and they're sending

somebody first thing in the morning.' The façade was
maintained, and he forced Maynard to wake up at 5a.m., and
dress himself. Then Ezra would sneak out of the house, cover
his face in a shroud and knock on the front door. Maynard
would answer, terrified, his pink-white knees held together and
quivering. 'I have come for you, Maynard Sloane!' he would
shout, and Maynard wet himself on the steps of their house
before Ezra revealed that it was he under the mask, and not the
Reaper of Alcatraz. 'I only did that to scare you,' Ezra told him
afterwards, 'because you do not want to end up there, son.'

As soon as the verdict on the case of his mother's suspected
murder was passed, the terror set in. Maynard had seen
pictures in the news, and read stories – about riots, about
violence, about racial tensions. Nobody in the courtroom
knew Maynard, so nobody sympathised with his fears. He
was, he reasoned, all alone, and that was maybe for the best.

The van that drove Maynard to his new home was black
and smelt of leather, despite there being nothing but hard
plastic seating, and his travel companions all glared at him as
they climbed in. Maynard smiled when they started moving,
but none of them smiled back. They flexed their tattooed arms
and bared their teeth, and Maynard looked at his feet and
prayed that they might, somehow, crash; that might be the
preferable result. After hours of bracing himself for corners
and listening to the snorts and gurgles of his fellow travellers,
the van stopped outside the gates to the prison and Maynard
was ushered out across the (surprisingly well-maintained) yard.
The other inmates filed out behind him, forming a line. They
passed through a larger courtyard area, wooden doors lined
with enormous concrete bricks, and stepped through into a
holding room filled with guards who sounded far more native
to New York than Maynard did. One of them called his name.

'You're in block twenty-three,' Maynard was told. 'Go and get cleaned down.' Through the door he was pointed towards was an overly bright tiled room with shower nozzles lining the walls. He stripped and the shower blasted him, the water so hot it stung. 'Stay in,' his guard ordered when he flinched away from it, so he let it slap against him, making his skin pink. 'Wash yourself,' said the guard, indicating a soap on some rope attached to the wall, so he did, and then stepped away. 'You don't look clean to me,' said the guard, who spat at him. 'Get back in,' Maynard was told as the phlegm rolled down his cheek.

After he was finally decreed clean he was asked questions ('Do you intend to commit a further felony whilst staying here?') and handed a uniform and a pair of hard rubber boots. He was then led through to his cell, past the rows of other cells, the inmates crowding around their bars. As he walked he realised that he didn't recognise anybody there; not just their faces, but the types of people that they were. His cell was in the middle of the rest, seemingly, and he took his place on the top bunk above a sleeping shape that didn't acknowledge him as he came in.

'Lights out,' shouted a guard at the end of the room, and the place fell into pitch-blackness. He could hear his cellmate breathing amidst the rattling from other cells, and the calls of the inmates into the darkness. He didn't sleep.

The resident of the bottom bunk was a bulky man with no teeth and a nose that was spread equidistant between his eyes. His name was Bruiser.

'You stay out of my bad books and I'll cover your ass in a fight,' he told Maynard, 'but I ain't no fag, so don't think you can come down here at night with your fag-Jew ways, or I'll snap you in two.' Maynard was going to inform him that he was neither Jewish nor gay, but decided against it. Bruiser invited Maynard to sit with him at breakfast. 'That way, the gangs'll know not to fuck with you. What are you in here for?' His voice was so squashed by his nose that it made him sound almost like he was deaf.

'I killed my mother,' Maynard said, 'or they accused me of it.'

'Momma's boy,' Bruiser replied. 'You want to keep that quiet. Almost everybody loves their mom, and it's an easy target. Say you killed your boss, or some fag, or a nigger or a wop or something. Get yourself in with a group.'

'Won't that annoy the other groups?'

'You're always going to put your dick up somebody here,' he said, starting a series of push-ups on the floor of the cell, 'might as well pick a side from the start.' His arms seemed to audibly creak with every push.

'What are you in here for?' asked Maynard, and Bruiser smiled, his grin curling underneath his flattened nose.

'Tax fraud,' he said, but Maynard didn't believe him.

Arnold 'Bruiser' Brudowski had been part of a gang of ex-boxers who attempted to rob a tax office that was temporarily holding hundreds of thousands of dollars of cash, all destined for the central tax offices. They were caught, and all killed by local police apart from Bruiser, who escaped, only to be caught four days later in Atlantic City, burning through the cash as fast as he could.

As promised, Maynard ate his breakfast of granola sitting next to Bruiser, and gossip about him quickly spread. Maynard never heard any of it, of course, but people started to mutter when he walked past them, and nobody caused trouble, not past the usual pandering for cigarettes and requests for – or offers of – sexual favours.

Weeks passed, and eventually Maynard applied for a job. The prison was looking for inmates to run music classes.

'I have no formal training,' he said in the interview, 'but I'm a quick study.' They gave him a week to learn how to read music, and at the end of that time he gave them a performance of 'Für Elise' that made the hairs stand up on the arms of the warden. He got the job, and from then on spent his days sitting in a makeshift music room – little more than a cupboard situated off the library with an out-of-tune piano against the wall. Soon students started coming, attending the classes as part of their rehabilitation, and Maynard taught them all 'Chopsticks'.

He never thought of home – not of the house, or of his mother and father, or Wendy, or Erwin – but he did think of Lia. He pictured Lia running, happy, the simplest image that he could conjure, a cliché, basic and pure. It was a recurring fantasy, and Bruiser started noticing him staring off into space, or facing the wall on his bunk, stroking the stone.

'Never gonna happen,' he would say, despite not knowing the dream. (He had seen the look on many faces before, many times. It was a sad, hard fact of prison; fantasies and dreams almost always went unfulfilled.) Maynard ignored him. He knew that Bruiser wasn't being cruel, but he wasn't ready to give up.

As well as teaching piano – and singing, after a while, then, as his own skills grew, basic guitar – Maynard took lessons in other classes. He started learning languages, French and Spanish and Italian, and he attempted pottery and art, areas in which he had not previously been given the opportunity to express his creative side. It was, he thought as his first anniversary of life in the prison rolled around, the most curiously productive year of his life. On his birthday he was given a cake. The wife of one of the guards had baked it, and he was guided blindfold into the family room where some of the guards sang 'Happy Birthday'.

'It's a brighter place with you here,' they told him. His name – or an approximation of it, 'Manyard' – was written on the cake in icing. He blew the candle out, and had a slice, cut by his own hand – a great sign of trust, he was assured, that he was allowed to handle a knife so sharp in a prison that was dedicated to plastic cutlery for fear of shivs – and they let him keep the candle, even, for posterity. The cake was sponge and jam, and was made, Maynard suspected, with powdered egg, but he didn't complain. He was far too touched by the gesture.

Before he knew it another year passed, and along came another cake, another set of cheers. This time he was handed a bottle of beer. He hadn't drunk alcohol in so long that it made him giddy, and he passed out in his bed, happy, dreaming of Lia. Bruiser was touched when he brought back a slice of the cake for him as well. The following week Maynard had a student pass an exam, and he was given a commendation by the warden.

'When you're up for parole, this will certainly help your cause.' Nobody liked to mention that it was still twenty-three years away. His third year started much as the other two had, with day-to-day activities keeping him busy, and the solace of the bunk and his thoughts – still of Lia – every evening. One night, however, everything changed. He was lying there, softly rocking himself to sleep, beginning to dream when he heard choking. He leant over the lip of his mattress and saw Bruiser hanging off the bed-frame, his face swollen and blue, his eyes rolled back, his mouth gasping. Maynard jumped down and shouted for the guards and put his hands on Bruiser's face, ready to puff air into his lungs if needed. The lights flicked on and the guards arrived and took over from him, and told him that they were sorry. They closed Bruiser's eyelids for him.

'The morgue guys aren't here at night,' they said, 'so he'll have to keep until morning.' They left the body there on the bed, and Maynard spent the night listening to it softly expel gas, the bed creaking as the insides shifted, just as Maynard had thought that they would.

It was nearly a month before Maynard got a new cellmate. The guards tried to send other prisoners elsewhere, diverting anybody that looked like they could give their friend – because that's what he had become, almost – a harder time than necessary, but there came a point of influx; twelve new prisoners arrived the same day and all had to be found rooms. The person who processed them was new to the job and didn't know Maynard, so his cellmate wasn't vetted.

'You've got company,' was the first that Maynard heard of it, waking him from sleep, and then the door opened in the darkness. At first, half-dreaming, he thought that Lia had come to see him. (He would never have told her so, but he always wondered why she didn't.) He saw her standing there, blurred, against the brick, but only for a second. The outline changed. 'This is John Maivea,' the guard said, 'he'll be bunking down with you.' Maivea was huge, and Maynard felt the whole bed-frame creak as he settled in below.

'Nice to meet you,' Maynard said, but his new cellmate just snarled like he was a cartoon.

The next day Maynard woke to John Maivea doing exercises in the same space that Bruiser used to use. Unlike Bruiser, the Maivea wasn't bulk; he was almost entirely muscle.

'What are you in here for, then?' asked Maynard, trying to emulate the role that Bruiser vacated, the old hand offering wisdom to the new man.

'I killed a man, and raped his woman.' He stopped and looked up at Maynard, whose head was hanging over the side of the bunk. 'I've killed lots of men, and raped lots of women.' Maynard shifted backwards, dressed under his covers (as he always did), and then ran to the breakfast hall. He didn't offer his new cellmate the opportunity to eat with him.

John Maivea was ex-Navy. He joined as a teenager as a way of escaping an otherwise mandatory prison sentence. He travelled the world and fought and killed many people, only a fraction of them as part of his duties. When he left – discharged, for raping and murdering a native girl in Vietnam, part of the first wave of troops sent there – nobody was sad to see him leave. He ended up in prison for killing a man in a bar, a man that dared to suggest that Maivea should stop licking his lips at his girlfriend. He killed the man, and then he beat the woman to within an inch of her life. It took four policemen to restrain him.

The Maivea – he liked his name to be referred to with a grammatical definitive, and everybody was terrified enough of him to agree – was brutal. He terrorised the other prisoners and ruined the guards' hold over the inmates. The criminals were afraid of him; the guards even more so. They stepped back when he queued for his meals, and they stayed clear when they heard that he was delivering beatings. This happened frequently as well, The Maivea often having to wash blood from his fists and clothes in the basin that he shared with Maynard. Maynard, for his part, never looked. When he found shivs, razors, knives, he left them where they were, and he avoided talking in the cell as much as possible.

One day, after The Maivea had been there for nearly a year, a body turned up in their cell, choked to death, a damp towel wrapped around the victim's neck. Maynard recognised him as one of the guards, the one who – coincidentally – logged him in at the start of his stay in the prison – but nobody saw who left him there. Both The Maivea and Maynard were interviewed by the guards – interim police in the matter, and baying for blood – and both were declared suspects despite their furious denials. (Maynard had been at a class, waiting for a student who never arrived, so had no solid alibi; The Maivea had been killing the guard, so had no alibi either.) Another guard, whom Maynard was close to, snuck in to see him after the interrogation.

'It's the strangling,' he said, 'like with Bruiser, and with your mom. Some people are saying that, maybe, it's a habit with you, a thing.' He left Maynard alone, watching the television – a repeating cycle of President Lyndon B. Johnson reaching his hand into a big glass bowl, performing the fourth Vietnam-war lottery in as many years – until the guards in charge of the investigation came back.

'You need to speak up,' they said, 'or we lock you down. Either you did it or he did it, and somebody's going to suffer.'

'I can't prove that he's responsible,' Maynard said, 'but I didn't kill anybody.' He thought of his mother as they dragged him to solitary confinement.

Maynard's seven days alone went with no real food, just dried-out bread and bowlfuls of dirty water. His diet, or lack of, led to vomiting at first, then dry-heaves, as all the nutrients had left his body. He was occasionally visited by guards, none from his wing, and all with an axe to grind. They kicked him and took a cudgel to his head, and when he woke from unconsciousness they kicked him again. Eventually Maynard was let out, dragged back to his cell in the dead of night and dumped on the floor. When he pulled himself to his bunk he found the mattress smeared in faeces, and all of his possessions – a photograph of his family (Erwin, his mother, Lia, taken at his father's wake), some books – at the side of the toilet, soaking wet with urine. He flipped his mattress and lay on it. The Maivea returned a few hours later and they ignored each other. Maynard spent the entire night praying that his cellmate had shut his eyes and didn't notice the soft stain that sat directly above his face through the slatted springs of the bed-frame.

The next day Maynard was woken early and escorted to the library, where the guards on duty threw books at him and flicked matches at his head. In his music room, the strings inside the piano had been cut. At dinner the cook spat in his food as he slopped it onto his plate. Maynard grimaced, and the cook spat again. Maynard ate around the spittle, and then returned to his bunk, only to discover The Maivea, angry.

'They're taking me in for more questions, about that guard,' he said, and he grabbed Maynard and threw him against the steel door. 'Maybe I say you did it, and you confess.' Maynard screamed and the guards ran in, pulled The Maivea back.

'He would have killed you,' one said to Maynard as he cowered on the floor, 'so count yourself lucky.' The guard raised his nightstick, slammed it against Maynard's body, and his arm cracked before he blacked out.

14

Erwin's memory of what had been before – before his father left, before he tried to kill himself, before his time on the streets – started to muddle itself. It began with the knowledge of how long he had been on the streets for, a frequently asked question when he met a new group of homeless.

'How long?' He thought, and discovered that he wasn't absolutely sure. 'Four or five years. Somewhere around there.' That night he dwelt on it, tried to count them down based on the Christmases that he had been through, but couldn't pin it down. And then, the next Christmas, whichever one that was, he caught dysentery.

As a younger man, Erwin had passed the homeless in the street and ignored them; or, at best, wondered what made them act the way that they did, what sent them spiralling into what appeared to be insanity, spitting and murmuring in alleyways, using newspapers as blankets, foraging through trash cans in the wide open as if they were bushes full of berries. He often wondered why they didn't just go to real berry-bushes, which were in casual abundance in the parks. His insistence on not completely abandoning his old ways when he actually found himself homeless meant that, as that winter hit and food became harder to find, he ate a handful of those real berries and was blessed with the worst bout of vomiting he had ever known, made worse by the lack of basic amenities. He found himself on a bench, shivering, resorting to using old magazines as shelter and to provide extra warmth, and then stumbling to dumpsters, an excess of spittle in his mouth from the illness. He saw himself in a shop window, and wondered who he had become before vomiting down himself and passing out. The fever hit hard.

He came to on the lawn, being tended to by a short black man, toothless and bald, like an over-grown baby.

'My name is Charlie Fallon,' the man said as soon as Erwin woke, 'and I'm not robbing you. I'm just cooking you something; some broth, get you warmed up.' He had a camping stove set up, and there were bones in the pot. When he handed it to Erwin to drink from a mug, Erwin found it one of the most wonderful things that he had ever eaten. It was delicious. 'You look like you need that,' Charlie said as Erwin gulped it down.

'I've been ill,' Erwin said, 'my stomach.'

'You haven't been doing this long,' Charlie said, and Erwin corrected him.

'I've been out for five years,' he said, which made Charlie shake his head.

'Like I say; you ain't been doing this long. I am, in comparison, a master.'

Charlie had grown up in the south in the 1920s, and moved north as soon as he was able. His was a classic story; he met a girl, white, in the 1940s, just after the start of World War II, and they had wanted to be together. They would meet in secret, in barns and in fields of corn, and they would kiss each other, and then, after a while, more. He got her pregnant, as always happens in their story, and was chased out of the town they lived in by men with pitchforks and hoods, the girl beaten in her church and forced to give up her child. He had nowhere to go, no money, no job, and few skills, so chose the path of least resistance, and spent every day of his life regretting it.

They bonded over the next few days, but Erwin's progress was slow, his stomach turning after every meal. It got colder and colder on the bench, and they hid from the rain as much as they could, though with increasing difficulty. One morning – after Erwin awoke with tears frozen on his cheeks – Charlie made an executive decision.

'We need to get you warmer,' Charlie said. 'How's about we head to Texas?' He begged for money for two days, saving enough for bus tickets, and they boarded a few days before Christmas. Erwin spent most of the journey in cramps, waiting for the next rest-stop. The bus was heaving with people and their gifts, all offering each other tidings of good-will, though none of them so much as glanced at Erwin and Charlie – not, at least, in a way that was obvious. Through the pain, Erwin wondered if they really looked that blatantly homeless.

When they arrived they were the first off the bus, and Erwin made for the toilets at the station. They were filthy – all of the toilets that they stopped at on the journey were – but he no longer worried about that sort of thing. Charlie waited outside, tapping his foot when Erwin was gone for fifteen minutes, then half an hour. When he reached the full hour Charlie went in and checked the stalls. He could see Erwin's shoe sticking out from below one of the doors, so he lunged at the door with his shoulder and dragged the body of his friend out into the bright daylight.

Erwin didn't wake up until he was in the hospital, Charlie sitting at his side. He opened his eyes, saw the drip in his arm and the beeping machine to his left, and panicked.

'Calm down,' Charlie told him, 'they just have you on fluids. You stay here until you're better.' Erwin fell asleep almost immediately, before Charlie could tell him that, as soon as he had his strength back, they were running like hell from that hospital and their lack of insurance or money.

Erwin had been on his feet for two minutes (to stumble to the lavatory) when Charlie told him that it was time and threw him his clothes, and then they ran down a fire escape, onto the street, down side roads, zig-zagging their way through alleys. Erwin stumbled constantly, weak as he was, but Charlie was there. Charlie soon flagged Erwin to stop running and they creased up together, gasping for breath.

'Happy Christmas,' Charlie mumbled.

'Well now,' came a voice from behind them, 'you boys look as to be running from trouble. What kind of trouble can that be, I wondered?' They looked at the man who stepped out from the shadows; at his lank hair and his floor-length coat, his fingerless gloves, his wafer-thin body, his white face and red eyes. 'I'm DeVere Arseneaux, and this here is my bridge,' he announced. All Erwin could think about was children's stories about trolls and tolls.

DeVere was from New Orleans, and was a hustler, a killer, and an addict. He left the city in the wake of riots and murders with his name on them, having started his career (such as it was) aged sixteen with street tricks and cons, working up to jobs for mob bosses. As soon as he could dive into the criminal underworld proper he did, and he made it ten years without getting caught for a single crime that he committed – crimes that numbered in the hundreds. Barely a day of his life went by without a felony of some kind being orchestrated with his hands. And then, it all crashed down. He killed a boy over a fifty-dollar debt, thinking that he was a nobody, but he was the child of a policeman, trying to get back at his father by dealing cheap – and bad – drugs to the nobodies in the seedier bars. The police swooped down on the city, shutting everything off, and DeVere was given up in the hope of keeping the police from arresting other criminals left, right and centre. He fled the city, and abandoned any façade of legitimacy, living under bridges and in deserted houses, dealing drugs whenever he could get his hands on them, cutting them cheaply, and making sure that anybody he dealt to got as hooked as he, himself, was.

DeVere showed them around the city of Austin, taking them to the best places to beg, to find money, or maybe even food.

'You hang round here, you want something, you got an ahnvee fo' something, the people, they see that, they give it to you.' He watched them, sizing them up, seeing how Charlie was suspicious of him, and Erwin was too weak to do anything for himself. 'You welcome in my home, if it'll help you recover,' he told Erwin, and Erwin nodded.

'We appreciate that,' Charlie said, answering for them both. DeVere's home was really just a house, abandoned and boarded up, situated just outside the city limits. It was, noted Erwin, rare to see a building so completely black, and it was as dark inside as it was out; there wasn't a window not covered in wood, the nails fastening the board with heads as wide as pennies. Here and there boards had been pulled down (or smashed) to let thin strips of light in, but for the most part they fumbled in the near-darkness.

'It's dark so as not to alert anybody that I'm here,' DeVere explained as their eyes adjusted. 'I'll go and cook something. You boys hungry?' As soon as he had gone Charlie leant in to Erwin.

'I don't like him,' the older man said. 'I do not like him one little bit.'

DeVere didn't live alone. He shared the house with Maura, an ex-prostitute (who Charlie suspected, had only left the business because her looks had deserted her slightly), and a young black man called Donald (who, DeVere informed them, was either a 'cooyon or a retard, but either way, he ain't worth a dollar'). Erwin and Charlie met them both that evening at dinner, as Maura cooked them a stew, and they ate it out of bowls that DeVere had stolen from a department store's bin, all slightly cracked but perfectly serviceable.

Maura's was a another classic tale: girl meets boy; boy beats girl; boy forces girl to start turning tricks for money; boy continues to beat girl; boy forces girl to commit some of the most hideous acts in the name of 'love' (but mainly in the name of money); girl kills boy when he's beating her so badly she can't see — she raises a fire poker and swipes, striking his temple, seeing his eyes fill with blood — girl runs, but needs to make money again, so turns to what she knows.

Donald was heavily autistic, to the point of near complete disability. He was born in the worst part of Houston – a part that rarely appeared on maps, and was notorious for the drugs that were trafficked through it. He was abandoned by a mother unable to cope with him; went into the foster system; was spat out the other end. He couldn't work, couldn't support himself, and ended up on the street. DeVere had found him, seen a possible source of begging income, and taken him in.

'Yous are perfectly welcome to stay here,' DeVere told them when they had finished eating, 'so find yourselves a room. I'm upstairs now. Fais do-do.' He led Maura off by the hand. She stared at Erwin as she went, and he, in turn, noticed that she had lovely eyes, and her hair – thick and dark – reminded him of Aurelia's.

The next morning she cooked breakfast. Erwin, having slept in the tiny box-room closest to the back door (and, subsequently, the outhouse), was up as soon as he heard her moving around.

'We've got bacon,' she said, 'and eggs, if you want them.' He did, his hunger back in full force, so she fried them on the same camping stove that they had cooked the stew on the night before, and they spoke as she cooked. They talked about the things you do when you don't know somebody: where they were from, how they ended up here (Erwin left out the part about faking his own death, just saying, instead, that he ran away from his family after his father died, and his relationship fell apart), and what their plans were.

'I'm going to get past this,' she said, rubbing at the inside of her elbows, 'and then, I don't know. I talk about going home, back to Indiana.'

'You and DeVere?' Erwin asked, and she laughed.

'We're not like that,' she said. 'It gets cold at night, and we don't have heating, so you take what you can get. He's not so bad.' She put the food onto a chipped plate and slid it across the floor to him, and they made eye contact again, and held it.

That evening, after dinner – sausages, thrown out of a restaurant, that looked stale but tasted okay – Maura let DeVere go to bed by himself, and then she and Erwin watched the others slope off to their corners of the house. She crawled across the floor towards him like a cat, and he kissed her so forcefully that he couldn't breathe for a second, having forgotten that art of taking air through the nose when in that situation. She pushed him backwards, straddled him and took her clothes off. It all came back to him over the next few minutes, and when they were done they lay on their backs and stared at the moon through one of the removed panels.

The following morning Erwin woke alone, and, when dressed, found that his other housemates were gathered in hallway, by the front door.

'We're leaving,' DeVere said, 'you got ten minutes to get your stuff together.' He didn't look directly at Erwin.

15

Maynard decided that prison hospital was – compared to regular hospital – desperately unpleasant. There were still disease cases and general illnesses – particularly stomach-related – but the majority of patients had physical injuries; in particular blood-letting seemed popular. As Maynard lay on one of the ward beds he watched tens of other cases come through the doors, from assorted broken bones (such as his own) to stabbings with knives, shivs, screwdrivers (one of which was through somebody's eye, and the victim convulsed like a lobster in a pot), all the way up to removed limbs and hideous burns. One of the nurses, when tending to Maynard's own broken arm, asked him – semi-rhetorically – how the violence got so bad.

'Don't the guards do anything?' she wondered, and Maynard didn't answer. She didn't push him. The bone was broken in four places, bad enough that a basic cast might not be enough. A doctor explained that they would watch it for a week, and then, if it needed help, pin the bones. Maynard asked for a book on the procedure and read about it as he lay in his bed, propped up, his left arm useless and agonising. Every day they took an X-ray of his arm, and every day the doctor looked at it, pondered.

'Sorry to have to keep you here like this,' he said, but Maynard didn't mind. He didn't want to go back to the general populace any quicker than he had to, and the guards that swung by to check on the ward every hour reinforced this. They never spoke to him; they just stared from the doorways, fingered the tops of their nightsticks. That was enough to terrify him. One afternoon, the guard that put Maynard in hospital – a filthy-mouthed older man, with a moustache that ran almost the breadth of his face – was watching the rest of the ward, but his attention flitted to Maynard whenever nobody else was looking. He stood behind Maynard's bed and leaned down to brush something from his shoe.

'You say it was me, I'll break all of you,' he said in a half-whisper. 'You tell anyone, and you'll never walk again.' He squeezed Maynard's arm when the nurse's attention was elsewhere, and then left. Maynard didn't sleep that night. A couple of guards were still kind to him, still on his side – the guard whose wife baked him his birthday cakes, especially – but not enough to offer him any sort of protection. They brought him things to keep him occupied, however, and to keep his mind from the problem at hand. Maynard awoke one morning to see a clutch of papers from his personal effects on his bedside table. It was a mess of photographs and letters, Maynard read them to the rest of the ward one night. They were quiet when he finished, but he read into it what he needed, and knew what he had to do.

Godwin Sloane was a quiet man. It was, people in the town believed, because of his parents, who were either dead (in the case of his father) or whoring themselves around (in the case of his mother, who, despite being close to death herself with cholera, was managing to turn a decent wage in the back-rooms of a local bar). Godwin kept to himself mostly, working for a local merchant. He was in charge of odd jobs and maintenance, day-to-day projects, and he had a reputation as a 'doer'. Physically, he was hugely intimidating, stocky and overgrown with hair.

'He'll do anything you want,' his boss would say, 'and he won't grumble. A fine man.' That was what followed him around town; that he was a fine man, and he was quiet, and he was strong. At night he would drink in the bars, and he would sit at a table with many raucous men, all gambling and swearing. They didn't push him as he kept drinking, and he was often in on their bets or games of cards, so they let him be. When anybody asked about him, nobody had a bad word to say. Godwin Sloane was, they agreed, alright.

Godwin's first girlfriend – of any serious degree – was called Eleanor Bittle. She was a plain girl, but kind, and she was gutsy. She made the first move on Godwin one night as he walked home. ('Godwin?' she asked through the darkness, having noticed his frame against the moonlight. He confirmed that it was he, and then she asked him if he wanted to take her for a meal. 'Only if you fancy it,' she said. He did, so they did.) She didn't believe in sex before they were married, being somewhat puritanical, so Godwin, having a real lust brewing, proposed. Her father gave his permission and they were set. From there, the wedding came and went, and then Eleanor fell pregnant on their wedding night.

'It's God's way of saying that this was right,' she told him. The baby was born before he knew it, and they called him Shaw. Shaw was strong as a child, and everybody who saw him predicted him a stoic and powerfully quiet man, like his father. That should have been the end of it, a happily-ever-after; but then, one night, walking home from a dinner with her parents without Godwin (who was working late), and cradling Shaw to her chest, Eleanor was attacked. The men had knives, and they threw her to the ground, discarding the baby to the sand, and then raping her in turn, the knife held up to her throat to prevent her from screaming. Shaw didn't cry as he fell, as he thudded face-first into the dust, and Eleanor spent the ordeal staring at him on the floor, not moving, not crying. She knew that he was dead before they finished, and when they finally ran off, she couldn't think about herself. She screamed for her child. Eventually somebody fetched the doctor, but it was too late.

Godwin blamed himself.

'I should have been there,' he shouted, which was true – the work that he had stayed behind to complete was unimportant, but he was a man of principles, and wanted to see it finished on time – but Eleanor told him to calm down. He was adamant. 'I should have been there!' He decided to avenge his son's death, his wife's injustice, and prowled the streets for days, searching for the men that Eleanor described – ratty, tattered, dirty, small, nasal voices, like goblins, almost – but found nothing. He gave up after a week, and tried to return to life as it was.

'We can have another,' Eleanor told him, and then seduced him, but his heart wasn't in it. She did all the work, and, sure enough, fell pregnant the first time they tried. This baby was called Theodore, and they treated him like he was a jewel. When he was an infant they rarely left the house with him – definitely not if they weren't both together – and Eleanor never let him out of her sight when Godwin was at work. If she did, Godwin would chastise her; on one occasion when she bathed and left Theodore playing in another room alone, Godwin beat her.

'What if he had eaten something he ought not, or fallen, and hit the soft crown of his head?' he roared, and Eleanor learned her lesson. Theodore was not left alone again. By the time he was sent off to school classes Godwin had his own business, fixing people's houses and installing drainage in the local villages and townships, and he was out for longer days. Eleanor was left in charge of Theodore's education, and she hated it, sitting with him, teaching him to count or to read, things that she could barely do herself to any high standard. When she realised that Godwin's day-to-day comings and goings were as clockwork – he left the house at eight, came back at eight, always, and regimented – she decided to send the boy to school with the other children. It took place in the main room of the local chapel, and was led by a nun, but it was better than what Eleanor had to offer. Theodore loved it, and agreed to keep it a secret between himself, his mother, and the other local children.

On the last day of his first week he left for home as usual, holding his mother's hand. They stopped for food with her family, and then, knowing that Godwin would be returning soon, rushed back. On the way they were stopped in the dark by a man with a knife.

'I'll take what you've got,' he said, meaning whatever jewellery or trinkets they happened to be carrying, or maybe even food, as he was poor and hungry. Eleanor screamed, having horrific flashes back to her first experience, and clutched Theodore to her. The man, startled by her howl, ran, and the streets soon filled with people searching for him.

'He tried to have his way with me!' Eleanor told them. When Godwin returned, he was incensed. He trawled the streets searching for the man – again, described by Eleanor as dirty, rodentish, shrunken, grotesque – and finally found him, down by the river.

'You monster,' Godwin said, and the man knew his fate. Godwin put the rape of his wife, the death of his child, and whatever act had just been committed on the man's shoulders, and held him by the scruff of the neck, beating him in the face with his fist until the man was a hollow mess of blood. When he was done he threw the body in the river and watched it float away, the water turning pink, fish picking as the body drifted.

He returned to Eleanor, and, when they were alone, told her what he had done. She cried all night, and when he tried to touch her she winced away. She stared at his hands as he did his handiwork and imagined the violence he did with them, and decided that, as much as she might still love him, they would never have another child.

Maynard's release from the hospital ward was swift when it was discovered that his wound would heal well enough in its cast.

'The arm will never be perfect again,' he was told, 'but it will work well enough, I suppose.' Back in his cell, The Maivea was nowhere to be seen – a second trip to solitary, having been caught raping a fellow inmate in the showers – but Maynard heard whispers that he was angry, ready to kill upon his return. The next morning Maynard got his breakfast as usual, but none of his old friends wanted to sit with him. One of them, an elderly man who had been arrested for fraud, spoke to him in the food queue.

'Watch yourself,' he said, mumbling as oatmeal was slopped into bowls. 'Remember: it's not a crime to step on a fly, swat an ant, squash a cockroach; not if that insect would sting you first.' That was the only warning that Maynard got. He knew, when the time came, that he would have to think quickly.

The time came that evening, after lights out. Maynard heard The Maivea being escorted down the corridor, the guard accompanying him being the same that broke Maynard's arm. He heard the guard's nightstick clanging cell bars as they walked; as they grew closer he heard the sniff of The Maivea's nose, a bloodhound on the scent. The door to the cell opened, and Maynard braced, tensed his body.

'Maynard, you got a visitor,' the guard sang, and The Maivea grabbed the nightstick from the guard's open hand. 'I've been overpowered!' said the guard weakly, faking a coup. The Maivea struck Maynard's bunk over and over, until he realised that Maynard wasn't in it. From his position under the bottom bunk, hugging the floor, Maynard smacked the Maivea's ankle with his cast, making him fall backwards into the guard, who reacted as Maynard predicted; with terror. Concerned that he was being roped into this murder attempt he struck out, hitting The Maivea in the shoulder. The Maivea retaliated, lunging backwards, crushing the guard against the wall. The guard smacked his far-larger opponent in the face, then The Maivea did the same, nightstick delivered by enormous hand to the temple. The guard was dead before he even hit the floor, and The Maivea just stood there, panting, gasping even, as the alarms sounded and more guards rushed up to tackle him to the ground. As soon as he was restrained Maynard slid out from his hiding place.

'I heard them fighting and I hid,' Maynard said, as meekly as he could manage. 'They came in, and The Maivea just went insane, smashing everything up. He said that he was going to make a break for it.' Maynard was absolved of all guilt, which was, he reasoned, absolutely fair.

(Except, it wasn't, he realised, when he tried to sleep. In his dreams, or the parts between being awake and being asleep, when he knew that he was dreaming, he saw The Maivea beating the guard's head – something he didn't actually witness clearly, but in his dream it was perfect, like a series of photographs, as if he had been there, poking around between them, somehow in the frame. The guilt roamed the cell as he tried to sleep, the bunk below him empty and yet still creaking.)

'You don't mess with Maynard Sloane,' became a whispered warning around the yard. Maynard was eventually given a new roommate, a timid old man called Dennis (who had killed his wife one night as she slept because of her incessant nagging). It was, the guards reasoned, unlikely that either of them would bully the other. Maynard watched his fifth, sixth, seventh years in the prison roll by. They were cakeless, and without ceremony, but he was being left alone. He did his washing; he taught his music; he read books; he exercised, sometimes with weights, sometimes walking, and once even in a swimming pool, when there was a day-release for well-behaved prisoners organised by the governor. He worked on his own music (which, he would admit, had suffered since being in prison, mainly because there was precious little inspiration to work from; grey stone bricks, tattoos and slop weren't conducive to creativity, he realised); he started to arrange his family stories into a book; he wrote letters to Lia, knowing that he would never send them, and he wrote letters to his mother, his brother, his father, knowing that they could never be sent; he learnt how to gamble; he started gardening, growing vegetables in the prison garden; he started going to church; he began watching television, something that had eluded him in the outside world, because he preferred the radio, and he discovered that he loved *The Mary Tyler Moore Show*; he became fluent in Spanish and French; he read law books, further than he had gone before, into criminal law, and started to put together a case for himself for his first parole hearing; and he met the warden, and was often invited to speak with him, to discuss the state of the prisoners, any tensions that had arisen, that sort of thing. Maynard's prison life was going, all told, as well as could be expected.

16

DeVere led the group. It was his natural position, walking at the front. (It let him run if they were chased from behind, and, if chased from the front, let him see the danger first, drop back into the pack, and then make a break. It was, for the criminal tracker, ideal.)

'You can't stay too long in one place,' DeVere told them, 'or you get complacent, and you settle. When you're like us, you never settle.' They stopped every few days and DeVere disappeared, returning with their money gone and a bag of food that never seemed as full as it should. He was both their de facto leader and cook, and they ate what he cooked for them and did as he said (which they were all fine with apart from Charlie, who scowled and frowned, but knew that he was, like it or not, better off with this group than he ever had been by himself). On DeVere's orders they would set themselves up as a group near the commercial centres of towns, places where people were likely to congregate, and they would beg, spreading newspaper on the ground and sitting Donald cross-legged on it, his slow voice and clumsy hands often netting more than the rest of them combined. They travelled for the best part of a year together, doing their job whilst DeVere went for their supplies.

The supplies he returned with became fewer each time, in

gradual increments. Eventually Charlie got suspicious and told Erwin to follow DeVere when he did his food run. Erwin saw DeVere swerve away from the market that he said he was heading towards and duck down an alleyway, and, from there, talk to two men in long coats. DeVere handed them most of the money and they gave him an envelope. When Erwin got back be told Charlie what had happened. The older man nodded.

'Okay,' he said. 'Okay.' That was the end of the matter, and DeVere soon came back with three days' worth of food. Charlie eyed him suspiciously and insisted on doing all the cooking himself.

Erwin and Maura had been sleeping together regularly. When they were done they would lie back and he would ask her if they were together.

'Not together,' she would reply, 'but we're not apart. Okay?' She had stopped sleeping with DeVere, but still her response irked Erwin. He told his worries to Charlie, who dismissed them.

'She's as keen on you as any woman in this situation could be. Maybe you could get her off that stuff whilst you're at it.' That stuff was the heroin that DeVere bought. Erwin couldn't bring himself to ask her about it, so he investigated her habit in other ways.

He watched her moods, how they swung violently, and then suddenly she became placid, slept, was back to being herself. When Maura slept, Erwin examined her body, crept around her body looking for where she was injecting it. (Charlie had described the process to Erwin – of cooking the heroin on a spoon, over a flame, and then sucking it into a syringe as a liquid, injecting it into the bloodstream, letting it mingle with the blood before it hardens – and explained that, if there weren't holes in her arms, they were somewhere else.)

Erwin checked in between her toes, in her armpits, behind her knees, and was ready to give up until, one day, whilst having sex, he looked down and saw the tiny holes lining the muscle and bone around her groin.

'Erwin,' she moaned as he stopped. He dressed and they argued, and he asked her why she took it. 'It makes me feel good,' she said. 'Everything is so hard here, and it takes the edge off.'

'Try and stop?' he asked her, and she nodded.

'For you,' she told him, with no intention of even attempting to give it up.

The group was heading towards Denver when the first throes of winter started to kick in, the roads and paths they were taking becoming noticeably more treacherous. After one particularly heavy period of sleet DeVere led them alongside a canyon so that they could avoid the main roads into a small town, and Erwin slipped. He went down the slope, crashing into a tree, and plunged through a thin layer of ice into the creek at the bottom. Charlie rushed down after him, DeVere just behind, and they dragged him to the side, shivering, his teeth clacking together like a wind-up toy.

'Take off whatever clothes you got spare, wrap them around him,' Charlie ordered the others, and they did.

'Shit,' DeVere said. They deduced that Erwin's arm was broken. (Maynard, as a child, was fascinated by the concept of precognition amongst twins, and often wondered if such a thing existed amongst normal siblings. He ran elaborate experiments involving flip-cards and other psychic tests, but never had a result. Had he known that Erwin's arm broke at roughly the same time as his did, he might have questioned whether it was, in some karmic way, a sympathy wound.) Erwin couldn't move the arm by itself, and howled in agony whenever he was forced to. They lay Erwin flat on the concrete floor of a warehouse, and tried to see where the break might be.

'If it is broken, we need to set it, wrap it in something really tight, get a sling on it,' Charlie told them, 'but first we have to see how bad the break is, get it back into position, stop infections.' They tried to feel the break but Erwin howled when they even touched his skin. 'We'll leave it until tomorrow,' Charlie decided, and they left Erwin to try and sleep; apart from Maura, who lay next to him and held him through the pain as the fever took hold.

The next morning he was green and sweating, burning up. Where he had been lying on the hard floor was an outline of his body, drenched into the concrete. Charlie told them that they needed to set the arm.

'If this gets worse, he might lose it.' They pinned Erwin down and Charlie felt the limb, Erwin bucking and howling underneath their bodies. 'We need to shut him up, or somebody'll call the police,' Charlie said, and DeVere had an idea. He gave Erwin some of the heroin as a sedative – only a small amount – and let it sink in. Maura decided that she couldn't watch (both because it hurt Erwin, and because it fuelled the nagging lust she had for the drug herself), and DeVere slid the needle, a needle that he had only used that morning on himself and Maura, into Erwin's inner-elbow. Erwin calmed immediately, his eyes rolling backwards, and Charlie straddled him, feeling the arm up and down, finding the crack, snapping it back into place. Erwin half-howled, but it was weak, and then they found a piece of wood and braced the arm with it, tying it off with bits of rope and twine. They left him to sleep, taking turns to watch him, but trying to give him peace.

'He needs to heal,' Charlie told DeVere tersely. 'For the next couple of days, you keep giving him that stuff, then you stop when I tell you too, as soon as the fever breaks.' In the corner Maura watched, and thought about whether his being healed might mean less of the drug for her next time around. It was a week before Erwin was rational again, able to hold a conversation, a week in which he sweated his fever out as DeVere loaded him up over and over, trying to prevent the pain from becoming too much, and everybody took turns watching him, making him semi-consciously drink water to keep his fluids up. It was a week, as well, in which Maura and DeVere slept together again one night, whilst they were meant to be watching Erwin. When they finished they shot up, and neither felt especially guilty.

'I feel sick,' were Erwin's first fully conscious words. Charlie and DeVere were attending, Maura having taken Donald off to find some fresh water in a local park.

'I'll get you some food, maybe,' Charlie said, and pottered off, whistling. DeVere moved closer to Erwin, sat on the floor in front of him.

'We were scared for you, you was making the worst noises. We thought you might need a noonie to suck on, get you through the other side.'

'I'm fine,' Erwin said, but he wasn't sure that he was. His head was blocked and his body ached, and he could feel the shivers running through him. 'The fever seems to be mostly lifted.' DeVere nodded.

'You come to me if you need anything, okay?' Erwin rubbed at the sores on his arms as Charlie came back with the dry toast that he had cooked over the fire they were keeping in one of the large, empty rooms of the warehouse.

From there, Erwin started feeling ill again. They were talking about setting off when he started regressing, the shivers back. He pulled DeVere to one side as they were packing and told him.

'I don't want Charlie to know I'm sick,' he said, and DeVere nodded. He pulled a packet of powder from his coat pocket and shook it in front of Erwin's face.

'You use this stuff till you get better, and then you stop using it. It keeps the pain in check, no?' Erwin agreed with that; the pain in his arm had been getting worse. 'This is only like painkillers, but stronger. Don't fuss; it's nothing to be hont about, boy.' They sat together in a room and DeVere helped him inject himself with the last of their stuff and then rolled his sleeve down for him, so as to cover the hole. Erwin rocked backwards and passed out, and when he woke the pain had gone, and he felt able to move off.

Over the weeks that followed, further segregation in the group occurred, DeVere and Erwin and Maura sneaking off in the evenings to sort themselves out, and then returning to Charlie and Donald. In Denver City they met a woman called Judy, homeless from her teens, and she asked to join them. She was an excellent cook, taking the duties over from DeVere (who, despite having another person to share his heroin with, found himself upping his dose, rendering him slightly more useless every day, and more dependent) and becoming a mother to the group, mirroring the fatherly role that Charlie increasingly inhabited. They had Christmas in Denver, spending the 25th in a restaurant that they found; it had recently shut down, but still had power running through the kitchens, and they cooked a turkey that DeVere stole from a butcher's shop and ate with knives and forks. It was, noted Maura, almost civilised. New Year came and they set off again, heading north. Maura began vomiting one morning, and they assumed a bug, so settled in, but the sickness didn't stop.

'Could you be in the family way, dear?' asked Judy, innocently, and Maura threw up again. Erwin swelled with pride when she told him, and cradled her. He had never realised that he wanted a child, but he did, and Maura's increasingly swollen belly only confirmed it. He would rest his head on it with pride and think about a future (a future where they left the streets, and he got a job under an assumed name, picking up his life. He would earn money and be able to pay to send his child – and subsequent children – to a good school, and they would be happy, and then, in later life, he could call Maynard out of the blue, tell him his story, and they could reconcile, away from the baggage that their family left them lumbered with). Then he would sleep, and he would wake only a few hours later needing more dope. 'You should stop taking that,' Judy told them both, and they nodded. 'It can't be good for the baby,' she would say, and they nodded again, both with the best intentions in the world, and yet not willing to sacrifice this thing that they were both so used to, and so dependent on.

A few months later into the pregnancy and they were starting to have trouble moving around as much. Maura found it harder to be on her feet, and Erwin found it harder to watch her struggle. DeVere insisted that they keep moving, heading nowhere.

'You can't be stationary, not when you live like we do,' he said as justification, but one day – when they were set up at the back of a smelter, with a constant supply of warmth, and a town just down the road that had no less than three supermarkets for them to shop for the cheapest goods from – Erwin told him that they weren't going anywhere.

'We need to rest,' he said, and DeVere got angry.

'You do enough resting,' he said, 'and there's better places than here.'

'Not that we've found, and not with the baby coming.' Donald, Charlie and Judy stood back as they argued, not getting involved, and Maura sat on the floor between them. DeVere clenched his fists.

'That baby is just as likely to be mine as it is yours, boy,' he spat, and Erwin swung for him with his good hand, connecting with DeVere's chin. The Cajun pounced, wrestling Erwin to the floor, and they rolled around, neither at full-strength, and both fighting more as an excuse for something to do until their next hit than for any real reason. When they were done DeVere agreed that they would stay for a while, because it was warm, and found himself a corner away from Erwin and Maura where he made camp and nursed his chin. The next day, Charlie called a meeting.

'There's less money coming in, and I'm taking charge of it. Maura needs food, and Donald. We all need food, so you can all do with less money for your little habit. I'll give you some every day, and you can make do with that.'

'Split it in three,' DeVere told him, 'I ain't shopping for these two no more.' Charlie gave him a handful of coins, and DeVere barked. 'That ain't enough to make a bill,' he said, and threw the coins down. 'I'll find the money my own way.' He stormed out, and they watched the big door swing.

'He'll be back,' said Charlie, but nobody believed him.

Months passed. They stayed in the factory at nights and begged in the days. DeVere returned, tail between his legs, but barely spoke, instead just watching them, watching Maura. Nothing changed. One day Erwin was hunting for the local dealers – his hands were shaking as he was spacing his habit out more, to conserve money so that they had something saved for when the baby was born – when he saw Charlie running through the town, waving his arms to flag him down.

'She's having the baby,' Charlie shouted, and Erwin ran back with him, the heroin suddenly the furthest thought from his mind. The labour lasted hours, well into the next day, and Maura screamed the entire time, Judy on her hands and knees delivering the child, Charlie and Erwin responsible for getting water and towels, and Donald staring, terrified at the noise that Maura was making. At the back of the room sat DeVere, offering only a scowl.

'I can see the head!' Judy shouted, and Erwin ran around to catch a glimpse of his heir. There, staring up, was the child's bloody face, as black as anybody Erwin had ever seen, eyes squeezed tightly shut, mouth already creasing up to howl. Erwin glared at Charlie.

'Don't look at me,' the older man said. In the corner Donald started to cry as well, but nobody went over to shut him up.

Erwin was standing outside in the cold, trying to keep his mind off both what he was going to say to Maura and the ache in his arm, when DeVere appeared. He offered Erwin a cigarette. Erwin shook his head.

'At least it's not yours either,' he said, and walked off.

Charlie found Erwin sitting on a park bench. In his veins he felt the warmth of the first part of the high, and he – for a few brief hours – managed to forget all about Maura and the baby, and the hopes that he had harboured. Charlie sat next to him.

'DeVere's gone. He said to pass on his condolences.' Charlie snorted. 'Maura won't stop crying, you know.' Erwin didn't reply. 'She's as messed up over this as you are, son, probably worse. She needs you, boy. Don't screw this one up any more than it already is.' Charlie left, but Erwin stayed until it got dark. From outside the factory he could hear the baby cry, and he just stood there, waiting for it to stop. Inside, Maura felt sick, and coughed, choked, found herself unable to breathe, smacked the floor for attention. Everybody else slept through the crying of the child as its mother died there, alone, behind the smelter.

17

At the start of his ninth year in prison, Maynard was called in to see the governor. It was an elaborate affair where Maynard, despite being offered coffee or tea when he arrived, and having it served in dainty china cups with elaborate floral patterns printed on them, had to keep his handcuffs and chains on the entire time. (The governor was terrified that any prisoner, given the chance, would attempt to kill him. He had recurring dreams when dealing with the prison system, of the prisoners launching themselves around his office and somehow tearing chunks from him. It was, he recognised, an utterly irrational fear, as any attempt made on his life would render them locked up for life at his behest. However, he still feared it, and with Maynard – quiet, non-violent Maynard – the fear was just as strong.) The meeting was short, and to the point.

'Maynard Sloane,' the governor said, 'your name has been put forward by some of the guards for this pardon. You have an exemplary behavioural record.' (The record was an official document, and didn't include rumours and hearsay. Therefore, neither of the deaths that Maynard was implicated in whilst in prison were included in it.) 'I think you're suitable for an early parole, don't you?' Maynard thanked him, and they shook hands (though the Governor's grip was far weaker than Maynard's, far more hesitant). 'There's a ceremony at Christmas, so hang on in there until then, and you'll be home by New Year.'

Less than a month away, Maynard realised. That night he

pictured his house looking exactly as it was when he left, and wondered if Lia would still be there with it.

His final month in the prison was quieter than most. He wound down his music classes, sending a couple of students through grade-diplomas in piano and singing. He finished the next segment of the Sloane family story, written up in his book with all the others. He said his goodbyes to everybody who affected him, good or bad, and he waited to leave, the days longer, harder to get through. He could taste his freedom, and he wanted it more than he ever realised.

Theodore Sloane worked for the new (and still shuddering) American government in Philadelphia, helping to build and prepare the first room for their congress to sit in. The day of the their first meeting he was putting the final touches on the benches, his calloused hands sanding the edges of the wood, when Josiah Bartlett, from New England, came in, congratulated him on the building.

'Would you sit in with us this afternoon?' he asked as Theodore finished polishing the tables.

'Would that not be inappropriate?'

Josiah laughed. 'It's your country too, Theodore. You can sit where you damned well like.' And so, that afternoon, Theodore sat in the room with representatives from all thirteen states as they spoke about, and signed their country away to, themselves.

Upon his return home that evening, tired and numb and more than a little drunk, Theodore decided to pack his daughter, Clara, off to bed early and spend time with his wife.

'I'm tired, and it's dark. That means it is time for you to sleep,' he told Clara, locking her door so that she couldn't disturb them. Pulling his wife Madelyn to bed, he tore her

clothes and prodded at her with those same calloused hands, proud of his achievements. Afterwards, breathing and coughing onto her naked shoulder, he slept without saying goodnight, and she lay staring at the ceiling for the next few hours until she finally drifted off.

At some point during the night Clara attempted to open her bedroom door. She stumbled in the darkness across the clear wood floorboards to the table next to the doorway, bumped into it, and grabbed the lamp in order to see her way to the gap between the door and the frame, that she might try and lift the latch on the other side. However, she didn't realise that the lamp gas had spilled when she nudged the table, and the match that she lit set fire to the small puddle, in turn making her howl and throw her arms into the air, sending the pool of flames up with them, across her arms, her face, her body. She carried on screaming through her father beating down the door, and through him hauling her body through the house and throwing her on the lawn, where she died. The first day that Theodore's family officially spent as Americans should probably have been somewhat less subdued than it was; but then, their first day as Americans should probably not have been celebrated with the death of their only child. The next day, Madelyn drowned herself to stop from crying.

Months passed, and Theodore's comeback was much awaited by the new elders of their country. They all knew of his plight and sent gifts – oranges, cherries, driftwood sculptures – and they held a party to announce his re-entry into polite society. He arrived late, full of apologies, his outfit gold and red and rich, and he stood by the grand doors in the hall and loudly cleared his throat to make an announcement.

'And now,' he started as he was passed a glass of wine by Jefferson's wife, 'I would like to introduce my new wife; Consuela Sloane!' The audience gasped as the doors flew open, and the ruddiest lady that they had ever seen flowed into the room. She swayed across the floor, her garish dress expanding and contracting with every kick of her slightly swollen ankles, her lips teasing half kisses at the wigged men and their primrose wives. 'We met in Plymouth, when I went to bury Madelyn and Clara, and we married almost straight away,' Theodore said. 'She is not much for our language, I warn you, but she has taught me many things, ladies,' he said, turning on the spot, smiling at as many of them as he could see, and smoothing his mustache flat across his cheeks, 'things that would ensure that your husbands will never want another!' Theodore and Consuela kissed, their tongues fluttering over each other, his hands wandering to her tied and presented bosom, and then they began the dancing. Later that evening the men gathered in the library over hand-rolled cigars and glasses of strong liquor. They all asked Theodore to tell them more about the sexual exploits that he now encountered. He smiled, showing a mouth full of wooden teeth, and, displaying none of his prior coyness, drew them pictures. That night, as they lay in bed, Theodore told his wife what he expected of her. 'I'm anxious that you fit into this society,' he had said, 'as I feel I could really go far here, with the right influences.' She nodded, and then slipped below the covers to show him another of her tricks.

Consuela started attending meetings with the wives of the heads of state, learning the subtleties of the language that had so far eluded her. She learnt the various ways to describe what she was cooking, and she learnt how to address strangers in polite company. More importantly, she learnt how to flirt with these gentlemen, who stared at her chest as she breathily said their names and curtsied her eyes. The gentlemen, in turn, learnt to hide their flirts with Consuela from the eyes of her husband and their wives. In this way, she began her affairs. Parties began to run as thus: they would enter, invited because everybody had been; greetings would flow, Theodore trying too hard to appease his peers, which would culminate in him leading them off to back rooms to throw whatever ideas he had gathered together at them, hoping that one would stick, and ingratiate him into the government; as he pitched, Consuela would sneak off to powder-rooms, and meet the sons of statesmen, butlers, drivers. She would let them take her there, immediately, biting her own hand to stop from screaming. She took to carrying red gloves with her to cover the marks. Hours later they would invariably reconvene at the foot of the large staircase in whichever hall or house the party was being held at, Theodore disheartened that his ideas had been rebuffed, and Consuela flowing behind the covered giggles of her friends.

'She's so daring,' they would whisper as she waved goodbye to them, 'so ignorant.' The next thing they knew, Consuela was pregnant.

Theodore had, until the announcement of the pregnancy, believed himself to have become infertile. Since Clara's conception he had engaged in intercourse on a number of occasions, with none of the encounters bearing any children. When Consuela missed her third cycle and was beginning to gain weight he was overjoyed. He showered her with the finest gifts that he could lay his hands on – a pony, a cherry tree, imported chocolates – and ensured that extra hands were hired to care for her. Consuela's labour came quickly and forcefully, taking them by surprise months before they expected it. She was on the table for twelve hours before she gave birth. The doctor in charge, one of Theodore's oldest friends, immediately came to see him.

'We're calling the baby Manuel!' yelled an excited and slightly drunken Theodore.

'The child's a negro,' the doctor said as Theodore lit his fifth cigar of the evening. His eyes fell black, and he found that he could not cry.

Thirty minutes later the doctor announced to a patiently waiting assemblage of friends that, unfortunately, both mother and child had died in childbirth. 'Theodore will need your well wishes, I'm sure,' they were told, and the room collectively cried in condolence. That evening the doctor arranged to have the bodies burnt, with a funeral to take place the following day, and weeks later he took delivery of a pony, a cherry tree and two slaves from the Sloane estate. Five years later, Theodore met a woman called Cecily, and they had a son together, who they named Damian, again disproving his infertility. He never loved Cecily as much as his other two wives (for their different reasons), but she did him, and that saw them through.

The press conference announcing his pardon was at midday, so Maynard spent the morning pacing his cell, eating his last breakfast in the prison – which was oatmeal, just as it had been every other day of his stay there – and worrying that something would go wrong, that the pardon would somehow be rescinded. In the truck that drove him to the conference he bit his nails furiously, and the escorting policemen made fun of him.

'You think he might make a break for it?' they asked each other, joking around. Maynard ignored them until they pulled up outside the town hall where it was all taking place, and one of them opened the doors. He smiled, and mocked starting to run when they helped him down from the truck. They all laughed together.

Inside the hall, the governor shook his hand slightly less warily than he had before, and gave a speech to the assembled press.

'Maynard Sloane came to this prison under a fog of confusion, confusion as to whether he was truly guilty of the crime that he was accused of – a crime that many didn't see as a crime to begin with.' (In his later years in office, the governor would become a staunch pro-euthanasia advocate.) 'His record throughout his time here has been exemplary, and his care and attentiveness has brought music into our lives where once there had been none. Everybody at Oneida State Correctional Facility is going to miss Maynard, and it is my pleasure to grant him his freedom today, and wish him all the luck in the world in this, his new life.' He shook Maynard's hand again, and they both posed for the cameras. Maynard cried through the flash-bulbs.

The paperwork took hours, Maynard signing documents in triplicate, waiting for them to be notorised, then signing more. The state, he knew, had to cover themselves. When that was done, his possessions were handed back to him, along with a pile of his now ill-fitting clothes, including a coat that hung from his body as if his shoulders were nothing more than a wire hanger, and he was set free outside the courthouse. A camera crew descended, a woman with puffed up and rigid hair pushing her microphone towards his face like the tentative opened jabs of a boxing match.

'Mr Sloane, would you like to say a few words for the people at home? How does it feel to be granted your release? Are you surprised?' Maynard looked around at the people, at how much even ten years could change the way that they looked, the technology they were brandishing.

'I'm always surprised,' he said.

He got into Penn Station just after seven. The city wasn't yet dark, still in that half-dusk that made it look its best. Nobody even contemplated noticing him. He decided to not head straight home, lugging his bag instead through Times Square, taking in the people, the feeling of being back, of being somewhere. The signs had changed, the frontispieces, the branding now spread further around the buildings, wrapping them in screens and billboards, over-sized and over-technologised presents. The whole place was brighter, and the streets were heaving with people either leaving – flowing towards the station, briefcases in hand – or heading out for the evening, tourists going to theatres and restaurants. He stood by the police-stand in the middle, the men and women in their blue uniforms making him feel slightly more reassured, and just soaked it all up.

The house was still in the same place, the same street, he was relieved to discover. (He had been afraid of returning and finding it demolished, or sold off, and having to pick through the rubble for anything that he had left behind and wanted to save.) The street was lined with cars now, all expensive, by the look of them, and the few people that he saw entering and exiting their houses – none of whom he recognised – were all well-to-do, all in suits or nice jackets, furs and leathers. The Sloane house stood out like a smear of dirt on glass; the rest of the houses – with their shiny new paintjobs and double-glazed windows – making it look like a relic, torn from another time and squeezed in between them. The steps needed a wash, old leaves turned to mush in the corners, and the door was greyed, aside from a few handprints where people had seen the gathered dust, tested its depth. His key – which had sat in the possessions box for ten years now – still fit the lock, and still turned, still with the same force needed, the same tricks to open it. He stood on the doorstep, the house unlocked and ready to enter, and marvelled at how he remembered the intricacies even after all these years.

The door jammed against the letters and newspapers that were piled up in the hallway. They spilled backwards to the doorway of the living room, and he could see that they had towered themselves (as more and more were added through the letterbox) and collapsed, multiple times. He managed to crack the door open enough to see in further, to see the years and years of print spilling inwards, like a sea somehow turned solid. He reached in and grabbed the closest, dated four years previous. After a while, he reasoned, the delivery boys wouldn't have been able to squeeze the papers in anymore, and they would have just stopped. He thought about where the money to pay for the subscriptions came from, how it must have eaten chunks from the family savings – if such a thing even existed – and how it was ironic that the subscriptions were maintained anyway, after Erwin's death; even before it, given how his brother had all but stopped reading in the wake of his relationship with Lia. He heaved the door more, watched the piles shift and tumble, and squeezed in, watching his steps as the mail slid around underneath him like loose ice. The house didn't reveal itself to him properly until he was past it (nearly at the stairs, so deep was the pile), and he could suddenly see it exactly as it was in his memories, only shrouded, wrapped in whiteness. Everything he could see that wasn't the wall or the floor was draped in a sheet, and then either – as with the banister – taped off to hold it in place, or – in the case of the pictures on the wall, the mirrors – tucked behind them. (He wouldn't know this, but before Lia left for London she went to a local upholsterer and bought all their white sheets, then spent the best part of a day wrapping everything up, ready for whoever came into the house next.) The piano still stood where it always did, tucked by the side of the stairs, the sheet running right over it, tucked into the lid like a mouth sucking on cotton. The house looked like it was full of Halloween ghosts.

'Hello?' he said, but didn't expect a reply; it was really to just hear himself, to be reassured that this was actually happening. Aside from the dust, the house was clean. The books were as he remembered, the kitchen – aside from the appliances, which all looked old – still homely, the bedrooms still as they were when he was a child. Nothing, he thought, moved on. Nothing changed.

The power and water were disconnected – he imagined that the increasingly colourful letters from their respective companies were in amongst the piles, as well as notices of impending court dates and legal documents. The mail, he knew, would have to be sorted another day, in case there was anything important – probably from the bank, informing him of exactly how dreadful a state his family finances were in – but right then, he didn't know where to start. He was hungry; he knew that much.

In Erwin's bedroom was a jar filled with coins, just spare change, so Maynard grabbed a handful of the largest denominations and headed out, walking to the nearest diner. There he ordered a dinner and sat, watching the people again, eating a roast that cost him over twice what it would have cost before he went to prison. When he was finished he paid and went home, stripped the cover sheet from his bed, found a blanket in the wardrobe and lay down. He stared at the ceiling all night, and found himself strangely longing for the clanging of nightstick on bars, the cat-calls of racial slurs ringing out through the darkness.

18

They had a funeral for Maura at the back of the smelter. Charlie spent some of their money on a shovel and dug a hole in the woods, and instructed Donald to make a cross from twigs and twine. (Charlie had been teaching Donald about God, about how he was all around them, and how he helped them in their day-to-day. This was the first time that he had been forced to deal with God and death in the same sentence, and Donald didn't understand. 'It's all part of a plan,' Charlie kept repeating, but as he wrapped Maura's body in a sheet that they had stolen from a building site, he wondered.) They had a service, Charlie reciting some passages from the Bible, Judy crying at the side of the grave. Erwin stood with the baby, not yet given a name, and jiggled it up and down, keeping it calm, cradling its neck, the back of its head. He watched the soft spots on her crown pulse as Charlie spoke, using them to stop himself from being overwhelmed. When the service – such as it was – was finished, they went inside, and Judy started gathering her possessions into a black bag.

'We're leaving,' Charlie told Erwin, 'we're done. With DeVere gone, Maura passed; this feels like the right time, we think.'

'You and Judy both?' asked Erwin, and Charlie nodded.

'We'll take care of Donald, if you want us to, but we're too old to go carrying a baby around with us.'

'We could leave her at a hospital.'

'She'll go into the system.' He embraced Erwin, which surprised them both. 'When I was younger, I thought of going back, to everything I ran away from, just taking what was coming to me. I didn't. You can. I'm too old to make amends, Erwin. You're not.' Judy came and said goodbye as well then, and Donald, who stood at the back and waved. Erwin waved back. When they had gone, walking south, Erwin went to the makeshift crib that Charlie had made for the baby, and found all of the money that they had gained from the past few days' collecting. He was so touched that he cried, and that started the baby crying, so he tried as best he could to calm them both down.

The bus took him East, because it was the first one to arrive. It was quiet, so he sat on the back row so as to have somewhere to change her if he needed to. Magically, she slept most of the way – Erwin assumed that it had something to do with the thrum of the bus as they drove, which, as he lay back with her at his side on the seat, felt like breathing, the pattern and roll of somebody inhaling over and over – and when they arrived at whatever town it was that they were in, Erwin found a cheap hotel. He put down the last of the money on a room, with a meal ticket for the diner out the front included in the price. He ate the meal quickly, devouring the sloppy burger that they gave him, the glass of ice cold Coke that tasted better than he ever remembered it tasting, and then he set himself and the baby up in the room, closing the curtains even though it wasn't yet dark, and had his best night's sleep in ten years. In the warmth of the room, even the baby slept through.

He awoke to a newspaper being thrown casually against the door. He mixed some baby milk with water from the coffee maker, made himself a cup of coffee, put himself through a rigorous and steaming shower from the overly-powerful faucet (which felt like hailstones on his sensitive skin). He had started to sweat and shiver from the lack of heroin in his system. He wrapped himself in a blanket and switched on the television. He flicked through the channels, marvelling at how many there were. And then he saw him, his brother, Maynard, shaking hands with a man in a cape, before being ushered down the steps of what looked like a courthouse.

'How does it feel to be a free man?' the reporters were all shouting. They did a recap on the screen of the case, flashing a picture up of the mother, the accusations originally thrown at Maynard. In the video, Maynard smiled and thanked the reporters for their interest in his story. He looks happy, thought Erwin. An hour later, unable to stop thinking about Maynard, Erwin picked up the phone handset and dialled the number of his old house, but it was dead.

People stared. At lunchtime, after finding a five dollar bill on the pavement, Erwin got a hot-dog from a cart, and the man who served him spent an age peering at both him and the baby, gauging their features, weighing up their relationship. (This was in case he was asked by the police to identify them. He couldn't be sure, but suspected that Erwin had stolen the child from somewhere. That is, thought the hot-dog seller, the sort of thing that people did nowadays.) In a launderette, where he washed the spare clothes that he had amassed – both for him and the infant – people muttered and shook their heads, and asked him general questions that probed deeper than he would like.

'Baby's momma not around today?'

'She's dead,' he said.

'She must have been one pretty lady,' one woman said. (By which she meant, 'She must have been black,' but was too polite to say that outright.)

'She was,' Erwin replied. (He didn't pick up on the undertones in the question.)

'What's her name?'

'I haven't decided yet,' Erwin said, which made the women by the dryers pull faces at each other.

'How did you say her momma died?' one asked, her voice overblown with hostility, so Erwin quickly gathered his just-cleaned (but not quite dry) clothes and left. Behind him, they jeered and called for him to come back. He didn't. At night, the baby missed the warmth of the hotel. Every time that Erwin found them somewhere to lie down she howled, and he was forced to move on as people stuck their heads out of their windows to see where the noise was coming from. She would sleep for an hour, and Erwin would drift off, thinking that they were safe, and then she would start again. He found it hard to get provisions by himself, not nearly raising enough money from his single-person begging job, even with the baby cradled in his arms. If anything, he thought, takings were lower, people sneering as they saw him. One woman – in her business suit, her shoulders as wide as her feet, dressed like she was just a rectangular shape, a box – spat in his hat that he used for begging.

'You should be ashamed, using the baby like that,' she said. He spent all of his money on a coffee from an expensive coffee shop so that he could get hot water for the baby's milk, and then had to rummage for his own dinner when the town had gone to bed, the baby crying the whole time. She started to run a fever, and coughed herself rigid on a few occasions, and he thought that he had lost her. (She had been born with the same blood as cursed her mother's veins; in this case, that blood had an addiction to heroin. This was her, as a baby, going through cold turkey.) She would recover in waves, and he would panic, and think about leaving her at a hospital, but he didn't know what that would accomplish, or if they would, somehow, track him down, imprison him for abandoning her.

'This isn't working,' he said to nobody. 'We need to change this.'

Erwin's skills from his time as an engineer were transferable. He could fix pipes, find heat sources when needed, and knew the best ways to insulate against the cold, even when faced with rags and scraps of clothing to use. They also helped him as he sat in a diner, cradling a single cup of coffee that he managed to make last for hours, and watched the people. He was looking for the ones most likely to do what he wanted, just as he used to when searching for the right place to dig a hole or lay some cable. He spotted a few different options – the family, husband, wife, two children, ordered ice creams, left laughing; the couple who were staring at an engagement ring on the woman's finger, the gay couple, holding hands semi-secretly, never stopping smiling – but the perfect choice appeared a little after four in the afternoon, as the waitress was starting to get impatient with him. There were three of them, a mother, a father, and a little girl, all well-dressed, all happy. They ate a meal, and the father teased his daughter about something or other. He heard them talk about a holiday they were going to book, and about the girl's school prospects – she had been put on the waiting list for a good one, and her chances were, the mother thought, good – and about the father's work. He was a doctor, a GP, and the rest of his week was full. They even looked like the baby that Erwin held close to his chest, all with light-but-dark skin, the little girl sharing his ward's huge eyes. They paid, so Erwin did as well, finishing his money again, just as he did every time he paid for anything, and they walked out and through the streets, stopping at a grocery store to buy a bagful of things, then heading off again. Erwin followed them all the way to their big home, in a nice area, and he saw their front room through the window, their nice things, their lovely furniture, their expensive car out front, their well-kept garden.

He waited a few hours in an alley around the back of the house, hiding in the shadows, shrugging himself down when they passed by their windows laughing and joking as they cooked a dinner that he could smell wafting on the air – and smelt amazing – and wrote a note for them, then kissed the baby goodbye. ('Dear Family,' the note read, 'Please look after this baby, as I cannot. Her name is Maura Evelyn, and she'll be no trouble. I wish this could all have happened differently, but it didn't. She's ill, and I don't know how to help her, but I think that you will. Please take her in, and give her everything that I cannot.') She coughed and shivered as he placed her on the doorstep with her tub of milk-mixture, and he knew as he pressed the doorbell and ran off, hearing her tiny mouth hacking in the darkness, that he had made the right decision.

Erwin found an area with other homeless people, and he spoke to them for a while, trying to find somewhere to score some heroin, but the only person who had any wasn't willing to share, so he lay under cardboard and he shivered as the need for more of the drug grabbed hold. When he woke up, drenched in sweat but still shivering, the people that had been staying with him were gone, and a policeman was standing over him with a flashlight shining in his face.

'You look like you need something to eat,' he said, and passed Erwin a sandwich from a pack at his side. 'Sit in the car – it's warm in there – and eat this.' Erwin did as he was told, afraid that he would be arrested, but needing the food. As he ate it he caught sight of himself in the rearview mirror, gaunt and white and dripping, his hair frayed and receding, what was there stuck to his forehead with sweat. His teeth were yellow and thin, his cheeks in-set, and his eyes paler than he ever remembered them being. When he had finished the sandwich he thanked the officer. 'No worries,' the man said, 'but get yourself cleaned up, yeah? That shit you're on ain't gonna keep you alive for much longer.'

'I know,' Erwin said. 'I've already stopped.'

Three days later, and Erwin's withdrawal was at its worst. He lay on the hard plastic chairs in the shelter, the TV in front of him playing episodes of *Taxi* back to back. He watched the short fat man and the foreign man, and, even though he didn't know their names, they made him laugh through the fug of the pain that he was in. Every time the scene changed they showed a static shot of New York, of different parts of it, and

Erwin recognised them all, and they all made him sad.

'I've got to go home,' he said, stuttering, his teeth chattering, and nobody there to listen to him.

It took Erwin weeks to pull himself together, to get to a state where he could stop himself vomiting, and stop soiling himself, and actually begin to think about travelling. Food wouldn't stay down, and he was barely able to manage water for a while, and he was unable to walk any great distance without getting tired, or feeling nauseous again. The people who worked at the shelter helped him as much as they could – they were thrilled to see somebody in his state so determined to pull themselves together, as most people going through withdrawal that ended up there only stayed until they raised enough money for another hit – and they cooked him supper when he was able to take it, and let him use their lavatory when the others were full, then let him sleep in the shelter at night, after they had locked up (something that was usually forbidden). When he stood up one day and told them that he was leaving, heading back to New York on the first bus he could find, they applauded him, and gave him a gift – an envelope with enough money for a one-way ticket.

On the bus he sat at the front, and watched as the road signs counted down the distance to New York City. He realised that, for the first time in years, he was excited about something.

19

The bank manager's office was almost entirely leather, from the chairs to the wipe-clean paneling that lined the walls. Maynard sank into one of the chairs, his suit scratching against the back, and the chair puffing out abruptly as he settled. The manager, an obese man who insisted on being called by his first name – Chuck – sat across from Maynard, behind his desk. His chair, Maynard noted, was not the same sort as the ones that the guests used, being wider, more secure. Chuck was, Maynard deduced from his accent, Texan.

'Mr Sloane,' Chuck said, 'your account hasn't exactly been a hotbed of activity these last few years.' He smiled, and Maynard smiled back.

'I know,' Maynard told him, and the big man nodded.

'Good. I mean, there were some huge withdrawls,' he said, pointing to some numbers on his screen, the blocky green font unreadable with Maynard's worse-than-he-realised eyesight, 'but that was over ten years ago.'

'Legal fees.'

Chuck raised an eyebrow. 'There's a few thousand dollars. There's been some interest on the account, but there's been a steady outgoing of payments to various organisations...'

'What payments?'

'Hang on.' He typed at the keyboard with his fingers, as thick as Snickers bars, and then rapped them on the table. 'Computers are slow,' he said, as way of apology, then the screen beeped, and he read the details. 'Looks like newspaper subscriptions, some fees to a funeral home, a mortuary, and that all leaves you with a little shy of ten thousand dollars.' He checked the screen again. 'And you don't have a cash-card, so we'll get you one of those.' Maynard fidgeted. 'Any other questions, Mr Sloane?'

'Call me Maynard,' he answered, 'Mr Sloane was my father.'

Maynard went back to the house, stared at the sheets, at the emptiness, at the particles of dust just hanging around in the strips of sunlight, waiting for something to happen, and decided to do something with the money. He went to 5th Avenue, to the high-class travel agents that his father once dragged them to in an effort to take a holiday, all of them, together, and sat in front of one of the bored-looking women behind the desk.

'I want to go away,' he said. She smiled and pulled out brochures.

'Where were you thinking of?' she asked.

'I'm not sure, really. Surprise me.' Maynard smiled.

Erwin's journey to the house was much like Maynard's, only more ponderous. He was terrified about the implications of his return, as to whether Maynard and Lia – if she was even still around – would accept him back into their lives. He wasn't even sure if he wanted them to. He walked past the house four or five times (trying to see lights, twitching curtains, any sign of life), then patrolled the whole neighbourhood, looking at what else had changed. New York was, as always, a few years ahead of everywhere else, but it was still the same, still the same steam from the streets, the same taxi cabs, the same shouting. When he finally plucked up the courage to go up to the front he realised that he didn't have keys, so he hammered on the door and waited for Maynard to answer. He sat on the steps and waited for night to come. When it did, and there was still no sign of his brother or Lia, he fiddled with the living room window, jimmying it open – he knew that it was loose to lock, it always had been – and clambered in, feet on the sofa. He saw the whiteness, saw the dust, and ran through the house, flinging open the doors. It was the most excitement that the dust had seen in ten years, and it danced around in his wake.

Maynard's travels took him all around the world. He saw the pyramids, and they looked as if they had been torn out of the books that he used to read about them, single colour totems laid flat on the sands; he saw the temples of China, majestic and painted in the brightest hues, with golden animals on podiums protecting them; he saw the snows of Russia, flustered and chaotic and tired, preparing for the Olympics; he saw England, Wales, Scotland, whistling around them on trains, stopping and buying cheese or meats, visiting castles, hiding from the rain and then moving on; he saw Italy, and spent a few days walking the woods and relaxing by a quiet swimming pool on a mountainside (and, quite coincidentally and unbeknown to him, staying only a few miles from where Wendy now lived); and he saw Morocco, and wandered the markets. His eventual flight home took hours, and he slept almost the entire way, waking with a new sense of self and purpose. He was, he decided as they landed, ready to start his new life, and he would begin by selling the dusty old house that he used to call home.

Maynard's key turned in the lock, as it always did, only the door opened with ease, the lock slightly cleaned, the hinges creak-free, the blockade gone. The mail and papers, Maynard saw, had been piled up against the wall in towers, simply and casually, and the white sheets were gone from some of the fixtures and fittings. The house was brighter, lighter, and smelt of cooking. It was a smell that Maynard knew, but couldn't place, it was so far in the back of his mind.

'Hello?' Maynard shouted, not expecting a reply – he didn't know what he was expecting – and Erwin stepped out into the kitchen doorway.

'Hello brother,' he said, and Maynard nearly died from the shock.

Part Three

Our history begins before we are born.
We represent the hereditary influences of our race,
and our ancestors virtually live in us.

James Nasmyth

20

Young Vito Sloane's favourite stories were the ones told by his mother, Lia, and invariably involved her escapades around Europe when he was far younger.

'When you were just born, weighing little more than a bag of flour, we were in London,' she told him, 'and then we moved to Crete, to the sun!' Vito loved stories about times past, about where they came from (even though he had no knowledge of his father).

Just after leaving New York with the Mandlebraums, Lia discovered that she was pregnant. Her belly barely swelled, but she delivered on time, having the baby in Hammersmith, in West London. She called him Vito, after her father, and when the time came to filling in the birth certificate, she didn't know what to put. 'Well, it's Erwin's, isn't it?' asked Joshua Mandlebraum, and she told him that she didn't know. He shook his head. 'Put Erwin,' he said. 'He's passed on, so there'll be no contesting legalities down the road.' She wrote the name in, filled the occupation box – engineer – and then wrote the date of his death in the little box. When the nurse took it she gave Lia a consoling hug. 'Just you and the little one now, then?' Lia nodded. They left immediately for Greece, with the Mandlebraums, and lived for Vito's first year in Crete. The day that he turned one, Lia spent the day walking around Chania, exploring the bookshops and jewellery stands along the front, Vito grabbing at every one of the orange rubber ballasts on the nets that lined the pavements along the front as he leaned out of his pushchair, and then they sat in a taverna for the evening, watching the sun go down over the harbour. At the time, Lia had just started seeing a man called Christos and that evening he proposed. She looked at Vito, how happy he was, and nearly said yes.

Vito would listen to the stories and then imagine how they might end as he drifted off to sleep, as Lia never got to finish them before his eyes shut. The eldest of the Mandlebraum children had just left for university, and Vito had graduated to his bedroom, ready to break into double-digits.

They weren't treated like household staff any more; Lia had taken to working for Joshua Mandlebraum's business, taking control of PA and secretarial duties, and was settled, as much as she could be. Every year or so it was announced that they were moving again, so she packed her bag – she had learned to pack light, learned what you needed to take with you, and what could be left behind – and they were off. Vito loved it – he loved seeing new things. That day after Maynard was released from prison they were informed that they were heading to Barcelona.

'Have you ever been there?' asked Vito as they packed. He bounced on the bed, excited by the books that Lia had shown him of sun-baked streets and parasols sunk into the sand. (They were leaving Berlin, which, whilst not without its charms, wasn't quite as picture-perfect as the Spanish city.)

'I have not,' she said, 'but I hear it's lovely. What are you most looking forward to?'

'The beaches,' her son said, 'I really want to build some sandcastles, and go swimming.' They finished packing and dragged their bags down the stairs, piling them up by the front door to wait for the car that was coming to pick them all up. As they rode in the car on the way to the airport he asked if they could go the beach that day, when they arrived.

'We'll see,' Lia told him.

'I really want to make some sandcastles.' He took out his book and opened it to the page that he had folded over. 'I think I want to make buildings when I'm older.' Lia heard him, and forced herself to smile.

Their house was right in the centre, next door to the house that the Mandlebraums – father, mother, daughter – occupied. Down the street was a market that sold fresh meat and fish and vegetables and fruit and a wide array of clothing, which was all they needed, reasonably. Lia taught Vito from the syllabus books that she had left over from the Mandlebraum children (as the amount of moving around that they did would have been hell for him in local schools, dealing with the language changes), and at weekends they drove down the dusty roads to Sitges and went swimming, built sandcastles, and she drank beer from bottles whilst sitting on the sand, men occasionally coming over in gaggles, introducing themselves. She laughed at their too-tight swimming trunks, at their glossy legs, their slicked back hair, but let them charm her, buy her drinks. Vito made friends with the other children on the beach, and at lunchtime they all ate burgers from one of the shacks, then picked ice creams from their rumbling freezers. When evening came they would visit local places and eat dinner, and then they swam in the warmed-up water, or they watched the tide lap at the walls of Vito's sandcastles, furrowing its way into the walls until they fell in on themselves, then Lia drove them back, still slightly drunk, but she drove slowly, and then she put Vito to bed and told him a story, just like always.

'Can we stay here?' Vito asked one night, after they had eaten paella with some of their neighbours, all crowded around a table in their tiny house, surrounded by almost non-stop laughter.

'Maybe,' Lia said, hoping that they could.

21

The brothers sat at the table and ate Erwin's stew. He had bought the ingredients (along with a large can of gas that was now plugged into the back of the oven) with some money that he found in his bedroom – which still looked as it had the day that he died. The stew tasted just as Maynard remembered, and he chewed at it stiffly, unable to stop staring at Erwin. The scar across his brother's neck pulled at itself as his jaw worked, stubble growing on either side of it, the stretch itself staying pink and clean. Erwin could only glance at Maynard; neither of them knew where to start, so they didn't say anything.

When they had finished eating they cleared the plates and stacked them in the sink (as there was still no water to wash them with). They wandered around each other until Maynard said that he was tired, after his flight.

'We'll talk tomorrow,' he said, and went to his room. He listened to Erwin bash around the house for hours, finally heading to bed close to midnight. Ten minutes later Maynard heard his brother's door open. He panicked that Erwin was going to run off again, so was starting to get dressed – to chase him down, tell him not to go anywhere – when he heard a soft rapping at his own door. Erwin came in and stood in front of Maynard.

'I'm sorry,' he said, and Maynard put his arms around his elder brother and held him as they both cried. When they were done with the tears they sat on Maynard's bed, and Erwin helped Maynard sort the next story from their family history into order as Maynard wrote it into his book. When he was finished Erwin was already asleep, so he joined him, both of them sleeping in the same room for the first time since they were children.

At his father's funeral, word reached Damian Sloane's ears that America had declared war on the United Kingdom in what was being hushedly spoken of as a Second War of Independence. As the body of Theodore Sloane was lowered into the ground, and his long life celebrated, his only surviving child contemplated what contribution he might be able to make to the war effort. That evening, he told his plans to Bryony, his wife, as they ate their dinner.

'I'm going to travel to Philadelphia and enlist,' he said, 'and I'm going tomorrow.' She flustered.

'So soon?'

'If I don't,' he replied, 'we could lose. One wave can turn the tide, dearest, and I could be that wave.' (She was petrified. Bryony's mother had died in childbirth, and her father had died a few years later, of heart problems. She had gone to live with her grandparents, and they had died of old age, and then lived with their neighbours, who also, just before she met Damian, fell foul to an accident involving a horse. She was terrified that it was her fault they were dying, and Damian reassured her that it wasn't. He proved it, she believed, by living when they married, and managing to stay alive through a burst of cholera

that, ultimately, had consumed his father. This, however, was something else.)

'Do you have to go?' she asked the next morning as he strapped on his boots, and he nodded.

'I will be staunch,' he said, 'because that's what Sloane men are, Bryony. Will you fetch me breakfast?' She nodded, and went into the garden to the apple tree, picked the freshest one she could see, and then mashed the apple in the kitchen into a fine paste.

'It's ready,' she shouted, and then, out of the corner of her eye, noticed the small jar that Damian had left on the side, labelled with a crudely drawn skull. It had come from a local trapper, and was designed to help kill the skunks that Damian hated, and patrolled their garden like attackers, waiting to strike with their musk. Having not yet heard her husband coming down the stairs, she grabbed one of the pellets from the jar and tore it apart, distributing the dust and juice inside it over his apple sauce. (She knew it was such a small amount that it wouldn't kill him, but it might play merry with his stomach, and prevent him leaving quite so quickly.) Damian came downstairs, his boots hitting the wood with the stride of determination, and he ate the bowl of fruit straight up. When he was finished he wiped his mouth.

'I should leave,' he said, and kissed Bryony, then dragged his pack behind him as he headed into the centre of town. He was just past the marker pointing him towards Philadelphia when his stomach gurgled for the first time, but he wrote it off as indigestion. By the time he was a mile down the road he began to taste bile in his throat, and another mile later he was on the floor in the dust, heaving the apple sauce from his mouth, smacking the dirt with his hands at the pain. He passed out as the sun grew stronger.

Assuming that her plan hadn't worked, Bryony cleaned the

house and wept until nightfall, when she went to bed early. She was woken by a hard knocking in the middle of the night. Peering from her window Bryony saw a group of merchants unloading something from their wagon.

'Mrs Sloane?' one of them shouted up to the window. 'We have your husband, we think.' Damian was in a bad way, propped against the well outside their house, his skin the colour of oats. 'You'll need to take him in,' they told her. Bryony dragged him to his bed as he murmured and rambled. She watched him sleep, hoping that he would get better, but not too much. The next morning he was feeling better, having exhumed most of his illness during his night-sweats, and he spoke about leaving as soon as he was able. Bryony knew what she had to do, and mixed his dinner that evening – a pie, the first food he had taken in since he first fell ill – with a thin squeezing of the poisoned berry. More illness followed, and the pattern was repeated another three or four times. Each time Damian was made weaker, and recovery took longer, but his resolve was still there.

'When I'm better, Bryony, I will leave,' he would say, and she would feel open another of the pellets and make some more dinner.

Eventually Bryony ran out of pellets, and couldn't find any more, as the trapper was out on a hunt. Damian recovered, and finally did as he was threatening, and left. He walked out of the town and towards Philadelphia, and Bryony sat at home and cried, going through grief before she even had cause to. The first night Damian slept at the side of the road, and was awoken by screaming in the morning as a horse-drawn cart pulled up.

'Do you need a ride?' asked the driver, the screaming coming from the back.

'What is that?' asked Damian, and the driver told him to go and look.

'They're just come back from the war,' the driver said, and

Damian saw them, their skin stained with blood, stumps and gashes and pus filling the tray of the cart like a bath. 'I'm to get them to their homes, for their final time. Nothing to save them, now. Will you have a ride, then?' Damian thought about it for a second – whether to plough onwards or quit, and which would be more noble – and then climbed aboard.

At the gate, Bryony saw him descend from the cart, which then continued on its way.

'You're home!' she yelled, and Damian clutched at his belly.

'The illness has come back,' he said, and he acted in pain for the next two days, forcing vomit into a bucket to maintain the pretence. Bryony, for her part, had to maintain the pretence as well, as she couldn't let on that she knew he was lying without exposing her own indiscretion. As he was – he claimed – getting better, he asked Bryony if she wanted to start a family. 'That seems a better way of supporting our country, in my state,' he said. She nodded and held him. Nine months later she gave birth to a son that they named Lord.

When Maynard woke up Erwin was no longer next to him. He panicked, thinking – again – that he had run away once more, and shouted his name as he headed downstairs.

'I'm here, making breakfast,' Erwin said. Maynard was shocked: his brother had never been good with anything but stews before he had disappeared. 'And I fetched the newspaper.' Maynard took the place that Erwin had set for him at the table, the knife and fork resting casually on Lia's tablecloth (which she had, in her rush to leave, forgotten to take, and missed terribly, but couldn't justify returning for). 'I had to cook for myself on the streets,' Erwin told him, lifting the bacon that he had fried onto a plate, then sliding an egg on next to it. 'You'd be amazed at the things that I learned.'

'Tell me,' said Maynard, so he did, telling him about the

running away, the scar, meeting Charlie, Maura, DeVere, the heroin – though he called it painkillers. He left out the part about the baby.

'What about you? And tell me about mother?' Erwin then asked, so Maynard did, talking about their mother's stroke and subsequent passing, but he left off the part about how he held his hand to the mother's mouth before she died, and then told him about prison, about the birthday cake, about music lessons, about The Maivea, about his early discharge. When he was done Erwin asked him about Lia.

'Where did she go?'

'I don't know,' said Maynard, 'she didn't tell me.' (Maynard hadn't yet sifted through the piles of letters that were in the hallway. If he had he would have seen three letters from Lia, explaining everything.)

That afternoon, Maynard hailed them a cab from the corner and they rode it to the graveyard that held their mother and father's bodies, alongside a tombstone for Erwin that had nothing underneath the soil. It rained, and they trudged through the mud to get to the spot that their father had chosen years before.

Ezra had presented it to them one Christmastime. 'This cost more than anything, but it's a good spot, and we'll have it forever.' He took them in a cab to the cemetery and they filed out, stood on their spots of land as people all around them lay flowers down on stones. 'I got a good deal,' Ezra said. When they got home, after they had eaten their dinner, Maynard – who was too young to know otherwise – complained that he didn't have any new toys. 'Santa didn't come?' he asked, and Ezra told him that he had, but that he'd given them the cemetery land. 'It's a gift for all of us,' he told his son, 'because we've all been good this year. You see?' Maynard didn't.

They huddled under an umbrella and Erwin read the names and dates of birth and death aloud. None of them had phrases on them – there were no epitaphs or mottos, just a record of who they were, so that future generations could know their relationships, or ignore them altogether. Ezra; Father, husband. Evelyn; Mother, wife. Erwin; Son. History had erased the divorce entirely, and rendered Erwin nothing but a singular footnote.

'We should get rid of mine,' Erwin said, and Maynard agreed. They tugged at the slim and elegant headstone, rocking it, trying to get it to move in the mud, then Maynard shut his umbrella and forced the tip into the ground, pushing it down and using it as a lever. They worked it until it was free, and together they strauggled with it back to the taxi, letting the rain wash the mud from it as they walked. When they arrived home they propped it against the wall in the hallway, behind the mail, and then Erwin went out to buy his second newspaper of the day. Maynard stared at the stone for minutes after Erwin had left, and then decided to make a start on sorting out the mail.

At half past ten that evening, just after Erwin climbed the stairs for bed, Maynard saw Lia's handwriting on a pale green envelope, the only one of the hundreds of letters that he had looked at that he was even remotely interested in. He pulled it open and read it.

('Dear Maynard,' she had written, 'I'm writing this from London, where I have been travelling with the Mandlebraum family. I have been looking after the children, who have a tendency towards being brattish, but I'll survive. I've included a picture. The baby is my son. I have called him Vito, after my father. I didn't even realise that I was pregnant, not until a couple of months before he was born, but, I'm told, that can be quite common. I'm writing this because I think I owe you something – I don't know exactly what – but I have to tell you that what happened with us, it was just between us. It didn't contribute towards Erwin's state of mind. Your brother, he just wasn't well, I don't think. You can never be sure, I suppose, can you? It must have been what happened with your father and mother, and her illness. Sometimes life is harder than it needs to be, for all of us. We're in London until the end of the year, and then we're moving to Greece, and after that, Joshua tells me, Italy. I have seen so many things on this trip, and truly think that my meeting you and Erwin – and that leading to this trip – must have been fated. When you get out of prison, you'll be an old man, Maynard, and it will be too late for us. But if you can, find me, and maybe, I don't know, there'll still be something there. I'd like to introduce you to Vito, as well. I think he'd like you. All my love, Lia.')

'When are you going to bed? Don't stay up all night,' Erwin shouted from the top of the stairs. Maynard folded the letter, put it in his pocket, and went to his room. There, he read it again, over and over. It was an hour before he thought to look at the postmark, and he saw that the letter had been sent nine years previously. 'Where are you now?' Maynard asked aloud, and then shut his eyes and tried to sleep, but he kept seeing Lia's face.

The next morning – after checking that the letter was still there, and still said the same things, and wasn't just a figment of his imagination – Maynard made breakfast before Erwin got up (mainly because the breakfast that Erwin had cooked the day before had been – in keeping with the rest of his cooking – fairly unpleasant). There was no answer, so Maynard panicked again, called louder. Finally, Erwin stumbled out of his room. He looked ill – pale, yellowed. (When he had first arrived home, Maynard hadn't liked to comment on Erwin's pallid features; gradually, however, colour had come back to his cheeks. Only now did he feel that he could say something.)

'You look awful,' Maynard said, holding his hand to his forehead to see if there was a temperature. (There wasn't.)

'I'm so ill,' he said, 'I think it's the flu. I'm going back to bed.'

'I'll bring your food up to you.'

'No,' Erwin said, coughing his way through the words like a stutter. 'No, I'm too ill to eat now. Later. If you go out, can you get me a newspaper?' Maynard sat in the kitchen by himself and ate both portions, then went to the closest newsstand, and left the paper outside Erwin's door.

Erwin stayed ill, so Maynard had to make dinner. They ate it in Erwin's room but he struggled, coughing on the meat as he chewed, finding the broccoli scratched his throat. When they were finished Maynard cleared the plates.

'We need to talk about money,' he said as he scraped the leftovers from his on top of Erwin's, 'and what we're going to do to get some.'

'We don't have enough?' asked Erwin, looking confused.

'We don't have any,' Maynard corrected him, 'we're broke.' Erwin nodded and rolled over. 'I'll let you know if I have any ideas, anyway.' His brother was snoring before Maynard had even shut the bedroom door.

In the middle of the night, Maynard awoke. The room was hot, so he opened the window, but then needed a drink. Downstairs, in the pitch darkness, he felt his way around, following the wall until his fingers ran over the cool wood of the piano. Quite without thinking about it he opened the lid and started to play. The song – piece, symphony, whatever it was – had mutated over the years, becoming more fluid, years of playing it in his classes in the prison. (He had even taught it to some of the students at the start, the simple but poetic phrasing being perfect for beginners progressing from 'Chopsticks' and 'The Entertainer'. They would ask him what it was, and he would tell them that it was 'nothing, just a little tune'.) He reached the point that he still couldn't get past, his stumbling block, and found that he was smiling as he hit it, thinking of Lia, and letting the music roll around the house, sinking into the sheets that still hung from nearly every surface.

22

The list of skills that might make Maynard employable were fairly small. His only actually qualification – in the practice of law – was rendered moot by his time in gaol. He had some graphic prowess, which might have aided him in the burgeoning design world, but no qualifications or actual experience under his belt. He was very good with words, but nobody wanted to take a try on a man with no previously printed proof of this talent. Whilst many would say that he could easily earn his keep as a pianist, perhaps just working in one of New York's many new bistro eateries that all advertised their meal-accompanying music on bill-posters outside their front doors, Maynard struggled with playing popular songs and so was resigned to playing what he had written himself (which, whilst being sometimes beautiful and occasionally mesmerising, wasn't what the society women of the Upper East Side wanted to hear whilst they bit into the crisp leaves of their Caesar salads). And Erwin was in no fit state to work: mentally, physically, living for so long on the streets had taken its toll, and his new illness – the flu, they assumed – was proving nightmarishly difficult to shake. Maynard could see the effects just by looking at his brother;

at the slight shake in his arm when he held his cutlery, in the stammer he had developed when he was tired. One day, at the end of his tether – and finally out of money, the bank account cleaned completely – Maynard decided that he had to go and talk to the family lawyer.

Frank Waits cut an imposing figure. Having been friends with Ezra for years he had known the family as they grew, and they had clung to him like dry rot. He was expensive, far more expensive than the Sloanes had any right to afford – his clients were almost exclusively celebrities, and, more than that, young celebrities, just into the city and desperate for advice – but he gave them a good rate due to loyalty, friendship, camaraderie. (In return, Ezra had always given him a very discreet – and free – service for his clients; even, on one occasion, taking care of what Frank had referred to as 'a tiny problem', when it was far out of Ezra's remit as a doctor.)

It was the biggest secret of Frank's life: that day, Ezra had banned his then-assistant, Michelle, from the examination room. She had asked why, and he had ignored her for as much of the day as he could handle. The only time he asked for her help was to prepare an anaesthetic (which they rarely did in his offices), which only raised her suspicions more. When it was all done, after Frank had arrived to take his lady-friend away to a private hospital that he had booked a room in for her, Ezra let Michelle in the room. She had no idea why there was so much blood there, or why Ezra was in tears as he cleaned his instruments, but at that second she knew that she couldn't possibly work for him any longer. After that he hired the much-neglected Wendy.

Frank's offices – he insisted all his clients call him by his first name – were located in a block to the east of Central Park that, were you to judge by address alone, would seem less than conspicuous. It had been chosen because it was the only building on that stretch with gargoyles; most prominent was the one above the front doors that stared down at the pavement. He ensured that all his assistants knew to wait a minute before buzzing people upstairs: he wanted to give them time to look around and realise that they, as he put it, 'aren't in Kansas any more'.

Maynard went by himself to see Frank. The family had never had to make appointments with him in the past, but Maynard had failed to take into account that Frank had no idea that he was out of prison, was innocent of killing his mother (whom Frank always had a soft spot for), and that Erwin was alive and not quite well and living in New York again.

Frank Waits' second biggest secret (in a life filled with them): one drunken night, Ezra working late, the mother pregnant with little Evelyn, and Frank stumbled to their doorstop where he told the mother that he had loved her since he met her, and that Ezra would only let her down and ruin her life ('Just look into his eyes! You can see the betrayal already!' he shouted on their doorstep). He tried to take her hand and told her over and over that he loved her, and that he was too scared to say anything usually, because this love that he had for her actually mattered. She shut the door in his face, and he sat on the doorstep crying. He hid when he heard footsteps and watched Ezra climb the steps, stop at the top, take a deep breath and enter. He always wondered, until the day that he died, what that breath meant.

Maynard pressed the buzzer and waited. (He didn't bother to look up – he remembered the gargoyle well enough from when he was a child.) The lock popped and he made his way through the elaborate foyer space, gold-leaf paint encircling reproductions of some of the world's most famous works of art, making them look both cheaper and more expensive at the same time. The assistant's desk was at the end of the hall. Her name was, according to the plaque on her desk, Penny.

'Hello, Penny. I'd like to see Mr Waits please,' Maynard said.

'And do you have an appointment, Mister?' She was already flicking through her book, moving from the page that represented that day, fully aware that there wasn't anybody on the page whose name she didn't recognise.

'No, no appointment. Can you just tell him that Maynard Sloane is here to see him, please? He'll want to see me.' He smiled at her, his best smile, and she sighed, only slightly charmed, and rose from her seat. She walked through to the office on her right, and Maynard could hear the faintest sound of murmured voices. Next thing he knew the doors had been flung open, and Frank Waits' enormous, hairy hands grabbed his lapels and pushed him backwards, sending him skidding across the polished marble floor. Behind Frank, in the doorway to his office, stood a well-known actress, horrified at what was happening, and Maynard thought that he must remember to tell her how much he enjoyed her work.

When she had gone, the lawyer apologising profusely, Maynard found himself hauled to his feet and frog-marched into the office, thrown into a chair. Frank Waits spoke before Maynard even had a chance to find out what was going on.

'Did you escape?' His voice was gruff, the sound of thousands of cigars smoked to the quick, their ash and dust washed into his lungs with glasses brimming over with single malt. He grabbed Maynard's shoulder tightly, the anger in his face running down to his fingers.

'No! They pardoned me.'

'Pardoned?' The lawyer half-laughed. 'Why the fuck,' Maynard fidgeted at Frank's use of the swear word, such was the power that he put into it, 'have you decided that you should come and see me now?'

'We're in a bit of a pickle.'

'Who's "we"? By my reckoning you're the only one left.'

'Erwin's alive as well. He faked his death.'

'Jesus Christ. What's wrong with you two?' He let go of Maynard's shoulder (Maynard was sure that he would have left an imprint as indelible as the tattoos that the gangs used in prison) and sat behind his desk. He had aged terribly, his once deep black beard and moustache now greyed and worn, his hairline having crept backwards, his scalp covered in deep purple spots that ran down his arms and nearly to the tips of his hands.

'Look, we're stuck for money. We've run out.' Frank laughed at this, and Maynard felt himself redden.

'And you want me to what, give you some? After what you've done?' Maynard didn't like to ask what it was that he was being accused of: he assumed that it was rhetorical. 'Look, I made a promise to your parents that I would help them, not you. I do this for them, not you.' (He was lying: he couldn't have given a damn about Ezra. He was doing it for Evelyn.) He reached into a cabinet under his desk and brought out a file. 'This is you, your family's file. There's some stocks; I'll free those up, but it'll take a week or so. After that you're down to assets. The house, your father's surgery.' He reached into his drawer and pulled out a handful of sunflower seeds that he pushed one-by-one into his mouth and played with between his teeth.

'And they're worth money, right? We could sell them, move into a small house somewhere out of the city.'

'I'm telling you this for your mother, because she loved that house. You can stay there: you just need to sell the practice.'

'That'll tide us over until we get jobs?'

'Haven't you got any idea what happened to property prices whilst you were gone, Maynard? Your father owned a building on the corner of 43rd and 6th: you won't need to work another day the rest of your life.' He offered to help them sell the property – for a cut of the profits far larger than he would usually take – and Maynard agreed. They shook hands and, as the door slammed shut behind him, Maynard found a freshly-pressed fifty-dollar bill in his palm, squeezed in during the handshake as if he were a doorman.

The walk back home found Maynard meandering through the park, wondering what might have been if he had done things in his life a little differently. What if he had stuck with his job, settled down with Wendy? What if he had never had feelings for Lia? What if Erwin really had died that day, or had never come back? What if he hadn't found himself in his mother's bedroom that day at the height of her pain? He stared at families as they walked their dogs or pushed their babies along in prams that became more extravagant by the day, at the single girls with risen hemlines and at the sharply-pinstriped businessmen, their hair growing longer and slicker, their shoes browner. He decided to not tell Erwin exactly how much money they were going to have: it could only complicate matters.

He took home a lunch of a freshly roasted chicken and fried potatoes from a local café and ate it with Erwin as they discussed the money situation. Erwin was still propped up in bed, his nose running and his throat ragged. In between mouthfuls Maynard spoke about his morning.

'I went to see Frank Waits.'

'Oh?'

'He said that there are still some of Father's business assets we can sell. Should get us some money, I would think, but it will take some time. He didn't say how much.'

'Alright then.' That was the end of the conversation. The chicken, which had been cooked in lemon and herbs, was excellent. Erwin didn't ask where it had come from, or how Maynard had afforded it, despite Maynard's having prepared an answer especially.

Erwin was getting better; or, at least, the flu that he had was, even though it had clung to him for far longer than it should have. What he didn't know about was what sat in his blood, rolling around his body, far worse than the flu; something that, no matter what he did, he had no chance of surviving.

23

Erwin sat in the living room when Maynard was out and contemplated their surroundings. Some of the sheets that Lia had draped around were still hanging, due to a combination of laziness and thinking that their removal was somehow pointless, as they never liked that painting – or whatever the sheet covered – anyway. The shapes that they made in the house were often nicer than what was underneath – Ezra Sloane having been one of those men with a lot of money and very little taste – so they were often an improvement. One day though, when he was feeling better than usual, Erwin decided that enough was enough, and stripped the sheets from everything in the living room, then moved the furniture that he disliked into the centre of the cleared space. He examined it from every angle, got a notepad – one of the old ones that he used to use in his engineering days, the pages now musty and slightly brittle from years spent on his bedside table – and started to draw, eyeing up the individual parts of the assembled pieces and marking them down on the pad in crude, quick drawings. When it was done he had designs for four new chairs, simpler and more casual, replacements for the stiff-backed and hard-cushioned seating that currently made up the rather pompous sofa. In the basement he found his old tools, still in his old tool-belt, and he sawed into the wooden legs of their old drinks cabinet and sideboard, and restuffed the chair cushions with the innards of the duvet that he took from his bed. From the rest of the wood he then made a coffee table, simple and ordinary, but tasteful. Maynard came in just as he was sanding the top of it, smoothing the corners.

'I thought I could sell this stuff, maybe,' Erwin told him before he had a chance to react. 'If we're short on money, that could really do something for us.'

'Okay,' Maynard told him, unwilling to disclose the truth about their finances, and glad to be rid of the furniture that he never much liked anyway, and that only ever reminded him of other times.

Over the next couple of months Erwin built his collection, like an artist readying for a show. He pillaged every room of the house – except for the mother's bedroom, which he still felt curious about entering, as if she might one day return like he did, a maternal Lazarus seeking her own bed – and raided parts from anything that could potentially work as part of his designs. Within a week the brothers were sleeping on mattresses on the floor, as their bed frames had become a dining table, a tasteful sideboard and the front of a chest of drawers. Soon parts of the banister went, and the skirting from the upstairs. The living room floor was covered in off-cuts, shards, wooden boards. (They had both taken to wearing shoes at all times due to the splinters.)

'We need all the wood we can find if I'm going to turn a profit on this!' Erwin would say when Maynard asked what had happened to the floorboards in the bathroom, and Maynard would just sigh.

As soon as Maynard got past working out their day-to-day expenses – putting aside a basic budget for food to tide them over until the sale of the surgery – he contemplated how best to spend the rest of the money gained from the sale of the family stocks. It wasn't until he lay in bed thinking about Lia that he realised; he could hire somebody to find out where she was.

Frank Waits, when told about the plan, was sceptical.

'I told you I didn't want any more to do with you, Maynard.' Outside his office waited an actress that Maynard didn't recognise. Apparently she had just been in a film that had done very well. 'This is unacceptable, you know.' He didn't seem angry, Maynard thought; just weary. (Maynard didn't know this, but Frank could absolutely see Evelyn in his eyes, his mouth. He hated seeing Maynard because of the reminder of what wasn't, but could – might – have been.)

'I just need the name of a good private investigator, and then I'll be off.' Frank threw him a card, beautifully made, slick and glossy. The embossed name crept along under Maynard's thumb.

'David Walls,' Frank said, 'he's expensive, but he'll find whatever it is that you're looking for.' Outside the office, Maynard dialled the number on the first payphone he saw.

'I don't meet in person,' The PI told Maynard, 'because people get too involved. Here's an address; post me what you're looking for, pictures, whatever it is, and a cheque for my retainer. I'll let you know if it's going to cost more.' The fee was exorbitant, but a letter, the cheque and a photograph of Lia went in the post later that day.

Maynard was walking through Harlem when he noticed a man – short, black, elderly, homeless by the looks of him – running towards him. The man shouted something that Maynard didn't hear, but then he apologised as he got closer.

'Sorry, wrong person,' he said. Maynard shrugged it off. When he got home he ran an inventory of Erwin's furniture. The downstairs of their house was cluttered with the furniture from every other room in the house, and it seemed to double every time Erwin built something else. The house was transformed with stuff that they didn't need, all piled up in corridors or against walls, and useless to them. To navigate to the kitchen required pinning oneself to the wall and inching past the empty frames of the wardrobes stacked there; to get out of the front required ducking under the protruding legs of upended tables.

'We need to sell this,' Maynard said, and Erwin agreed with him.

The letter from David Walls, PI, came as they were eating breakfast, some weeks after he had been booked. Erwin got to the post first, and passed the envelope to Maynard, who opened it, read the first line and then closed it. (The letter said that Lia and her son were in Barcelona, in Spain. There was no date or signature on the letter, and no return address.)

'It's nothing,' Maynard said to his brother, who couldn't have cared less. (Erwin's attention was wavering, wandering; neither of them noticed this.) As Maynard ate his oatmeal he couldn't think about anything but what the letter might say, and where Lia could be. As soon as he was done he went upstairs, shut the bedroom door and read it. 'Barcelona,' he said aloud when he was done, and then went to his atlas in the living room and stared at the outline of the city until he swore he could almost see her.

That evening, Erwin decided that he could improve on one of his pieces, a table that he had made from their dining table, this new one smaller, with a join in it that made it extendable, and varnished a lighter shade. As he did it Maynard worked on another of the Sloane tales until it got dark.

His parents' plan had been to name him with a grandiose flourish in order to give him a head-start in life, and to that extent they had succeeded: Lord Sloane was treated differently as soon as he came of age, as many assumed that it was a title and not a name. He began to amass a reputation as a bounder, born firstly from his attitude towards women and secondly from rumour and myth. Word would spread from township to township that 'Lord Sloane is not to be trusted with your daughters!' and this turned into a belief that he was an actual Lord, which, in turn, meant that the less than salubrious daughters instantly wanted to meet – and often bed – this man. The title suggested money (though he did not have a penny to his name), and Lord played on this, only ordering the best when he found himself in courtly situations, and then refusing to pay for it because of his status. He would take women to rooms that he blagged from barmen and make them call him by his name whilst he promised them the world before he stole it from them, leaving them penniless or destitute or, worse still, pregnant and alone.

In his moments of weakness, after sex perhaps, Lord would occasionally be asked what he really wanted from life. He would usually give stock answers – jewels, property, women – though on one occasion, after sleeping with a woman called Betsy (whom he was especially fond of), he told what he believed might have been the truth.

'What do you really want, my Lord?' she asked, stroking him, both of them naked as they lay, sweaty, on the bed.

'I know not.' He always adopted a stricter vocal tone when he was in character.

'Oh, come now,' she sighed, 'surely you've given it thought, quiet contemplation when with one of the many women who were with you before I.' Women frequently said this to him, hoping that he would tell them that they were individual, special. He never did. She pressed his chest with the base of her palm, kneading it.

'Fine. I want a house, a family. Is that what you want to hear? Jesus, woman!' he snapped.

'A family?' she asked, surprised, and slightly disappointed. They went to sleep then, or at least she did; Lord couldn't stop thinking of what he had said to her quite without meaning to. When Betsy awoke in the morning Lord was long gone, having left nothing for her, and taken all the jewellery she had in her cabinet.

He moved on the following day, as he always did, travelling across the middle states of the country, moving from town to town. He had dressed his wagon in fine fabrics made up from various beddings owned by women that he had slept with, and had stolen an expensive saddle for his horse, all plaited leathers. Gold paint lined what had been a simple design on his wagon, which now included a crest that he claimed to belong to his family (and actually came from a sign hanging outside a public house that he had passed, and, having an excellent eye and steady hand, had copied in the middle of the road). That evening he met a woman, as usual, and, after drinking for hours, took her into the nearest barn that he could find. When they were done he left and cried as he walked, naked, carrying his clothes. He dressed by a river, in the finery that he acquired throughout his travels – knee-length coat, tricorne, shoes with the largest silver buckles that he had ever seen – and mounted his wagon. As he left the town everybody bowed and called him 'Lord', and he felt sick and, for the first time, repentant.

The following day he arrived at a town called Linger. The

local tavern was nice and clean, and had rooms available. When they asked him to sign the guestbook, he surprised himself, writing only 'Sloane' in the box, and then answering to that over the first day that he was there. Nobody asked a surname, so he didn't offer it. The potential, he realised, here, where nobody knew him, was enormous; the potential to stop his old ways, to start afresh. The first few days there he just sized the place up, and then, quite by accident, met the most beautiful girl that he had ever seen.

'I'm Lacey,' she said, and he kissed her hand. She was dark and exotic and yet homely all in one, and her skin seemed to tingle as his lips touched it.

'I'm Sloane,' he offered, and they had dinner together, enormous steaks, and drank wine – all of which he paid for – before he walked her home.

'Will you come in?' she asked, and he shook his head.

'Another time,' he said, and kissed her. Her breath, he noted, tasted more exciting than that of any of the hundreds of women that he had been with before her. The next day he took a job as a junior accountant – he was exceptionally skilled with money, mainly from his experience of gambling – for a local firm, and, that evening, took Lacey out for dinner again. They courted for weeks before he went to bed with her, and even then he was gentle, uncustomarily so, he thought. He told her he loved her as they went to sleep, but didn't know if she heard him. It was the first time that he had ever meant it.

They were together for months, and then, one day, he saw a ring for sale on the cart of a travelling salesman. It was beautiful and shiny, so he spent some of the wages that he had saved on it, and proposed that evening. She said yes, and they set a date in the summer, then went to tell her parents so that he could ask permission, however posthumous that might have been. That night, in bed, he noticed a lesion on his groin, sore and red. He didn't alert Lacey to it, however, and just crossed his fingers that it would go away of its own accord, as they had whenever one had troubled him before. This one didn't. Instead it grew over the following weeks, and he made up an excuse – that of saving themselves for the nuptials – so that Lacey didn't see it.

A month later, fever hit, and he struggled through until it faded. The lesion turned into a growth, and it grew, spreading across the inside of his thigh. He hid it right up until his wedding day, when he shuffled down the aisle so as not to irritate it and cause himself further pain. He used his father's first name as a fake surname for the ceremony, and then feigned illness that evening so that his new wife wouldn't have to see the untended sores that reigned over his lower abdomen. After a month of married life he still hadn't slept with her, or undressed in front of her, and she was getting worried, so they argued, and he found himself in a bar, shivering and in pain. A woman came down the stairs and slid across the bar to him, sitting next to him.

'What's your name, sugar?' she asked, her accent pure Southern charm, pealing out over the noise of the other drinkers. He thought about it, then slurred at her.

'Lord,' he said, 'Lord Sloane.' They had sex in the pitch-blackness of one of the upstairs rooms, so she couldn't see his sores, or the pain that he was in as she worked on him. He went straight home afterwards, still drunk, and told Lacey everything about the whore. 'Leave me,' he told her, and she did. As she left she told him that she was pregnant, four months in.

'It happened that first night we were together,' she said, and he wept, watching her walk away, his unborn child in her belly. Everything that he longed for was gone, and he was left, syphilitic and alone.

Over the coming months he watched from a distance as his son was born, and, as his back slowly seized up, the child grew.

The boy – who was named Sinclair, through no choice of Lord's – crawled, then walked, then talked, but was allowed no contact with his father. Lord's disease took hold, bulbous sores growing on his face, under his skin, making his features swell. He stopped leaving the house that he had bought for his family to live in before it all fell apart, and he stayed alone. He eventually stopped being able to recognise Sinclair and Lacey when he saw them from his window, as the fevers ran to his brain and interfered, and then he stopped thinking altogether, waiting alone in his chair, his back rigid, his head shaking, his mouth drooling, his groin and brain a mass of ruinous sores. One day Lacey took pity on him, and introduced him to his son. Lord couldn't speak, or gesture. He sat there as Lacey explained to the young Sinclair that a horrific accident had taken Lord away from them. Sinclair couldn't stand to look at his father, and hid his eyes from Lord's gaze, which was as focused on his offspring as it had ever been on anything else his whole life.

Later that day Lord Sloane died.

When the story was finished it was pitch black both out and inside the house and the Sloane brothers were forced to go to bed. (Maynard, having spent nearly all the money on finding Lia, was discovering that the wait for the property to sell was longer than he had anticipated. He had pushed them to adapt, using many of the skills that both he and Erwin learned in their years in the wilderness. They were relying on daylight, barrels of campfire gas, and water from the local community pumps in the park. They ate oatmeal every breakfast and the cheapest stews every dinner, made with vegetables that were being binned from the back of grocery stores. It was serving them fine.) They both lay in their beds and thought about the story, and Erwin found himself coughing in the darkness, a tickle in his throat that refused to stop.

Maynard awoke to banging, and found a sickly-looking Erwin downstairs, weakly lifting books from the fixed shelves that ran around the perimeter of the living room.

'I think I can use these for something,' he said, as he pulled the books down. He took them into the hallway and piled them up next to the unopened mail and years of subscribed newspapers and magazines that he hadn't yet touched. The hallway was brought inwards, Maynard realised, with something akin to fake walls making it a foot shallower on either side.

'We should throw these newspapers, you know. Take them somewhere.' Maynard began counting the piles, but stopped at twenty.

'No. I'll get to them,' Erwin said, 'eventually, I will. For now, leave them. Help me with these books.' Maynard did as he was told, working on the engineering section of the shelves next to Erwin, who was deep in pulling the medical books down. He placed a copy of *The Journal of Minimally Invasive Gynaecology* on top of a book about World War II aircraft and steadied the pile to stop it toppling over as he coughed up something black and viscous. 'I'm sorry,' he said, and Maynard waved the apology off. They both tried to ignore the thick liquid that Erwin had hacked onto the floor between them.

The books seemed to take up more room than they ever did when they were on the shelves, running around the living room and hallway like an internal fence. Erwin had built them to head-height and then stopped, unless there was a fixture that he had to avoid – the in-built hallway table, for example – but the walls now looked like they were made from the books themselves. Maynard just looked at them, at the newspaper covering the floor (that Erwin had laid down to protect the floorboards from his furniture building), and shook his head.

The next morning, another letter arrived from David Walls, hand delivered, and still with no date or return address or signature, and after Maynard had read it, he ran straight out of the house to find a payphone. ('I've found her,' the letter read, 'and she's in Barcelona, definitely. This is her phone number.' There was, again, no signature or date.)

It rang. Maynard, at the payphone outside the Rockefeller Center, broke into a sweat just at the noise from the receiver. The sound of the ring was totally different to the one he was used to hearing: it was a solid tone, long and muted, like the low burst of a trumpet. Then a click and a pause and finally he heard the distant voice of Joshua Mandlebraum.

'*Hola*.' The word was Spanish, but the accent was pure old-New York, sharp and nasal.

'Mr Mandlebraum?'

'Hello?'

'It's Maynard Sloane, Mr Mandlebraum!'

'Is there anybody there?'

'Can you hear me?'

'Hello?'

'Can I speak to Lia? Mr Mandlebraum?'

'I can't understand a damn word they're saying, you try.' The noise of the phone being passed, then:

'Hello?' It was Lia; her voice older, deeper, the effects of the sun, maybe, of the heat, but definitely her.

'Lia!'

'There's nobody there,' she said. There was another click, a full-stop, and the line went dead. Maynard shouted, tried to dial again, but it wouldn't connect, just kicking him back to the initial tone every time he keyed in the number, swallowing his dimes and forcing him to get more, to keep trying. After an hour he gave up, and walked across to a bar

– a tourist trap, decorated in garish red and white stripes, waiters covered in buttons and badges, with funny hats – and he sat and drank cocktails that he had never heard of, spending far more than he had rationed for that day. (Maynard had broken the money that they had gained from the sale of the stocks into 365 chunks, then halved each chunk, giving them a daily budget designed to last them two years. His cocktail splurge cost them a week of dinners.) As he sipped at his fourth, yellow and cream based, like it had curdled, the twenty-four-hour news show updated with a story about a storm that was headed for the Barcelona coastline. They showed video of trees being uprooted and sand being thrown in the wind.

'Not now,' he said, so quietly as to be almost inaudible, but the barman still thought that he was talking to him.

24

The worst of it began with a cough, deeper than it had been before, coming from the chest; and then a realisation that his nose was streaming. The cough was brutal, hacking and slashing its way through his throat.

'Maynard?' Erwin called out, but there was no answer – Maynard was still out, frantically trying to dial Spain to no avail – so he pulled himself up, stumbled to the bathroom. He was streaming from his nose and his eyes, every crease in his skin sore and red. He wiped himself down, splashed water on his head, dried it off. Wrapped in a blanket he made his way downstairs, sat in the kitchen and peeled an orange for himself, the segments stinging his throat as he swallowed them almost whole. 'Maynard?' he called out again, wondering what the hell was wrong.

Needing water, he heaved the bucket that Maynard filled nightly – Maynard having fallen wholly into the role of The Hunter in the wake of Erwin's sickness – and dragged himself to the edge of the park, to the water pump. He filled the bucket until he could barely lift it – his arms were much weaker than he remembered, which meant that this must be some strong virus, to affect him so badly – and then made it back to the house, gasping for breath. He lay on the hallway flooring, more out of necessity than choice, and lifted his shirt at the back so that the cold of the floor could touch him, cool him down as much as possible.

Maynard drunkenly opened the door to the house and found it sticking, just as it did when the mail was still piled up there; only this time, when he peered around it, he saw his brother on the floor jamming the entrance. He didn't say anything, just heaved the door so that Erwin's foot shifted, and pushed his way in. His brother, he thought, looked like he was already dead. (Maynard had experience with finding his brother that way: the look on Erwin's face, or, rather, the lack of a look, was almost exactly the same as when he had been found on the bathroom floor, knife covered in the blood from his throat.)

As soon as Maynard started to pull him to his feet, in order to then work him over the shoulder into a fireman's lift, Erwin stirred.

'I'm okay,' he said, then repeated it a few more times, 'I'm okay, I'm okay, and I'm okay.' Maynard watched Erwin stand and sway in the hallway, colour coming back to his face, knowing that he was anything but.

The doctor took his blood samples and sent them off with the nurse, then pulled Maynard to one side as Erwin put his shirt back on. The doctor was a giant of a man, with a stalactite of a beard that made his face appear to be more hair than skin, and he rocked as he spoke, backwards and forwards, heel to toe.

'Your brother is very sick,' he said, and Maynard nodded. 'It's getting more common. I think you both have to prepare for the worst.' He outlined the disease to Maynard in his office, as Maynard watched his brother through the window in the door, propped up in bed, sipping from a cup of water that they provided him with. 'There isn't a cure,' the doctor said. 'This won't end the way that you want it to.'

'Does it ever?'

'No. This will get worse, and it won't get better.'

'Okay,' Maynard said.

They caught a cab home, Maynard helping his brother in and out of the back seat. When they were home Maynard watched Erwin climb the stairs, weaker than he'd ever been before, an old man without the years. He wondered why they hadn't see it coming, why it had just sprung up on them, and he repeated, as Erwin coughed and asked him to fetch him a drink, the doctor's final words.

'This will get worse, and it won't get better.'

That night, as he lay in bed, Maynard realised that he hadn't thought about Lia at all that day. On the radio he listened to the BBC World Service – which sounded as if it were a million miles away – where they mentioned that the storm had passed without incident. He was able to hear Erwin snoring from his room so he crept out, downstairs, pulled his shoes on, left the house and headed for the nearest working payphone that he could find, close to the edge of Times Square. The phone was answered on the first ring.

'*Buenos Dias.*' It was that same New York voice, clumsily bluffing through the Spanish pronunciation.

'Mr Mandlebraum?'

'Speaking.'

'It's Maynard Sloane, Mr Mandlebraum.' There was silence, far longer than Maynard would have liked. The only way that he knew he was still on the line was the noise from a television or radio in the background. 'I wanted to speak to Lia, please.'

'You're out of prison?' His voice was hushed, so quiet that Maynard could barely hear him.

'Yes.'

'Listen, I think it's for the best that you don't speak to her. She's happy, here. She's seeing somebody.' (She wasn't, and his reasons for saying this were ambiguous, at best. He would tell his wife that he said it because he was under the impression that she was; he would tell himself that he said it because, when he dreamt of Lia in her swimming costume, dancing around their pool at night-time parties, and she flirted with him gently, it could be him that she was seeing.)

'I just want to talk to her, Mr Mandlebraum, tell her –' He was interrupted.

'She's happy here, and you shouldn't call again. I shan't tell her that you've been in contact, Maynard. I hope that you keep well, and yet keep well away from us here.' Maynard heard the tone as the line went dead, and stood there holding the handset until the man behind him, waiting patiently for the booth, asked if he was finished. Maynard handed it over, heard him dial somebody, laugh, say something sweet.

At the house Erwin woke up and called for his brother in the darkness. He was coughing something up that he was sure was blood.

'Maynard?' he shouted, but there was no noise coming from anywhere in the house. It was pitch black, darker than he had ever seen it; the middle of the night, surely, on a night with no moon.

When they were children, Ezra had gone through a period of time wherein he made Erwin and Maynard sleep with their curtains open. With them closed at night the house was pitch black; there were no street lamps on at that time, and nothing got past the heavy-set curtains that their mother favoured. 'Think of what you can learn about the stars just by seeing them more often!' the father encouraged. They hated it; the moonlight caused them to sleep fitfully and their schoolwork suffered the following day. They started a habit of training themselves to stay awake until Ezra went to bed himself, at which point they would draw the curtains and sleep properly, waking up before he did and opening them again. It meant that they had less sleep, but it was constant. Ezra caught Erwin one day with the curtains drawn. 'Why did you lie to me?' he asked his trembling, terrified son. 'I didn't want to disappoint you,' Erwin said. Ezra asked Maynard the same question. 'I wanted to get some sleep,' Maynard answered.

Erwin made his way through the house, feeling along the walls to find his way downstairs, his fingers fluttering against the slightly fraying edges of wallpaper by the dado rails, then clinging to the corners of doorways. He made his way around in the darkness of the house on countless occasions, and yet it now felt utterly different. The distance between doorframes, the number of steps that it took, the feel of the banister under his clammy hands, all felt different. Each step creaked, he was sure, not the floorboards, or even his legs, but the air, creaking as he pushed through it. He lowered himself to a sitting position and shuffled along until he found the edge of the stairs, then eased himself down them one by one. His nose was streaming again, and his eyes, like tears but thicker, and soon he was – he guessed – halfway down the stairs, so he stopped and tried to catch his breath. It was so dark he couldn't even fathom where he was, and he was gently hyperventilating. He shouted for his brother but the words just sank, absorbed by the stacks of paper at the foot of the stairs. (Erwin briefly wondered if he was dreaming, so foreign to him this all felt; if he would just fall and, all of sudden, wake up.)

He started moving again after a while, shuffling from step to step, keeping his back against the wall. As soon as he reached the bottom – and he had very little room, as there was a chest of drawers only a foot away from the base of the stairs, with two dining chairs sitting on top of it – he began to crawl, following the floor straight ahead, turning left, down to where he knew the kitchen to be, feeling in front of him the whole time for obstructions; for papers, for books, for furniture. Splinters of wood constantly jabbed at his palms, but he had no choice but to ignore them. He passed the piano and then felt the frame of the kitchen door. Across the kitchen floor was Lia's tablecloth, the sink, and then finally the bucket, the water. Erwin put his hands in, pulled water out, splashed it over his face, let it run off into the sink. His face stung.

'There's something really wrong,' he said, and then realised that he couldn't see the moon though the kitchen windows, even though those windows didn't have curtain; that he couldn't even see where the kitchen windows were. It wasn't just dark, Erwin realised. His eyesight had gone. He hauled himself to a chair (that he had constructed from the legs of his old bureau and shards of the bathroom flooring), and he blinked his eyes furiously, trying to make his vision kick back in. Then it did, and he saw his father, sitting at the kitchen table, somehow.

He looked young, Erwin thought. When he had died his hair had been grey, mostly, and he had a moustache. He had always looked young before that moustache, and they never knew if it was a concession to his age, or a statement.

It was a mixture, of course. Ezra had been watching a film with some of their friends, one of the classics, a trip to the cinema a couple of years before he left his wife, and the women, upon leaving, had all noted how dashing Clark Gable had looked. 'He was young,' they said, 'but he had a worldliness.' Ezra wanted that quality, so casually started to grow the moustache in, first as a beard – 'It's something I'm trying,' he told his clients when they remarked upon it – and then shaving the bottom half, leaving only the thin but strong upper lip.

Ezra was wearing a shirt and slacks, the sort that he would wear to the office, or around the house at the weekends. He only really had one outfit outside his surgery, and this was it. Ezra smiled at Erwin until there was a click, as the front door opened, when he just disappeared.

'I'm in here!' Erwin shouted, and he heard his brother come through the hall. 'Maynard,' he said, 'I think I've gone blind.'

Erwin could see flickers of light, they discovered. As Maynard helped him through the house he would occasionally snap his head towards a source and order that he be taken that way, invariably to a window or doorway – once to a mirror reflecting a window – but by the time they got there the light had gone from his vision and he was back to black. He didn't tell Maynard that he had seen Ezra; Erwin had reasoned that it was either a ghost or a fantasy, and the appearance of either wasn't something that he wanted to share with his brother. After Maynard had made them some cheese sandwiches, and then helped Erwin eat them by cutting them up smaller for him and wiping his shirt when he spilled the mayo down himself, they went upstairs. It was a slow process, step by step, Erwin shaking when he didn't immediately find his footing.

'You used to be more daring than this,' Maynard said as they reached the half-way point, and Erwin just snorted. Maynard helped him to bed, then sat next to him. 'I'll read to you?' Erwin wondered if he had much choice, but didn't say that, so Maynard started, and by the time he was finished it looked like Erwin was asleep, so he left him to go downstairs and work out what he was going to do to help them both.

Having been persuaded by his friends to join the war effort, Sinclair Sloane was quickly discovered to have excellent vision, and was soon enlisted into the naval side of the battle. The day before he shipped out, his wife Alana sat him down to check he knew what he was doing.

'You're sure that this is the fight for you?' she asked, and he nodded.

'It means a career.'

'But what about our starting a family?' she asked. They had been trying for over a year to get pregnant to no avail, and Alana had begun to wonder if it was ever going to happen.

'There'll be time enough for that when I return,' and he kissed her forehead, and that led to her lips, and that led to their making love, which, in turn, led to the birth of their first child, Rusty. But Sinclair wouldn't be around to see his birth, or even to know that he was conceived: the following week he was stationed to the CSS Shenandoah, *and sent off on his first mission.*

Whilst he was gone, Sinclair's wife had brought their first child to term. She had named him Rusty, after the colour of his hair, and had persuaded her father to build them a cot. When she received word that the ship had surrendered, and that the crew would be coming home, she was overjoyed. That evening Rusty coughed and died in his crib, and, amongst her waves of mourning, she decided to never tell Sinclair what had happened. She persuaded everyone that they knew to keep her secret, and buried the baby in an unmarked plot south of their house next to the river, where she could secretly visit it and pray that it found its way to heaven, even though it wasn't yet old enough to crawl.

Sinclair was thrilled to be home. He told his wife all his tales of being at sea, which were considerably less full of derring-do than he would have liked. After two weeks of skirting around the issue, Alana was sure that she had gotten away with the birth/death of the baby. Sinclair had taken to telling people that he had learnt the skills of cartography whilst at sea (which was, basically, a lie, his only experience being that he had finally seen some maps), and was offered an apprenticeship with a map-maker only a few miles away – and across the state border – in Washington. The cartographer was an old man, all too willing to pass on his knowledge and skills to Sinclair. Sinclair was equally willing to learn. Two weeks after starting his job, Sinclair had a conversation with Alana, offering her the opportunity for a child now that he was staying at home. She smiled, and they made love, but she prayed, when they were done, that nothing came of it. Nothing did, and weeks later she had her period, and sighed, grateful.

'We'll try again,' Sinclair said, and they did, repeatedly. Each time Alana prayed that it wouldn't take, and she was always thrilled. Months passed, and then, one day, Sinclair went fishing. He caught a trout, pulled it from the river, lay it on the ground, gutted it, then started to build a fire to cook it for his lunch when he saw that it was blackened inside, dying from some disease. Knowing that he couldn't eat it, and he couldn't leave it for anyone – or anything, as there were bears in that wood – to find and eat, he decided to bury it. He fetched a stick from the brush and carved a groove in the ground, then stumbled upon (what he didn't know was) his son's foot, skeletal and rotten. 'Oh, what fresh hell is this?' he asked, to nobody in particular.

Alana saw him carrying the body from the window, and ran out to talk to him before he could get to the house, to explain. It took her a few seconds to realise that he didn't know who the boy was, and a few more seconds to overcome her initial impulses; to vomit, to scream, to clench the child to her chest.

'This poor child,' Sinclair said, 'it must have only been months old, not even able to talk, I'd wager.' Alana nodded and swallowed back bile. 'I should ask in the town, see if anybody knows where he came from.' So Sinclair set about asking his questions, the body of Rusty left in a box in their back yard. Nobody told him anything, but he knew that they weren't as ignorant of the child's identity as they let on; each of them hurried him away, and wouldn't look him in the eye. Eventually it was the local doctor who gave the game away, as Sinclair looked impassioned, and told him that he desperately wanted the parents to know that their child was buried there. 'After all, they may have been victim of some horrid kidnap,' he said, and the doctor shook his head and told Sinclair all that he knew.

Sinclair stewed. He went home and told Alana that he hadn't found the child's parents, and he ate his dinner and went to bed, but he didn't sleep. He lay with his eyes open, staring at his wife as she, herself, feigned sleep, and they both thought about the child lying outside in the makeshift coffin.

Over breakfast the following morning Sinclair asked Alana if they could try for another child.

'Not now,' she said.

'Why?' he asked. 'You were always desperate for a child before I left. What's changed?' She told him that nothing had changed, and he stood next to her, leant in close to her ear. 'Do you not long for that attachment?' he asked, and she cried. 'There's something you're not telling me,' he said, leaving her in tears. She sobbed all day. When he got home from work he continued to play with her, trying to make her confess. 'I am sure that the corpse is of a boy, a baby boy,' he said as they ate dinner, and then, as they lay in bed – both of them, again, not sleeping – he asked her if she could hear crying. 'It seems to be coming from outside,' he said, and she started sobbing. The next morning he asked her again why they couldn't have a child and she didn't have an answer, so they had the worst sex of their lives. (This time, miraculously, the pregnancy took, but neither would know for weeks.) Over the next few days, at his most spiteful, Sinclair claimed to be able to see a child through the trees, down by the river. 'He can't get home, he's saying,' and this was enough to make Alana howl, and confess all to Sinclair. He hit her, repeatedly, and they went to bed. He slept, and she sobbed until she slept as well.

Sinclair couldn't tell what time it was when he woke up, but he knew that it was still the middle of the night. Standing at the foot of the bed was, he realised, a vision of his child, Rusty, barely able to stand. He was older than the skeleton was, and he pointed at his father and howled. Sinclair screamed as well, and then Alana woke up, and the phantasm was gone. Sinclair couldn't stop talking about it.

'He was there!' he shouted, and Alana cried.

'Why are you still punishing me?' she begged, 'I have told you the truth!'

'This is not punishment,' Sinclair insisted, 'it was a visitation!' Alana didn't believe him. They buried the skeleton on their land again, and then Alana found out she was pregnant, and chose to not tell her husband until, physically, she had no choice. They took to sleeping in separate rooms, Alana with their new boy, Quaid, and Sinclair by himself. He woke up every night, shaking and sweating, occasionally insisting that he could see their son, staring, open-mouthed, at the foot of his bed.

Erwin woke up. He realised that he could see again –
everything was blurred, yes, but it was still there. Through
the darkness came his father, by the side of his bed, tucking
him in.

25

Erwin's sight came and went, and when it came, he used it.
(This was, the doctor told Maynard when he phoned him to
ask for advice, one of the many ways in which Erwin's
sickness could manifest itself. 'If it's doing this now,' he said,
'he will go completely blind. It'd be best for you prepare for
that, make any changes you can make to your house.')

'I need to read as much as possible,' he told Maynard, so
Maynard went out with the money that they had and bought
magazines and newspapers. He shifted their diet to one that
was cheaper, resorting to cooking up the stews that Erwin
used to favour, using watered-down stock and cheap
vegetables that the grocers were nearly ready to throw away,
and would spend the money, instead, on as many of the
dailies as he could find, as well as a hearty mixture of
specialist magazines (engineering, cars, architecture) and the
occasional comic book, as Erwin showed an increasing
appreciation for the funny pages. (The most disturbing aspect
of Erwin's decline, for Maynard, was the speed at which he
seemed to be ageing. He was barely in his fifties, and yet
seemed thirty years older than that. Maynard knew that his
brother was not quite right in his mind.) And when Erwin's
eyes were working, he did as he promised and read almost
constantly, willing to read whatever he could lay his hands
on. When the eyesight went, Maynard read to him until it got
so dark that it was impossible. They would go for walks, but

never too far, as Erwin couldn't count on being able to see for any extended period of time, and he was never allowed – Maynard's rules – out by himself, just in case.

'You could go under the wheels of a bus,' Maynard said, and that seemed to make it gospel. The newspapers that were read were left in the corner, and new ones were brought in every day. At the weekends, Maynard struggled under their weight. The piles of discarded papers covered everything, stacked on the furniture, the floor, each other. They formed bridges, Erwin conducting their arrangement in ways that would stop them collapsing. (Left to Maynard's watch, a number of them had toppled; their contents lay strewn across the floor like litter.)

Ezra's appearances didn't have a timetable or a schedule, Erwin discovered. He came without warning, and it didn't seem to matter if Erwin was in one of his blind moments or not, or if Maynard was around. Maynard couldn't see him, that much was clear, so Erwin ignored his father as much as he could – as much as he could without appearing rude – when his brother was in the room.

'I can't talk right now,' he would whisper if Maynard's attention wandered, and Ezra understood. (Maynard, not being stupid, noticed these little conversations, but just assumed that they were another by-product in an increasingly long list of his brother's symptoms.) They didn't have actual conversations. Instead, Erwin spoke to him, and Ezra listened. In life, he hadn't been good at that, Erwin recalled, but now he was excellent, giving his son his full attention, standing or sitting near him and letting him speak until he was done. When they were finished he would sign off, always with the same phrase.

'I'm so proud of you, son,' he would say, the only phrase

that ever left his lips, the only phrase that Erwin could actually remember him saying when he was alive. Erwin would swell as his father left the room and disappeared.

Ezra said it to Erwin when Maynard was born, to reassure the jealous older child; on his first day of school; when he graduated; on the first day of every contract that Erwin was hired to work on; when Erwin went on dates; on the day before he left the family, so that Erwin would carry that pride with him.

Maynard hadn't completely forgotten about Lia. He tried phoning again, hanging up when he heard Joshua Mandlebraum's voice at the end of the line, and looked into ways to write to her, finding out the address of the Mandlebraum shipping company, and composing the letter. He didn't put the stamp on the envelope because he worried about what would happen if the envelope didn't make its way to her first, or at all, or if it actually did. (The letter, incidentally, didn't mention Erwin.) Everything else, though, was Erwin-orientated. He became a cook, an assistant, a reader. When the blindness was in full effect, he had to make sure that Erwin was bathed properly, and that his food was cut up for him, his pills always ready to be taken. (Erwin occasionally questioned the worth of the pills, as there was no cure for his disease; Maynard reassured him, as he had been reassured himself by the doctor, that it would make his life easier. All Maynard could think of, as he handed the pills over every morning, was their mother, and the thought that anybody would trust him to deliver medicine to another person ever again.) Erwin stopped speaking as much, at least to Maynard. He chattered to himself and to Ezra, but Maynard found conversation wanting, and frequently spoke just to fill in the silence. A couple of months after Erwin went blind, Maynard's voice was all but gone, and he started gargling salt water so that he could still speak.

'That would be all we need,' he croaked to Erwin, 'one of us blind and one of us mute. Add in a deaf brother and you'd have the set.' The only time he spent to himself was when he went to sleep, to the bathroom, to the shops or cooked, so he did those things a lot. When left alone, Erwin worked on plans to make their lives easier, and then roped Maynard into putting them into effect when he finally reappeared.

'Move my bed down here,' he said, in the throes of one such idea, 'and then you won't need to help me up and down the stairs every day.' Maynard dragged the thin mattress down the stairs – he had to fold it at the bottom and heave it nearly to the ceiling in order to get it past Erwin's furniture, still piled up and waiting for something – and placed it in the corner of the room, where the bookshelves had been before, then guided Erwin to it, leaving him sitting there just above floor level. He made them lunch and, upon his return, saw that Erwin had taken some of the magazines from the far side of the room and piled them next to the mattress, stacked neatly. 'Bedside table,' he said. Maynard set his sandwich down on it and sat on one of the chairs that Erwin had built before, and they ate.

He left Erwin to sleep and went to see Frank Waits. He explained that they needed money, and soon, as they were almost completely out, and Erwin needed help.

'What's wrong with him?'

'Just his eyesight; he's going blind,' Maynard told him, choosing to not explain about Erwin's condition further (in case Frank Waits thought badly of him, as there were rumours about his disease and how you caught it, and the slang that went along with it). Frank explained that the surgery still hadn't sold, so he was going to drop the price again.

'It's the markets,' the lawyer explained, 'they're dreadful, and nobody has any money at the moment. It'll come.' When Maynard returned home he set about doing the washing, and hauled their clothes and bed-sheets to the nearest launderette, seven blocks away. They were all stuffed into black bin bags, four of them, and he packed the machines as tightly as he was able (in order to save on quarters) then sat and watched the drums struggle to turn under their loads. On the wall was a poster, a picture of a man, pale and unshaven, his skin pulled down on his cheeks, his eyes glazed over and sunken, surrounded by yellow skin. They looked, he thought, not unlike the stones of apricots. 'Get Yourself Tested Today', the poster read. Maynard turned his attention back to the clothing, which had finished washing, so he loaded it all into the dryers and then stared at the poster again, wondering how long Erwin had left now that he was finally starting to look like the man on the poster.

Erwin woke up one day and realised that winter had arrived. He was shivering in his sleep, and could hear the rattling in his head clearer than ever before. He called his brother's name until Maynard ran downstairs.

'Is there no way we can get the heating on?'

'I'll have a look.' Maynard wasn't noticing it, as he took to wearing more layers, or leaving his coat and gloves on indoors. (It was incredible, he thought, how rapidly he stopped caring about his personal appearance when the only person that ever really stood a chance of seeing him was not only related to him, but also blind.) There wasn't enough money for that week's food even, so he suggested instead lighting the fire. The chimney was blocked, though, and nothing would take in it, the house instead filling with smoke.

'Can you get an oil drum?' Erwin asked, so Maynard did,

from outside the firehouse down the road, and Erwin told him where to punch holes in it, and how deep to stuff it with newspapers, and they lit it and sat in the room, letting it warm them, rubbing their hands together close to the warming metal.

'This isn't going to work tonight, you know,' Maynard said, 'I can't leave you alone in here with this thing lit.'

'Okay.' Erwin wasn't going to argue, as he was distracted by the appearance of Ezra in the doorway.

'We'll have to find another solution.'

'I know,' Erwin said. That afternoon, as he sat furiously reading newspapers in case his eyesight suddenly went again, Erwin found it.

The door to the living room was closed as Maynard went down the stairs, which was odd, as Erwin usually left it propped open in case he needed anything. Maynard hadn't heard a peep all night from him, so called to him as soon as he saw that the door was shut. (He had a horrendous vision of Erwin propped against the wall, somehow bloated and gaunt at the same time, his eyes dulled and lifeless; or, perhaps, of his body burning in the fire in the middle of the room; or that he had killed himself again, perhaps by drawing the sharpest edge of a magazine cover across the scar that ran the breadth of his neck, spilling it open in the cleanest, neatest cut ever made.)

'Come in!' Erwin shouted back, so he did. Inside, the bed area – in fact, the entire corner of the room, almost – was gone, or covered, at least. All he could see was a pile of magazines and newspapers, walls built across, six magazines deep, hundreds of magazines high, making something akin to a shed or an igloo out of paper. There, at floor level, was a hole, an entrance, and in it lay Erwin. He had made an archway in the stacks. 'You wouldn't believe how warm it is in here!' he shouted. Maynard shuffled in through the hole after him, finding an enclosure only slightly larger than the mattress that lay on the floor. Inside it was grey and dark but was, as Erwin promised, warm. 'You can help me, help me build the walls up to the ceiling, really trap the heat in,' Erwin said. He patted one. 'They're sturdy, really. What do you think?'

'It's nice,' was all Maynard could manage. Propped up against the back wall, Erwin grinned.

26

Wendy Cotscombe (née Bathulur) hadn't thought about the Sloane family for over ten years. When she came close, something else drove into her mind, a bouquet of flowers or a kitten or something that one of her daughters was doing, and she moved on. This holiday, her first in as many years, was a return to her roots; a way to show her children the place where she grew up, the things that she remembered before they travelled to LA, where Joshua, her husband, grew up.

A few weeks after Maynard's incarceration, Wendy had decided that she wanted to get as far from New York as she could. She didn't want to be reminded of Maynard any more, and the way she was just forgotten from his life when it got difficult. She weighed up her options and decided that she wanted a career change as well; the medical world had shown her everything, and she didn't want a part of it any more. One day at the job centre she met a travelling businessman called Carl Johnson. He worked for a talent agency, and told her that he could get her some sort of contract doing some modelling.

'You really are pretty enough to do some modelling,' he told

her after buying her a breakfast of waffles, and she decided that a future with his company might be interesting. She took the Greyhound to Los Angeles, every other seat on the bus occupied by other pretty young girls. Due to the cost of living in LA she was forced to share with four other would-be models/actresses/singers in a two-bedroom apartment, taking it in turns to use the beds. The girls' careers weren't going as planned, so they mostly worked in restaurants or as strippers in some of the seedier parts of town. Wendy decided to wait until her first modelling job before worrying about money, though: Mr Johnson had chosen her personally.

It transpired that Mr Johnson chose all the girls personally, and after putting Wendy on his books, getting her drunk and having sex with her (sex that made her cry) he grew bored and moved on quickly. She booked a couple of small jobs: one was advertising cat-food in a mall, dressed as a giant dog and surrounded by hundreds of mewling kittens in pink-ribbon bow ties; the other posing for photographs dressed as a waitress for a new menu to be used in a diner. It was in this diner that she also saw a 'Help Wanted' sign, and soon she had a job and an apron to carry around alongside her rather thin portfolio. The girls that she lived with disappeared one by one over the following months, usually to return home – often with talk of a sweetheart that they had left behind rather than an admittance of defeat. Soon Wendy was the oldest girl in the apartment– but she wasn't really a girl, not any more, she was a woman – and she took the others under her wing. She had modelled for a few more jobs, but had also been promoted at the diner, and was dating a nice man that she had met whilst pouring his coffee. They had even gone on holiday to Montana, and they had made love in a way that she and Maynard never had.

Ten months into their courtship Wendy's boyfriend, whose name was Leonard (and who was the manager of a local department store), became her fiancé after leaving a nice-sized ring inside his coffee cup one morning in the diner. They gave her the rest of the day off to go and celebrate. Wendy soon told the girls that she was leaving, and they were all thrilled for her – it meant that there was one less person in the bed rotation for a short while. Their wedding took place the following summer in a hotel on Sunset – Len knew the owner and got a good discount – and they decided to honeymoon around Europe. There, Wendy fell in love with Italy, and they decided to move there on a whim. After informing all their friends and family they had a garage sale of all the possessions that they couldn't take with them, and were soon left with two trunks of clothes and heirlooms. They stayed in a hotel in Umbria whilst they looked for houses and work. They soon stumbled upon a house that had been converted into a small hotel, and it fitted all of the criteria that they had made – nice garden, room for expansion, close to a lake – and they spoke for hours with the owners – again, on a whim – about whether they could maybe make a go of running a hotel. So they made an offer on the property, which was accepted, and two weeks later they were moving their trunks in. They chose a new name for it – Posto Poco Piccolo (which means 'Little Small Place' – they liked the onomatopoeia) – and started stripping the fading wallpaper, painting the outside, visiting antiques fairs for nice furniture, and investing much of their money into animals and vegetable patches for the garden so that they could be close to self-sufficient. By the start of the next season the hotel was open for business, so they told everyone in the local town to let visitors know – Wendy had learnt an astonishing amount of Italian in the time – and very soon they had their first customers. With the money that they made from the customers they bought some advertising space in the back sections of some Italian newspapers and wrote to travel agents in the United States to ask for inclusion in their *brochures. Business was so good that they were soon able to build another wing onto the house, adding an extra five rooms, and Leonard began planning for the addition of a swimming pool for the following summer. That summer came and went, and whilst the pool wasn't completed quite on time, it did get done as winter rolled around. Wendy made a show of braving the cold water to emphasise her joy at having the pool, and that evening the two of them made love on a sunbed.*

Nine months later, like clockwork, she gave birth to a little girl that they called Carolyn, after Leonard's mother. Carolyn liked, as she grew: flowers, ponies, cats (she really loved cats, and would, when she owned her own house in later life, own six of them) and her little baby sister, who was born when she was four. This sister was called Joanne, and she liked the ponies and cats that Carolyn liked. The business went from strength to strength, and they opened another hotel in Tuscany, which was run by a friend that they had met on a weekend trip to Rome, another US-ex-pat by the name of Mark Dyson, an ex-prison guard from New Jersey (who, they would have discovered had they dug deeper, had been one of Maynard's few friends in prison). The second hotel, called Posto Piccolo Più Grande ('Slightly Bigger Small Place'), was even more successful than the first, and they were able to employ a full-time cook and two maids to work in both, giving them some much needed time off, and the chance to take their first real family holiday.

Wendy's family spent their first few days in New York doing the sights – the Empire State Building, the Statue of Liberty, riding to the top of the World Trade Center and staring down at the crowds of people going to work, or just milling. They shopped at Rockefeller; ate cupcakes; walked through – and took a carriage ride in – Central Park; and went to a musical. The girls had a wonderful time. They all did. Wendy thought about when she lived here, and thought about Maynard briefly, remembering how he looked, vaguely, how he moved. What he liked. The children asked where Wendy used to live, so she showed them her old house and then her old workplace, Ezra's offices (which had a FOR SALE sign in the window). They ate at Tavern On The Green, and they wandered around Times Square at night. It was a proper holiday. On their fourth day, Carolyn, the youngest daughter, fell ill with the flu.

'You likely caught it on the plane,' her father said, and she coughed and spluttered enough that Wendy decided to get her some medicine from the local pharmacy. It had changed since she lived there – it was now a Walgreens, rebranded and bought out by a larger company – but the layout was mostly the same, and she soon found the appropriate aisle. As she was heading towards the counter she stopped at the candy, bought some bags for them all to share, and then saw him: his slightly stooped back; his hair, receding, but still his. He was talking to the woman at the counter about something, and she couldn't totally see his face, but she knew that he was Maynard. She stalked around for a better angle, going down the drinks aisle, then doubling back, heading down by bandages, and, whilst she couldn't get a profile look, she felt confident in his identity. She made her way to the sunglasses rack, checked herself in the tiny mirror – she hadn't really changed, apart from the lines around her eyes and mouth, and her perpetual tan – but she smoothed her hair, put on lipstick, and then dashed back, sliding in behind him in the queue. She listened as he spoke – definitely him, definitely his voice, confirming that he understood how the medicines were meant to be taken – and then watched as they were handed over in a bag, five or six bottles of pills. He turned, and then, all of sudden, they were standing face to face.

'Hello,' she said, and he smiled pleasantly, as you would

at a neighbour or a shopkeeper, stepped to one side and walked out of the shop.

'Can I help?' asked the woman behind the counter, already impatient at seeing Wendy's slightly incredulous expression. Wendy shook her head and wandered the aisles for a while, before leaving with the sweets and drugs in her hands, completely having forgotten to pay for them. She only remembered when she was too far gone for it to matter, with no security guard chasing her, and she opened one of the bags of candy and ate it and continued walking the way she was heading, away from the store and back to the hotel and her children, her husband, her new – and much improved, far more enjoyable – life.

The rest of their holiday was tempered by her moods, and their trip to California was positively disastrous as one day they chanced upon her old café and she saw that she was still the model being used on their menus. She cried over her hash browns, and they had to take her back to the hotel, where she remained for the following two days. When they finally persuaded her to leave, to watch a film at Mann's Chinese Theater, she sat rubbing her wrists with her thumbs the whole way through, leaving her skin sore. The next day they set off for home. She cried the whole way home. Wendy and Joshua stayed in Italy and grew old, and absolutely nothing of consequence happened to them until the days that they died. Wendy never returned to New York City.

Maynard was nearly home by the time that he realised that he recognised the woman from the drugstore. He sat on a wall and tried to grab her name from somewhere inside him, but struggled. Eventually a woman passed him speaking Italian to her dog, a small thing on a pink lead, and he thought about Lia, and forgot all about Wendy once more.

Lia, for her part, was getting restless. She loved Barcelona, loved the city, but was beginning to feel frustrated at the hold that the Mandlebraums had over her, so handed in her notice.

'I've learnt enough of the languages to get by,' she told them one day after breakfast, 'and I think I want to move on.' Joshua Mandlebraum looked like he was going to be sick.

'What will you do?' he asked, his voice trembling as much as his legs, and she pulled a pad from her handbag, flipped to a page and placed it in front of them.

'I'm thinking of opening a restaurant,' she said. 'I've got some money saved, and it would be nice, you know? Hire a chef, run it from the front. It'll give Vito something to do as well, in the evenings.'

'You can't leave!' Joshua said, laughing nervously, but his wife corrected him.

'Of course she can. You must be bored with us; bored to death with the children all grown up. I'm bloody bored with us! You should do what makes you happy!' She hugged Lia, and then insisted that they open a bottle of champagne to celebrate.

'Don't leave,' pleaded Joshua quietly as he opened the bottle. Nobody heard over the pop-smack of the cork flying out and hitting the ceiling.

Most mornings Erwin would get woken up by Ezra. The elder Sloane would suddenly appear in the igloo, and Erwin would soporifically greet him and then tell his father everything that he had been doing. Sometimes – unbeknownst to Erwin – Maynard would approach and peer in through the door to the igloo.

'Who are you talking to?' he would ask, and Erwin would make an excuse. After it happened a few times he took to whispering to his father, speaking in as hushed a tone as he could physically manage, which let him hear Maynard's approach better and hide what he was saying. (On one of the occasions that Maynard nearly overheard what Erwin was saying, the conversation revolved around the mother, and her death. 'I don't know if he did kill her,' Erwin was saying, 'but I don't think he would have let her suffer. I don't know how I feel about that.' Maynard caught the very tail-end, and Erwin was grateful for that; he didn't want to have to talk about the mother's death in any great detail, in case he didn't like what he learned.) Still, every time Ezra left he told Erwin how proud he was. In those moments, his voice was exactly how Erwin remembered it; measured and calm and persuasive. Even in death and near-silence, his father was utterly charming.

Maynard would bring dinner and pills and watch as Erwin took them. He cut them in half so that they were easier to swallow (as Erwin's throat was almost perpetually ragged and hoarse, and far more closed than it used to be) and made sure that dinner was overcooked, to make it easier to chew. Erwin had lost a tooth during one breakfast; he had been biting into some toast with jam spread upon it, the tooth pulling away with the bread and leaving a thick trail of saliva in the air, bridging the two. Maynard wanted to make sure that he cut down on the chance of it happening again. It was one of a series of losses: the hair was going from Erwin's head in great clumps, coating the floor of the igloo as if it were a barber's shop; the skin around his joints was flaking and caked white; his eye sockets were dark, despite how much he slept, and pulled downwards to the point where it seemed as if his eyes could just spill out and tumble to the floor. Maynard looked at his brother as he ate and wondered if Erwin had any idea just how much he was falling apart.

27

Maynard didn't see the letter that appeared from Frank Waits that morning (informing them that their father's office had sold for just shy of the asking price, and asking where he wanted the money transferred to, as well as chastising them for not having a phone line to instigate contact), nor did he see the letter that appeared from Lia the day after (a letter intended for Maynard when he got out of prison, telling him that she was happy in Barcelona). The post instead piled up along with the newspapers, towers of white with occasional bursts of yellow or brown, pushed up against the wall and nearly as tall as Erwin's shelter.

'We need to do something with all of this,' he said as Erwin lay on his back with his head in the passageway to the paper hut.

'I can use it,' Erwin said, 'I've been thinking about building something else.' Maynard told him that was fine, that he could do whatever he liked; he was desperate to please him in case whatever he requested ended up being his last. He moved the letters into the living room so that Erwin could find them – and, at one point, his hand was on the letter from Lia, and he was so close to seeing her handwriting, but was distracted by Erwin asking for help to stand up – and then rounded up all the rest of the newspapers and magazines. 'It's funny,' Erwin muttered as Maynard carried the tied-off bundles in and stacked them in the window bay, 'I always wanted to build for myself, and now, here I am, and I can't even see what I'm making.' Maynard didn't think it was funny at all, but his brother grinned as if they were co-conspirators. (It was, Maynard thought, one of the small mercies of Erwin's blindness: he never knew what face Maynard was pulling, so always assumed that Maynard was grinning along with him. In this situation the almost-constant look of pity and concern and sadness on Maynard's face had no effect.) That night as Maynard slept, Erwin worked again. By the morning he had completed another hut, this in the shape of a kidney, with a tunnel running between the two.

'What's it for?' Maynard asked him, and Erwin shrugged.

'It's nice to have another room,' he said, 'somewhere else to do things. I thought I might put some chairs in there.' They dragged footstools that Erwin had made from table legs and drawer-innards through the entrance and arranged them. 'This way I can have somewhere for visitors to sit.' Maynard didn't ask him which visitors he was expecting, but knew that there probably weren't any coming.

That evening, he sat in the second hut with Erwin, acting like they were somehow far more normal than they were, and read him the next Sloane story, this time about their grandfather, Quaid Sloane, a man that neither of them had ever met, or even really heard about. When he was done he went to bed, turning the lights off in the house, and lying in bed trying to not notice just how dark it really was. Downstairs, however, Erwin had visitors.

In 1914 Quaid Sloane was one of the richest men in America. Nobody was aware of that, of course, as his money was tied up in factories and research and developments and shares. His family (a wife and son) knew that they were well-off, certainly, and they never wanted for anything. There were clues to their enormous fortune: they were the first family on their block to have a car (though the Mandlebraums across the road swiftly followed suit); they got fresh fruit and vegetables thrice weekly; Quaid would buy new shirts every few weeks to prevent having to over-wash the old ones. But when the war began, they suddenly had riches the likes of which they had never even contemplated. Quaid opened a vault at the back of one of his factories, and filled it with gold bullion, just to fulfil a fantasy. He invested money in military weaponry. He was the largest (silent) investor in Hollywood's early years. And for all of this, he didn't have a clue about what he wanted from life.

With his mother and father clearly hating each other, and spending as much time as possible out of each other's company, Quaid had spent a lot of his childhood by himself, or wandering between the two. He learnt how to play them off one another perfectly, how to make them distrust each other more than they already did, and he learnt how to milk them for money. He invested the money in himself, buying a bicycle and working deliveries for local companies, and then, when he had earned the investment back twice over, bought a better bicycle, and so on, always managing to save. When he was fifteen his father died, and Quaid told his mother that he was moving to the city. She didn't try to stop him.

Upon his arrival in New York he went straight to the first office block that he saw outside his bed and breakfast, and asked if there were any apprenticeships available. There weren't, but Quaid (being Quaid) persisted, and was offered a job in the mail-room, where, he was reliably informed, 'careers begin'. The man that offered him the job, Colonel Alfred Workman (where the title was an affectation, rather than an honour or a first name), expected that this young man would become head of the postal division of WM Corp. (the name of his company) one day, or possibly move into another division – marketing, maybe. Within six years Quaid was telling 'Colonel' Alfred (and he spat the prefix as he said it) that the board of directors – of which Quaid was the newest – had decided that the 'Colonel' was to leave for pastures new. He would be kept on as a placeholder, a figurehead, he was told, but his power was gone. That evening, the board held a private metaphorical crowning for Quaid, and he moved his boxes of papers into the largest office in the building.

One day Quaid was inspecting a factory that the company owned, a small outfit that made bolts vital in holding together axles. He had finished his tour of the shop floor and was being spoken to about productivity when he saw a calendar on the far wall, next to a grimy window into the staff canteen. On it, a woman posed in a black bathing suit. He had never seen anything like her before. Upon being told that the calendar came from Italy, Quaid tore it off the walls, and ordered that nobody look at filth like it again on his premises. He took the picture, and told work that he needed a few weeks off. They agreed – he had done so much already for the company – and he boarded a boat for Italy.

The country agreed with Quaid, and he grew fat and complacent over the months that he searched for the woman that he knew he would marry. He found the publishers of the calendar, in Rome, and they pointed him down a side street, to a small diagonal house that barely stood. Quaid knocked on the door and when the model answered – and she looked better in person, he thought – he went down on one knee and showed her the enormous diamond ring that he had to offer her. She saw the ring and his clothes and said 'Si'.

They travelled back to America the next day, and married on the ship, Quaid slipping the Captain a handful of banknotes to perform the ceremony. At night they would lie next to each other as they didn't speak the same language. (Quaid wondered, out loud, if they would have anything to talk about if they could.) Then, ten days into their trip Quaid's new wife – he thought her name was Filomena, but it could have been a variation, her accent was so thick and impenetrable – sat with him on the bed before they slept. She kissed him on the side of his face, on his unkempt sideburns, and he could feel her saliva in the hairs. They had sex then, sex that neither of them would ever remember, frantic and disquieting. This was how Ezra was conceived. During Filomena's pregnancy she learnt American (Quaid refused to call it English, so proud was he of his heritage). Her favorite word was 'Tomato'.

Ezra was nearly ten pounds at his birth. His mother couldn't walk for a week, developing something that Quaid referred to as 'the shuffle'. (They only had sex once more their whole lives, and neither of them thought it a particularly pleasant experience.) The second that Ezra could read – he was three, or thereabouts – his father was plying him with books on medicine. Quaid wanted so much to have a doctor for a son; it meant stability and intelligence, a job with its own title, and power. Quaid began predicting his own illnesses as only a burgeoning hypochondriac could. They would sit at the dinner table and eat steak and Quaid would moan.

'My guts are rotting, you know. Food will soon drop clean through to my bowel.' Or, if Filomena ever cooked pasta: 'I hear that this can slip down the wrong channel, and into the lung. The other morning I coughed up spaghetti. And blood.' He wanted Ezra to be able to fix him for free in his twilight years, which he was convinced he was heading towards faster than the trains and aeroplanes that his company were starting to invest in. And Ezra didn't know better for the first few years of his education. Being home-schooled by a variety of different tutors that Quaid had paid to come in and teach well above his own natural reading level meant that Ezra by-passed the traditional fairytales and went straight towards medical textbooks and encyclopaedias. Aged seven he was reading literary fiction heavyweights, Dickens and Hardy and Tolstoy. He usually gave up after a couple of chapters, wondering where the facts were to be found.

In the months around Ezra's eighteenth birthday Quaid fell

to the floor frequently, clutching at his chest. He was convinced that every bout of angina was a heart-attack, every twinge of indigestion a stroke. He used to breathe against a pocket mirror that he carried to reassure himself that he was alive when he spent long stretches by himself.

'I have so many dreams,' he would say, 'that I have died, and floated upwards from my body, naked.' He started to try topical heart remedies, and developments to change the blood in his system, and even invested in medicine from a travelling salesman (that he knew to be nothing more than water and vinegar and salt). There was, of course, a bitter irony, as the one facet that Quaid believed to be fine – his mind – was the one thing that others believed to be failing him. The irony continued when the doctors told him that he had a cyst on his brain, physical and mental injury mixed up in one. 'But I am a businessman!' he cried, and keeled over in the corner of the doctor's office, trying to break for the door as if he would be wiped clean and this visit declared null and void were he to make it back into the stale air of the reception room.

Quaid spent months in the hospital then, as his health got worse and worse. His mind always stayed one step behind his body. 'I need the bathroom!' he would declare five minutes after passing. 'I hunger!' he shouted as the nurse wiped the apple sauce from his mouth and washed his plastic spoon. 'My son! Bring me my son!' as Ezra waved goodbye from the doorway. Filomena liked to pretend that she was fine, and that she had dealt with Quaid's deterioration in the proper way, maintaining her home and ensuring that baby Ezra was well looked-after. Inside, she was destroyed.

Quaid Sloane finally died one morning after eating a tub of hospital pudding, witnessed by his wife, who slept in a chair at the side of his bed. His will-reading took place before his funeral, and not a single one of the vultures that appeared for the will *stayed for the service. Two years later his name appeared at the end of the credits of* The Wizard of Oz, *thanking him for the money that helped make it glorious Technicolor.*

Erwin recognised his grandfather almost immediately from the descriptions in Maynard's story. Quaid was the same height as Ezra, and looked exactly like him, only older, fatter. He didn't say anything, but sat down opposite Erwin, next to Ezra, and Erwin told them all about his day. Ezra smiled when he was finished.

'I'm so proud of you, son,' he said. Erwin didn't sleep that night. By the time that Maynard woke up he had already dragged himself into the main part of the living room and was rearranging the bundles of newspapers, stacking them against the side of the igloo. Somehow he had managed to make the most of the original room almost disappear.

'It's better for insulation,' he said. Maynard just accepted it and made breakfast.

The doctor came to the house, and Maynard shut the front room off so that he couldn't see the shelter. He had moved Erwin, sitting him on a chair in the kitchen. The doctor made a face at the furniture stocked up in the hallways, and at the dust, at the sheets still hanging from the banisters and the pictures in the hallway. (Truth be told, both brothers had completely forgotten about the chaos, really, treating it as you would anything that stayed in one place for long enough; part of, ironically, the furniture.) He climbed over the tables, holding his briefcase over his head – a briefcase which, Maynard thought, seemed curiously small for a man of his size. Erwin had his sleeve rolled up already.

'He can't see anything?' the doctor asked as Maynard followed him into the kitchen.

'Not any more. He used to have good days.' The doctor nodded.

'Hello Erwin. I have to take some bloods, okay?' He spoke loudly, as if Erwin's hearing were affected as well. 'We need to see how you're doing, how far along the disease is.' He rubbed the inside of Erwin's elbow, opened his little case and unwrapped a sterilised needle. 'We count the blood cells, you see,' he said as he slapped Erwin's skin, bringing one of the incredibly pale veins to the surface, 'and that way we can see how your body is doing with the disease, if it's coping alright.' (It was a speech that he gave relatively regularly to patients with HIV and AIDS. He usually told them how well they were looking as well, but he couldn't do it with Erwin, not in good conscience.) He poked the needle in, drew out the blood – it wasn't really as dark as it should have been, Maynard thought – and then sealed the syringe in a bag. 'We're done,' he told Erwin, patting him on the shoulder. 'You'll need to watch that, check that it congeals okay. Take these pills – they'll help.' He put a bottle of tablets on the table, but Erwin didn't react. He was distracted; down the hall, Ezra was welcoming his great-great-great grandfather into the house, shaking his hand. Erwin marvelled at his clothes and shoes and hairpiece.

The results came days later, hand delivered by the doctor. Maynard didn't have time to get Erwin out of the shelter, but met the doctor on the doorstep, pulling the door to behind him.

'My brother's asleep,' Maynard led with, and the doctor nodded.

'I'm not one to dilly, Mr Sloane, so I'll get to the point. Erwin needs more care, I think, than he might be getting here.'

'He's fine.'

'He's dying.'

'Give him medicine, then.'

'There's nothing we can give him, not to cure this. All we can do is up his dose to try and make it all easier for him. He's dying, Maynard.'

'Then he won't go anywhere. He's fine here with me.' Maynard's voice was raised.

'I can't force you,' the doctor said, and he left. Maynard panted when he was gone, his chest heaving; he rarely got angry, or defensive. In the living room, Erwin hadn't noticed their discussion, even with the mildly raised tone of Maynard's voice; he was taking tea with a number of his ancestors, and they were all telling stories, but only Erwin was talking.

28

The final parts of his family's story were fragmented and cluttered, many written in a language and hand that Maynard barely understood, even more with little point or purpose. He sorted, read and discarded them as Erwin sat in the living room amongst the towers of papers and books and minutiae. Maynard had all but stopped caring. He gave Erwin his medicine, made his meals, read to him when he wanted it, but then left him to his own devices, made the most of the daylight. When dusk fell Maynard did the water run, dashing to the park with his bucket. Occasionally, when it was darker, he would bathe his brother, or light a candle and continue working on emptying the box, reading each piece of writing and either marking them potentially interesting or just piling them on top of all the other paper that now comprised the interior of their house. Sometimes he sat at the piano and put his fingers on the keys and pressed them gently, so gently that they barely made a sound. He shaved his beard off and then let it grow again. He wrote letters that he would never send, and watched the incoming mail pile up in the hallways. He wandered the neighbourhood, stopping in shops and looking at their stock, talking to lost tourists, taking advantage of the museums. He went to the library and searched for as much as he could find on all of his ancestors, piecing together the actual dates of their births and deaths, and started drawing up a family tree, mounting it on his bedroom wall. There were gaps, but it was nearly complete.

Through all of this he watched Erwin collapse. His brother's pose fell, his body hunched constantly, more used to sitting on the floor or crawling. Erwin's skin looked paler than ever before, the colour of the faded paper that lined their nest of a home, the colour of wallpaper paste. Maynard would sit with him after they ate dinner and stare as Erwin rearranged himself into the position in which he would spend the rest of the evening, propped against the wall, slumped down slightly, his back unable to support him as it should, his neck lolling slightly. Maynard watched dust settle on him, the air full of the stuff, caught in the rays of light coming through the windows. It clung to what was left of Erwin's hair; to his shoulders, to his shoeless feet. Erwin spoke to himself more, mumbling as he built the living room up. He began tearing the books on the shelves apart, yanking the pages out to build his towers, sticking them together with water, smoothing the edges. Erwin's teeth were falling out at an alarming rate, so Maynard adapted their diet, completely changing what they ate. He bought masses of apples, shop-bruised or old and ready for being thrown out, boiled them down to their maximum softness for apple sauce and let Erwin eat it with a spoon, the chunks of the fruit dissolving to nothingness in his mouth, under the pressure of his gums.

'I'm feeling better,' Erwin told him one morning. Maynard looked at him and thought about their mother.

The launderette was a source of pleasure for Maynard. He enjoyed the routine, the cycle of the drums, and the people. There was always chatter, always a thrum of enjoyment – everybody in there had a shared purpose, and they all wanted to be there as much as everybody else. Everybody was there, rich or poor, and nobody cared about anybody else above the level of basic nosiness, secure in the knowledge that all they wanted from the place was the ability to leave with their clothes cleaned. Maynard would fill his machines and watch them spin and listen, and, for a few hours, he was somewhere else entirely.

One day he had just loaded the dryer when he was approached. The man was black, elderly – very old, by the looks of him, his hair white, his lips chapped – he walked with a stick. Maynard recognised him, but wasn't sure from where.

'Erwin?' the man asked, and Maynard shook his head.

'No, Erwin's my brother,' he replied. 'How do you know him?'

'My name is Charlie Fallon,' the man said, 'and I know Erwin real well.' Charlie got them coffee from the machine and they sat on the wooden benches as he told the story of how he knew Erwin, how they travelled together, how their friendship ended.

'How's the baby?' Charlie asked.

'The baby?'

'Maura's baby; Erwin was taking care of her?'

'Erwin's never mentioned a baby.'

'He didn't bring her home?' Maynard shook his head. 'Must have been adopted then. I'd love to ask him.'

'You can try,' Maynard said, 'you can certainly try.'

'It's been a few months since we've had a visitor,' Maynard pre-emptively apologised as they walked up the steps to the house, 'and we've let things go, because, you know.' Charlie was shocked when he saw the state of the house. The front door opened to darkness, the walls lined with newspaper towers that loomed over them. Charlie stepped backwards before he could go in, sized it up. The furniture sat piled up as tightly as it could be, chairs on top of tables on top of chests of drawers. 'Erwin made these,' Maynard told Charlie as he gawped, 'and we didn't have anywhere to put them.' (This was an absolute lie: they could have gone back into the rooms that were emptied in order to make them. Nearly every room in the house was bare, looking like little more than a squat, with mattresses on the floor and anything that used to be in drawers strewn across the partially torn-up floorboards.)

'He's through here,' Maynard said, indicating the living room, opening the door to let Charlie through. Charlie noticed the smell first, the smell of water and libraries and – for some reason – hay bales, and then saw the piles of paper, standing everywhere, tall enough to touch the ceiling in places. He saw the shapes of the shelter and the other room. The main shelter, now built, sat bluntly swollen from the floor like an abscess. Outside it sat Erwin's oildrum fire, long extinguished. The light that used to come in through the living room windows was blocked by Erwin's towers. 'Erwin's in there,' Maynard said, indicating the entrance to the tunnels that started at the line of the doorway. Charlie bent down and peered in, then stood up again as he heard Maynard crying. He led him by the arm to the kitchen (over the tables, under the chairs) and sat him down.

'This place is a housefire waiting to happen,' Charlie said. 'What happened?' In between sobs, Maynard let it all out.

Charlie sat with Erwin for hours. Maynard watched them speak sporadically, stopping when Erwin got distracted by something else. When that happened Charlie would rub the inside of the igloo, running his hands along the flattened print, the still-visible headlines telling their own askew and disordered version of history. When he was done he shook Erwin's hand, and then shuffled backwards down the tunnel, towards the (relative) light of the hallway. He stood, dusted himself off, and led Maynard to the kitchen.

'Was he pleased to see you?'

'Maynard, he didn't have a damn clue who I was.' Charlie fingered the corner of the tablecloth. 'When did he get this bad?'

'I don't know,' Maynard told him, 'I don't know.'

'He needs help; serious, serious help.'

'I'm helping him,' Maynard said, and Charlie forced himself to smile. He stayed for a dinner of hastily constructed stew and told Maynard about his life, both before and after being homeless. (Erwin had his dinner in the shelter, served in a bowl.)

'I live and work at the 52nd Street shelter, now. We try and put people into housing, get them set up.'

'That sounds like good work.'

'It's nice to help people, you know. It makes me feel good.'

'I think if I had been homeless for as long as you,' Maynard said, 'I'd be totally selfish once it got better.'

'Who's saying that I'm not?' Charlie asked. They went for a walk, offering to take Erwin, but were turned away. (Erwin was meeting Shaw Sloane for the first time, and telling him about engineering.) They ended up at the shelter, and Charlie showed Maynard how it worked, that they let people stay there, pick themselves up, tried to get them into a room. 'We own seven brownstones,' he told him, taking him down the street and showing him around their largest. 'Each one has four or five families in it, one family to a room. They share the bathroom, the kitchen, take turns making dinners. We give them the houses, and they don't have anything else – I mean, they look like this, all of them sleeping on the floors – but it's warm, and it's better than the streets, especially for the kids.' They met a family in one of the rooms, Maynard sitting on the floor with the youngest boy who was blasting on a recorder, and he showed him how to place his fingers over the holes properly, and how to play the first few notes of 'Frère Jacques'. When they were done Charlie took Maynard back to the shelter. They sat in the dining room, empty because it was being prepped for that evening's service, and drank thick black coffee that stuck to the rims of their mugs and scalded the roof of Maynard's mouth. Charlie introduced Maynard to Judy and Donald, both of whom worked there with him, and remembered Erwin.

'He was a lovely boy,' Judy said.

'Say hello to Erwin,' Donald said, which made both Charlie and Judy laugh hysterically.

'He doesn't say much,' Charlie explained as his (now) wife went off to start preparing for that evening's meal.

'Why did you bring me here, Charlie?' Maynard asked.

'You seem like a good person. I thought you would want to see this, that maybe you would want to help.'

'We don't have money, Charlie.'

'Time, then. You have time.'

'I have Erwin.'

'Erwin should be in care.' Charlie delivered his statement factually, as if reading the news. 'He needs more help than you can give him.'

'Maybe, but we don't have the money. All he's got is me.' Maynard stood and excused himself, and left Charlie sitting at the table.

'Call on me if I can help!' Charlie shouted, but he wasn't sure that Maynard heard him.

That night, as Erwin slept, Maynard got out of bed and dressed himself. He propped the front door of the house open with a splintered chunk of wood and dragged Erwin's furniture to the street piece by piece, clearing the hallway of the house completely. The sidewalk was like a showroom, all the pieces lined up. Maynard heaved the first table onto his back and tottered down the street with it, around the corner, walking to the shelter. He left it outside, and then, after mopping his brow, headed back to the house to get the next piece.

The following morning, Charlie was woken up by a phone call from Judy, who had arrived at the shelter for the morning shift.

'You need to come down here,' she said, so he did, and they spent the morning distributing the furniture throughout their houses. Everybody that received a piece agreed that, whilst the design was somewhat abstract and unconventional, the quality was exceptional.

Erwin, when he woke up, didn't even notice that it was gone.

Maynard kept working on his translation. He'd reached the final piece of writing in the ancestral chest. It was a letter, the handwriting ambiguous and scrawled, the words colloquial and hard to understand. The pillars of paper seemed to keep growing somehow, despite Maynard only buying one newspaper a day. They were consigned to the living room. The house appeared divided; the living room was jammed full, cramped and creaking under the weight of the papers, whilst the rest of the house was all but empty, vast and dark and spacious. It looked, Maynard frequently thought, as if it were abandoned, or being prepared for sale.

By the end of that year Erwin had lost control of most of his senses. He could only tell if Maynard was in the room if Maynard shouted, and would only respond to being touched if Maynard's hands were at extremes of temperature. Sometimes he had good days, when he could gather himself together and move around, work on his home, and when he would become convinced that he had seen something, a flutter of light in the corner of his eye. He would be overjoyed and mumble as such.

'Maybe I'm getting better!' he would twitter, laughing through the orange segments stuffed into his mouth. Maynard would have to lean close to hear the words, and one glance at Erwin's face told him all he needed to know. His skin looked as if it were now made of tissue paper, ready to flake off if brushed; his lips thin strips of pinkish-grey (like veal, Maynard thought as he pulled himself in). Maynard knew that Erwin's time was coming: he just didn't know when.

Erwin had stopped moving, almost completely, some time around that November. His bones creaked, and his muscles atrophied, and he decided that it was easier to sit still as much as possible because of the pain that he was in (a pain that the tablets had wholly ceased dealing with). He was hurting everywhere now, the aches running around his body in a relay, swapping between his head, his stomach, his legs. December gave way to January – they had a Christmas celebration dinner of a variety of fruits, including pear, grapefruit, lemon and blood orange, and Maynard sang hymns to Erwin, hoping that he would suddenly join in (which he did, with all the other members of the Sloane dynasty, though Maynard couldn't hear them) – and January gave way to February snows.

Maynard was being affected by the house as well, and he knew it. The almost perpetual darkness they lived in had made his eyesight worse; the diet of apple sauce and other soft foods that he ate with Erwin made his stomach ache every night; his fingers shook from the cold that he felt when he stayed outside Erwin's dens, unwilling to give himself entirely over to his brother's whims. He occasionally thought about trying to play the piano, to play his piece, but his memory – and his fingers – always failed him even as he was warming up. The piano ended up out of tune and eventually dusty. Maynard would fall asleep at random times, sometimes propped on the piano stool, sometime whilst sitting on the stairs, forced between *Time* magazine and the *Daily Bugle*, and trying to remember if the task that he was currently attending to was upstairs or downstairs, and then forgetting what it was entirely. And then he would see Erwin, and he would remember that it was dinner time, or time to change him, and he would retreat to the stairs to cry and pray that something would happen to save him, and begin the cycle all over again.

'You should leave me,' Erwin said one day, out of the blue. 'I can't,' Maynard said. They sat together and Maynard, for just the briefest of seconds, wished that Erwin would just finally die.

29

One day, a week before he died, Erwin very briefly got his eyesight back. He woke as usual, only this time he noticed that he could see his brother though the tunnel, sitting at the base of the stairs reading a book. Maynard looked, Erwin thought, much smaller than he remembered. He looked frail and alone. Ezra came into the shelter.

'Is it because he's been looking after me?' Erwin asked, and his father smiled, as he always did. 'Is there anything that

I could do for him? He's done so much for me.' Quaid entered and sat with them, then the rest of the family. 'He looks so sad.' His ancestors all nodded in agreement. 'I wish I could do something to help him.' He coughed and Maynard looked up, just in time for Erwin's sight to leave him again. He could still see Ezra, of course, who bent down and told his son, again, how proud he was of him.

Erwin's last few movements culminated in him propping himself up against a pile of old issues of *The New Yorker* in the window seat, one arm jauntily positioned at his side – 'Like a little teapot,' Maynard thought – the other hanging limp on the floor, palm up, occasionally twitching. Maynard read to Erwin for most of the daylight hours. He read many of the books over and over again. The books left in the house – the whole ones, at least – were few and far between, or covered by paper sheaths, so Maynard read what he could and filled in the gaps where pages had been torn out for Erwin's walls. They started with technical books, Erwin's old collections of engineering manuals. Soon they moved on to the magazines, with Maynard trying – usually vainly – to find articles that Erwin hadn't already read. He read Erwin the Sloane family stories over and over, making them neater, tidying them each time. He edited and picked, and began to realise who his ancestors really were; what they did, what made them the men that they were. Erwin didn't care about the continuity, about getting closure to the stories. There was no indication that Erwin ever even listened to what he was being read. Ezra was sitting with Erwin constantly, as devout as Maynard, smiling. Erwin couldn't remember a time when he had seen him so happy.

Erwin's cough became a hack, a jab. He spat blood with every lurch of his chest. The noise growled and threatened constantly, an angry dog living in his throat. He woke up when he coughed, and he coughed constantly. Maynard didn't keep track, but he estimated that, over that week, Erwin only slept for a few minutes at a time, and less than a few hours in total. (Maynard only had a few more hours than that himself.) He had stopped being able to swallow his pills, clenching his jaw shut as they were offered to him, so Maynard took to crunching them with the same pestle and mortar that he used on their mother's pills years before, and using the same technique: holding the powder in a handkerchief up to Erwin's mouth and letting him inhale the dust. Maynard had to mash his food into a paste and mix it with water and hold it up to Erwin's mouth, though the amount that he actually took in was negligible. Over that week Erwin got thinner and thinner, his skin dragging itself across his face towards the floor, and Maynard, for the first time, wished that his brother would, now, just die. He held the tissue with the powder and he thought, for the briefest of seconds, about how prison wasn't so bad the first time around, and he wondered.

On his final day, Maynard woke his brother by shaking him. Erwin was slumped against the wall of the shelter, and Maynard initially thought that he was dead, the approach across the room being one of pure nerves and terror, but a still quiet of inevitability. (Maynard remembered a time when that walk towards a maybe-corpse was almost impossible for him to achieve.) He shook his brother by the shoulder, and Erwin opened his blind eyes.

'I've made you breakfast,' Maynard said, bowl of apple sauce in his hands, but Erwin shook his head and pointed to his throat. Behind Maynard, he could see Ezra smiling with the rest of the family.

Maynard got his brother to drink water and then spent the

morning clearing the rest of the box. The final few scraps were nothings; letters from names that he didn't recognise, shopping lists, pictures of people that he would never meet. When the box was empty he sighed.

'It's done,' he said, and then noticed that there was something else, jammed deep down in a crack where the wooden sides met the base of the box; a folded piece of paper. He drew it out, unfolded it, read it, and when he was done he asked Erwin if he wanted to hear it. Erwin nodded, but pointed at his throat (jabbing the pink strip of scar), indicating that it was time for his medicine. 'When I've read it to you,' Maynard said.

I am sad to say that I'll soon be gone; I know that I'm not long for the world. I can feel it all coming toward me, far too quickly. I wish I could end all of this now, leave you all to your lives, and that you might know how much I love you. It is so easy to repent in impending death; or when your life collapses, and you can only see one way to pick up the pieces. Far harder is repenting when you know that others might judge you because of it. You won't read this letter until I'm done; know that I repented, or even that I tried. I'm proud of you.

Maynard didn't know who the letter was from, so folded it and added it to the piles at their side.

'I'll fetch your pills,' he said, and left Erwin alone. He crushed them with the pestle and mortar as always, folded them into his handkerchief, went back to Erwin and held his hand to his brother's mouth. Erwin watched over his brother's forefinger and thumb, pressing onto his lips, and saw every one of his ancestors appear with his father; they came towards him and Erwin smiled.

When Maynard pulled his hand away the powder of the

pills was all gone, and his brother was limp, jaw lolling. There was no air pulling from his mouth, nothing being drawn, so he sat with him until morning, and, for want of something to do, read him the letter again.

30

Morning rolled around, and Erwin was still dead. His body was cold, even in the comparative warmth of the shelter. Maynard lay next to his brother and stared at the ceiling, glossy and smooth, and he shut his eyes and held him until he couldn't bear it any more.

He pulled himself from the tunnel and looked at the room, seeing it for what it as for the first time. Piles of newspaper and cardboard and magazines and torn-up books lay everywhere. Rats ran around in the rubbish that had accumulated in the corners. The room was dark, dusty, in desperate need of cleaners, exterminators, gutting.

'This is who we became,' Maynard said, and climbed over the piles, through tunnels, towards the windows. He wrenched down the furthest tower, pulling at it with all of his might, and bringing the first sunlight into the front room in what felt like – and could have been – years. The towers dominoed, crashing into one another, thudding down and throwing up dust as they did, clouds of the stuff filling the room and swirling like a hurricane in the light of the sun. Maynard panicked for Erwin's body, but the towers had covered him already, the shelter collapsed. Erwin's feet were sticking out of the pile, and next to them lay a letter, bright white, with a handwritten envelope. Through the tears Maynard noticed Lia's handwriting, the letter that she had sent to him years before, never really expecting him to read it.

'Jesus,' he said. Underneath Lia's letter was a letter addressed to him from Frank Waits, so he opened that as well, and read the final amount that their father's offices had sold for. 'Jesus,' he repeated.

He packed a bag of shirts and underwear; along with the stories of the Sloane family, and thought about how he might try to get them published somewhere, that somebody might want to read about them. He sat at the kitchen table, wrote two letters, and then folded the tablecloth neatly into his bag. Then, after saying goodbye to Erwin one final time, and telling him how proud he was of him, Maynard thought about how they had lost all track of how long they had been been cocooned in their house. It wasn't, in the end, really that important, the length of time. He left Erwin there alone, struggled over the sea of paper, over the piles of discarded fiction he had read to Erwin, over piles of issues of *The New Yorker* and *Time* magazine and *National Geographic* and the daily newspapers that echoed with time.

The letters Maynard had written and posted arrived at their destinations over the course of the next few days. The first went to Frank Waits, apologising for not being in touch sooner, and informing him that Erwin had, finally, passed away. It explained that the money from the sale of Ezra's surgery was to go to the 52nd Street Shelter, to be used to help rehousing people in New York, and the deeds to the house that he had just vacated were to be left to the same. He thanked Frank for his time, and for the time that he gave to his family, and told him that he was leaving the country, and wouldn't ever come back.

The second letter went to Charlie Fallon, care of the 52nd Street Shelter. It simply told him to be at the Sloane house early the following morning, and to bring men. Charlie assumed that there was more furniture coming, so gathered seven of his best, along with Judy, and they marched through the streets. They smelt the smoke before they saw it, and when they turned the corner they saw the flames climbing out of the window frames, creeping up the walls like weeds. By the time the fire engines arrived the paper labyrinth inside had burned away, taking Erwin's body with it. By the evening the house was dripping wet and black inside, though the solid brownstone structure remained strong and defiant. The following morning Frank Waits turned up at Charlie's door and handed him the keys, and the cheque that Maynard had failed to pick up. The house was covered with yellow tape, but the police let Charlie in, and explained that they had found a body.

'Must be Maynard Sloane,' they said, consulting their clipboards. 'He was the only one of the lot still alive.' The house was completely empty; everything stripped from the walls, all the interiors gone. Charlie pictured how it would look cleaned, decorated, given over to people who needed it, and he started to cry.

As he was leaving he saw a grey slab by the front door, turned it over and saw Erwin's headstone. He picked it up and carried it home and, one week later, directly after the funeral held for Maynard at the family plot, he placed the stone back into the ground that it had come from.

Epilogue

Maynard got off the plane into the heat and struggled to find a cab, looking for yellow cars. He eventually realised that he needed white ones. He showed his driver an address, scrawled onto a scrappy piece of paper – courtesy of David Walls, Private Investigator – and watched the streets as they went past, faster than he would have liked. He caught himself clinging to the leather door more than once; he squinted when other cars manned their horns with terrifying frequency; he braced as they screeched to a halt outside the small restaurant. The windows were dark, but he could see inside, to the tables of people, the candles lighting their faces. Through the door he found that the tablecloths were all yellow gingham, just like the one that he had in his bag. He was served by a young man, fresh into his teenage years, his golden skin at odds with his bottle-green eyes and his blond hair. Maynard ordered a bottle of red wine and a steak, and then he sat and watched as Lia came out of the back room, told her staff what to do, ruffled the boy's hair. She looked the same, almost; grey streaks in her hair gave her age away, but her face was the same, the way that she moved. Maynard got up from his table and moved to the back of the room, where there was a rickety old piano and a stool. He mocked putting coat tails behind him as he sat down, and cracked his knuckles, and then played his piece right the way through to the end, discovering what had been missing for so many years as he played. When he was done the people in the restaurant applauded, because the opus was, finally, complete.

Acknowledgements

There are some people who helped force this novel into shape over the course of the past six years; Stephen Knight, who had invaluable and guiding thoughts about it as it gestated and progressed; Holly Howitt, who read more drafts of this (filled with dreadful apostrophe use) than I dare to imagine; and Lucy Llewellyn, who helped me bash it into the vastly more accessible format it has now than the one it had when first written. Thanks all.

PARTHIAN